SIREN
Publishing

Ménage Everlasting

LAW OF DESIRE

DESIRE, OKLAHOMA 13

The

Leah Brooke

Collection

Law of Desire

Krystal Kane lived with memories of the men she loved and been forced by family obligations to push away.

Her fantasies kept her going, but she knew that the two men who wanted to share her couldn't want any more than an affair.

When her mother died, she wanted nothing more than to get away, not wanting to hear from them the words that would end the fantasy.

Needing them more than ever, she fought the overwhelming desire to call them, only to look up, and find them standing there.

Rafe Delgatto and Linc Barrett had waited for Krystal for years, unable to forget the woman who'd stolen their hearts.

They rushed to her side as soon as they learned she needed them, and quickly whisked her to the home they'd made for her.

She could heal in Desire, Oklahoma, while they proved to her that their love was real—and protect her from a threat they hadn't anticipated.

Genres: Contemporary, Ménage a Trois/Quatre, Romantic Suspense
Length: 73,191

Law of Desire

Desire, Oklahoma 13

Leah Brooke

Siren Publishing, Inc.
www.SirenPublishing.com

A SIREN PUBLISHING BOOK

Law of Desire
Copyright © 2018 by Leah Brooke

ISBN: 978-1-64243-534-4
First Publication:October 2018
Cover design by Les Byerley
All art and logo copyright © 2018 by Siren Publishing, Inc.

Siren Publishing, Inc.
www.SirenPublishing.com

ABOUT THE AUTHOR

When Leah's not writing, she's spending time with family and friends, and spoiling her fur babies.

For all titles by Leah Brooke, please visit
www.bookstrand.com/leah-brooke

Law of Desire

Desire, Oklahoma 13

LEAH BROOKE

Chapter One

Rafe Delgatto stood leaning against the wall of his boss's office, eyeing Ace Tyler with narrowed eyes. "Are you sure you're ready to come back?"

Ace, the sheriff of Desire, Oklahoma, had recently been run over by a car in a freak accident, something that would have put most men down for weeks.

Ace hadn't even had a broken bone.

Despite being given the day off, Rafe and his best friend, Linc Barrett, both deputies in Desire, had come in to see for themselves that the stubborn sheriff could handle coming back to work so soon.

Behind his paper-strewn desk, Ace sat back with a smile, his hands clasped over his flat stomach. "Do I look like I'm not ready?"

Rafe couldn't hold back a smile. "The truth is that you look better than you did before you got run over. You got a secret I should know about? Vitamins? Supplements?"

Ace's lips twitched as he sat forward again. "Hope takes good care of me." He gave Rafe and Linc a sympathetic smile. "I hope the two of you know that feeling one day. You're getting ready to go visit her again, aren't you?"

Rafe inclined his head and glanced at Linc. "Yeah. Linc went last month. It's my turn to go. I'm leaving first thing in the morning."

Ace sighed and shook his head. "I don't know how the two of you do it. I would go nuts."

Linc sighed. "It hasn't been easy. It's the way it has to be, and right now there's not a damned thing we can do about it. We can't be there with her because it hurts her and her mother too much, but we can't stay away. We need to see her and for her to know that we're waiting for her."

Shaking his head, Ace got up to refill his coffee cup. "I have to admit I keep expecting the two of you to come in one day and tell me you're resigning to go back to San Diego."

"No." Rafe sipped from his own cup. "One of the roadblocks we were running into with her was that she didn't take our relationship seriously because we wanted her to belong to both of us. She couldn't—can't—believe that we both love her. She tries to put distance between us each time we go to see her. When she couldn't afford to keep her cell phone anymore, we got her a new one, but she wouldn't even take that."

"She said she wouldn't take charity and told us to find someone else. We thought if we could find a place to live the way we wanted with her, she would realize just how serious we are." Linc smiled faintly. "When we came here to apply for a job, we didn't know what to expect. We like the small-town feeling, the fact that everyone's intent on protecting the women, and the friendliness of the town. It's safe, and that's something we very much want for her."

"It's the perfect place to be with her and bring up a family." Rafe had imagined it many times, the mental image of Krystal heavy with their child making his arms ache to hold her.

Even now, his dreams of her had him reaching for her in the night.

Ace inclined his head and went back to his seat. "And that's why you bought the old Cooper house when it went up for sale."

Rafe smiled, thinking about the work they'd already had done to the bathrooms and kitchen. "It is. It's a nice house with a good-sized backyard." He glanced at Linc. "As soon as she's free, we're going to her and bring her back here. She should be happy here."

He hoped that bringing her to a place where men and women lived happily, and very much in love in ménage marriages, he and Linc could show her just how well it could work.

Ace sat back again, his eyes slightly narrowed. "I've never wanted to pry, but you've been waiting a long time. One of you goes somewhere every month. You're gone one day, and you come back again, looking like shit."

Linc glanced at Rafe and dropped into one of the chairs in front of Ace's desk. "Her name is Krystal. Krystal Kane."

Ace smiled encouragingly. "A beautiful name."

Rafe straightened and went to the coffee pot, more for something to do than because he wanted more coffee. "She's a beautiful woman—inside as well as out. She's got a good heart, but she takes care of everyone around her instead of herself."

Ace reached for his own coffee and leaned back in his chair again. "How did you meet her?"

Rafe turned with his cup. "When we were working in San Diego, Linc and I were on a call for a domestic disturbance, well, you know the story."

Ace frowned. "Yes. I read the reports. You were shot. Please don't tell me she's the one who shot you."

Rafe smiled at that. "No. She was one of the nurses in the emergency room."

"A nurse." Ace smiled. "Taking care of others instead of herself. It makes sense."

Rafe nodded. "Linc and I had been sharing women on and off for some time, but when we met Krystal…" He sucked in a breath, blowing it out in a rush. "Well, that was it. We both fell in love with her. It hit us hard."

Ace smiled at that, looking down into his coffee cup. "Yeah. That's the real kind. If they don't make you crazy, you're not in love."

Linc rose as if too restless to sit. "We wanted to marry her, but we couldn't convince her that we were serious, so we didn't even get the chance to ask her."

"We'd only known her for forty-seven days when her father was diagnosed with cancer." Rafe set his cup aside and scraped a hand through his hair, his stomach in knots at the memory. "Her mother and father both needed her."

Ace's lips thinned. "Understandable. Hell on all of you, though."

"She's been through hell." Linc went to the window, staring out. "She told us not to wait for her."

"And of course, neither one of you wanted to listen to her, but here you both are." Ace finished his coffee and set his cup aside. "One of you visits her every month, which means that each of you only gets to see her every other month. Other than the few days you took off when her father died, you both hoard your days off and vacation time, so I can only assume it's so that you can spend time with her when she's free. Does her mother still need her so much?"

Rafe dropped into one of the chairs, the image of Krystal the last time he saw her forming in his mind with ease. "Krystal worked during the day and went to her parents' house at night to take care of her father and help her mother. Two weeks after her father died, her mother had a stroke."

Ace stiffened. "Jesus!"

"That was three years ago." Rafe jumped from his seat again. "Krystal had to give up her apartment and move in with her mother. Her brother, a troublemaker, disappeared before her father died, leaving her to handle everything on her own. We tried to help, but our presence just upset her mother, so Krystal made us promise to stay away."

Leaning back in his seat, Ace sighed. "Let me guess. Her mother didn't take kindly to her daughter having two lovers."

"Exactly. She didn't think we were serious, either, and after her stroke just became more agitated whenever she saw us." Linc scraped a hand through his hair. "Which upset Krystal. We keep visiting her because we want her to know that we're still here for her." He chuckled humorlessly. "She keeps telling us to find someone else."

Ace smiled. "And to you, there is no one else. Neither one of you has even looked at another woman since you got here."

"There is no other woman." Rafe clenched his jaw in frustration. "We'll wait as long as it takes. We'd hoped her mother would recover, but with her husband gone, she doesn't seem to want to go on. She's been going downhill for months, and Krystal can't do anything but watch."

Linc sighed and turned from the window. "She needs us with her, but she won't allow it because of her mother. She gets more distant each time we go, but there's a yearning and sadness in her eyes that rips me to shreds. She leans into us, but then pushes us away as if she's afraid to just let go—even for a minute. We're giving her what she asked for, but it costs us, and worse, it costs her."

Inclining his head, Ace blew out a breath. "Of that I have no doubt. You told me once that you were saving your vacation time for when you needed it. It makes more sense now."

Rafe rose again, too restless to sit still. "Our regular days off are more than enough to visit her. We haven't even bought much furniture for the house because we want her to pick it out."

"We're hoping it makes it feel more like her home and will help get her mind off of things." Linc sipped from his cup and grimaced. "She's gonna have a lot to work through. Her mother ended up in a nursing facility when her condition continued to deteriorate. Krystal's with her every day. Her mother got agitated when she wasn't there, and she lost her job because she spent so much time with her mother."

Rafe's cell phone rang, and he paused in his pacing to dig it out of his pocket. One look at the display and he froze in place. With his heart in his throat, he lifted his gaze to Linc's. "Hell."

His stomach clenched, his throat going dry, and, to his surprise, his hand shook.

Linc froze at his tone. "Is it her?"

"No. The facility. I'll put it on speaker."

Ace rose. "I'll give you some privacy."

"No." Rafe shook his head, his heart in his throat. "It'll save time." He sucked in a breath and answered. "Delgatto."

"Mr. Delgatto, this is Dr. Smith. You wanted me to call you about any change."

Rafe swallowed heavily, his hand tightening on the back of the chair closest to him. "Yes, Doctor? What happened?"

"I'm sorry to inform you that Mrs. Kane suffered another stroke this morning. She's been made more comfortable, but I'm afraid it's just a matter of time."

Meeting Linc's gaze, Rafe saw the same worry for Krystal. "How's Krystal?"

"Stoic. I'm more than a little worried. It's clear that she's exhausted and staying here twenty-four-seven has taken quite a toll on her."

Linc stepped closer. "You said a matter of time, Doctor. How much time are you talking about? Days? Weeks?"

"Hours. To be honest, I'm surprised she's hung on this long. You asked me to call you, and we've all become very fond of Miss Kane. She's going to need you."

Rafe stared at Linc. "We'll catch the next plane there. Is Krystal's brother with her?"

"I'm afraid we haven't seen him in months."

A muscle worked in Linc's jaw. "So she's alone."

"A nurse is with her."

Rafe glanced at Ace who'd stepped aside, his voice low as he spoke into his cell phone. "We'll get there as soon as we can."

"She doesn't know that I'm calling you. I have to admit that we're all a little worried about where she'll go when she leaves here."

"Probably to her mother's house."

A pregnant sigh followed. "She hasn't told you?"

Rafe stiffened. "Told us what?"

"She had to sell her mother's house and belongings to pay for her mother's care when the insurance ran out."

"Where the hell has she been living?"

"She sleeps in a chair next to her mother's bed. Showers in her mother's bathroom."

Stunned, Rafe circled the chair and dropped into it. "Jesus!"

"We've tried to help her as much as possible. The women in the cafeteria have been making sure she gets enough to eat."

Linc flattened both hands on the desk and bowed his head, his eyes closed in agony. "And she didn't tell us a thing."

The doctor blew out a breath. "I should have known that neither one of you knew about it."

"We didn't. Thank you, Doctor. If she tries to leave before we get there, can you see if you can delay her?" Rafe rose, dug his keys out of his pocket, and glanced at Ace, who looked furious. "We're on our way."

Disconnecting, he turned to Ace. "Ace, we need—"

Ace tossed his phone onto his desk in an angry gesture, his eyes sharp. "You're already booked on the next plane to San Diego. Move your asses and go get her."

After picking up the bags they kept packed, along with their black suits, Rafe drove toward the airport with Linc. "Christ, I've got butterflies. What the hell are we going to do if she refuses to come with us?"

Linc sighed. "We beg, and if all else fails, we kidnap her. I don't give a damn what we have to do. I'm sure as hell not coming back without her."

Chapter Two

Krystal Kane sat next to the bed she'd been sitting beside for months, holding her mother's frail hand between hers.

It was almost over, but Krystal was too numb to cry.

She knew that she should, but it was like a huge bubble had formed around her, separating her from the rest of the world.

She'd expected this—knew it would happen—and had dreaded it.

Now, a sense of peace settled over her.

Maggie, the nurse on duty for her mother, came into the room again, placing a hand on Krystal's shoulder. "She's comfortable. I promise."

Krystal nodded, staring at her mother's face. "I know. She looks so peaceful. It's been a long time since I've seen her looking this way."

The lines of worry and anger that had been so much a part of her mother's features for years had smoothed out, the faint smile on her lips a stark reminder of days gone by.

Maggie patted her shoulder and moved away to approach Krystal's mother from the other side. "We tried to call your brother. The number was disconnected."

Krystal nodded again, not at all surprised. "He changes his number all the time."

Her brother, Kevin, always had a scheme to make fast money, and his schemes always seemed to manage to get him into some kind of trouble.

She hated to admit, even to herself, that his presence wouldn't have made her feel any better.

Maggie smiled kindly, her eyes filled with concern. "Are those handsome men coming?"

Krystal shook her head, pushing the mental image of Rafe and Linc ruthlessly aside. "No. I'll call them when I get settled to tell them I'm all right."

A lifetime ago, they'd been her lovers, and it had been the happiest time in her life.

Just knowing they were only a phone call away gave her a strength she'd desperately needed.

It had taken every bit of willpower she could muster to resist making that call.

Still, the ache for them had only grown stronger.

Rafe and Linc had to be the handsomest and most masculine men she'd ever met. They were gentle and kind and had taken her virginity with a tenderness she would never forget.

Both had a strong moral code that she respected and admired, and she knew she would never love anyone the way she loved them.

It hurt to think of them with another woman, but she wouldn't try to fool herself.

After all, she hadn't expected that they'd been celibate since the last time they'd made love to her.

Three years was a long time, and Linc and Rafe were highly sexed men in their prime.

She had to admit to being surprised that they kept coming to see her and attributed it to their sense of loyalty to her because they'd taken her virginity.

She couldn't allow them to tie themselves to her out of a sense of duty or guilt that they'd taken her virginity and felt they couldn't abandon her.

She didn't know where she would go yet and would probably take a bus headed east and stop when the mood struck her.

When she did, she would call them. She owed them that. She still had their cell numbers on a piece of paper in her purse written in Rafe's masculine script.

She would never call them again after that but knew she'd keep that small slip of paper until the day she died.

It would relieve their sense of guilt, and they could get on with their lives—if they hadn't already.

Maggie adjusted her mother's blanket. "One of those handsome men shows up every month. I hear them asking you if they can stay.

You should have taken them up on it. No one should have to go through what you've been through alone."

"I couldn't do that to them." Krystal forced a smile, something that had become harder and harder over the last several months. "What kind of life would they have? Hell, I'm not even the same person I was when we were together."

"We all change."

Krystal sighed, so tired that even carrying on the conversation with the nurse exhausted her. "They haven't." Rafe and Linc were still as handsomely rugged and loving as always, and Krystal knew it wouldn't be fair to lead them on when she had nothing to offer. "It would never work."

They'd told her during their visits that they'd made a life in a town called Desire in Oklahoma, a place, they claimed, where it was accepted for a woman to be married to more than one man.

She didn't believe them, of course, but had to admit she'd fantasized about it during the long days sitting next to her mother's bed and watching her sleep.

She'd rather live on the memories and the fantasies than risk being with them and falling even deeper in love, only to have it end when they realized it wouldn't work between them.

She'd wrap her memories around her like a blanket, hoping they could warm her on cold and lonely nights.

Determined to put Rafe and Linc out of her mind, she focused on her mother and the memories of the past and happier times.

During the next hour, her mother's breathing slowed even more.

Krystal focused on each breath, each time wondering if it would be her mother's last one, sucking in another breath each time her mother did.

It hurt, but she didn't cry.

She didn't even know if she could anymore.

She'd known this time would come, but now that it was close, she felt so distant from it all, as if she dreamed it.

She pinched her own hand several times over the next few hours, half believing that she was dreaming and would wake up to see that her mother had woken from her nap.

She ached for Rafe and Linc, but she vowed to herself that she wouldn't call them until she'd settled somewhere.

The doctor appeared again, using his stethoscope to listen to her mother's heart. "Are you all right?"

Nodding, Krystal ran her thumb over the top of her mother's hand. "I'm fine."

"I'm sorry. You've been so strong."

She felt like a fraud. She wasn't strong at all. Lifting her gaze to his, she shook her head and forced a polite smile. "I wish I was."

Dr. Smith smiled and lightly patted her hand. "You are. Most people wouldn't do what you've done."

"She's my mother."

He gestured toward her mother's tray. "It looks like Maggie brought you some soup."

Krystal barely glanced at it. "That was nice of her." Turning back to her mother, she eyed Dr. Smith. "Is there any chance?"

Straightening, he tucked his stethoscope into his pocket, his sympathetic smile bringing a lump to Krystal's throat. "I'm sorry."

Forcing another smile, Krystal nodded. "Thank you for all you've done. You've been very kind."

Minutes after the doctor left, Krystal's mother drew her last breath.

Krystal waited, expecting her mother to take another as she had for the last several hours, but it didn't come.

Her mother had passed away.

Still holding her hand, Krystal sat there, wondering why she didn't cry.

Time stood still for her, her mind blank.

She stared at her mother's hand in hers, suddenly feeling completely alone.

When thoughts of Rafe and Linc started to creep in, she ruthlessly pushed them back, her throat clogged with the tears she couldn't shed.

She needed Rafe and Linc more than she'd ever needed anything in her life, but she wouldn't call them.

Calling them would be the most selfish thing she could have done, and she wouldn't burden them any more than she already had.

They would come if she called. All she had to do was pick up the phone and they would be on their way.

Knowing that made it even more difficult to resist calling them.

The feeling of having her entire life ahead of her hit her hard, the enormity of it overwhelming.

She couldn't let herself think of anything except the next step.

She had to finish taking care of her mother.

She'd already pre-paid for her mother's funeral and had only to make the arrangements.

Her mother had lost contact with all of her friends when Krystal's father had been sick, and she didn't really expect anyone to come.

She would get a taxi and go to the funeral home. She didn't relish the thought of lugging her three suitcases along with her purse, but she would just have to figure out a way to do it.

She kissed her mother's cold hand and tucked it under the covers, just as Maggie appeared on the other side of her mother's bed. "She's gone."

"Yes." Maggie tucked her mother's other hand under the covers. "She's at peace now."

"I hope so. She's earned it."

Her mother would finally be with her father again, the man she considered her soul mate.

Krystal had never believed in such a thing, but after experiencing the kind of happiness she hadn't known existed with Rafe and Linc, and the empty loneliness since she pushed them away, she wondered if it could be possible to have two soul mates.

"So have you." Maggie smiled and wiped away a tear that Krystal couldn't shed. "I hope you find the happiness and peace that you deserve."

"Thank you." Krystal glanced at Maggie and started to stand, surprised that her legs wouldn't support her. "I have to go to the funeral home and make final arrangements."

Maggie frowned and shook her head. "I wish you would call those men of yours."

Krystal shook her head, glancing at the three suitcases that stood in the corner, dreading the thought of trying to carry them. "They're not mine anymore."

"We beg to differ."

With a gasp, Krystal spun, her knees giving out at the sight of Rafe and Linc striding into the room toward her.

She had to be dreaming. It was the only explanation.

She must have fallen asleep while thinking of them.

Rafe's dark brown eyes and Linc's hazel ones never left hers as they moved closer, the concern in them just like she'd imagined.

The dream was so real that she could even smell the light, fresh, masculine scent of them.

Instead of comforting her, it just made the ache for them unbearable.

Linc caught her when she would have fallen, lifting her high against his chest. His hard arms closed around her, enveloping her in his warmth and strength. The concern in his eyes sharpened as he stared down at her. "I'm so sorry, baby. Are you okay?"

Looking up at him, Krystal blinked and reached up to cup his jaw, gasping again and jerking her hand back when she found it solid and warm against her palm. "I'm not dreaming. You're here."

Rafe closed in on her other side, running a hand over her hair and bending to kiss her forehead. The warmth from his lips lingered when he lifted his head again to smile down at her, his eyes also dark with concern and anger. "No, baby. You're awake, and we're definitely here." He turned to Maggie, who smiled, tears welling in her eyes. "Are those her suitcases?"

Nodding, Maggie wiped away a tear. "Yes. She's kept them hidden in the closet so you wouldn't know. Take good care of her."

Linc caught her hand again and held it against his chest. "We thoroughly intend to."

While Rafe collected her suitcases, Linc carried her out of her mother's room and down the long hall, seemingly oblivious to the attention they drew.

Krystal stared up at Linc, knowing that no dream could feel so real. "I didn't call you. I wouldn't do that to you. I know I didn't call you."

"No, baby. You didn't." Linc pulled her closer, silently urging her to lay her head on his shoulder.

Pressing a hand against his chest, she tried to push away memories of other times he'd carried her. "Please put me down."

"No." Even carrying her didn't slow him down, his long strides taking them quickly toward the front door. "If I do, you'll fall. Besides, I've waited a long time to have you in my arms again and I'm not about to let go."

Chapter Three

Linc carried Krystal down the long hall of the nursing facility and out the door, alarmed at how thin she'd become.

Her clothes disguised most of it, but holding her close, he felt every missing pound.

"I can't believe you're here." Blinking against the bright sunlight, she buried her face against his shoulder. "She's gone, Linc."

Linc paused next to the car they'd rented, easing her to her feet, only to gather her against him in case her knees gave out again. "I know, baby. I'm so sorry."

Cupping the back of her head, he held her close, bending to press her face against his neck. "I'm so sorry, sweetheart. Rafe and I are here for you. You're not alone. We'll get through this."

She lifted her head, glancing up at him before staring at a spot on his shoulder. "Thank you for coming, but I can take care of it."

Her skin looked too pale, her blue eyes dim, with dark circles under them. Her long blonde hair had lost the shine it once had, and she'd pulled it back into a ponytail, which emphasized the increasingly sharp angles of her features due to weight loss.

"Don't." Linc tucked her into the front passenger seat, handing her the purse the nurse had given him, while Rafe slid behind the wheel.

Shading her eyes from the sun, Krystal frowned up at him. "Don't what?"

"Don't try to push us away. That's over. Things are gonna be different from now on." He handed the end of the seatbelt to Rafe, who snapped it into place. "Are you warm enough?"

Despite the warm day, Krystal shivered, probably from nerves and reaction. "I'm fine, thank you." She reached down to unbuckle the seat belt, frowning when Rafe stopped her. "I can't go with you."

Wondering how long it had been since she'd been outside, Linc bit back a curse. "Why not?"

"I have to go to the funeral home. I have to make the arrangements to bury my mother." Her voice was so low he had to strain to hear her.

Concerned by her sluggish movements and speech, Linc shared a look with Rafe, unsurprised to find that his friend appeared just as worried. "We know that, honey. You didn't really think we were going to leave before the funeral, did you?"

Krystal frowned. "I don't know. You really don't have to stay, but I'd appreciate a ride to the funeral home. My suitcases?"

Rafe checked that her seat belt was secure. "I already put them in the trunk, honey. Just relax. We've got you now."

Linc sighed and crouched down next to her, taking her hand in his. Slightly alarmed to find it cold, he closed his other over it to warm it. "Baby, we'll take you and stay with you. We'll help you through this, Krystal. You're not alone, and we're damned well not gonna let you push us aside anymore."

Frowning, Krystal stared down at her purse. "It's for the best. You shouldn't have come. I would have called you when I got settled to let you know I was okay."

Rafe turned her face to his, his jaw clenched in anger. "Just like that, huh? A phone call to tell us that you were gone?"

Dropping her head against the headrest, Krystal closed her eyes with a sigh. "Things with us never got serious enough for you to go through all this trouble."

"Bullshit." Linc closed her door and got into the seat behind her and then slid to the other side so he could see her. "Things between us were very serious, but you couldn't get that through your hard head. I'm damned glad we asked the doctor to keep us informed. Visiting you once a month wasn't enough for us, but we followed your wishes. Now we're going to do things our way."

She sat up abruptly, whipping her head around to stare at him, her features paling even more. "Linc!"

Irritated at himself for taking his frustration out on her at such a time, Linc blew out a breath, nodding in understanding at Rafe's warning look. "I'm sorry, baby. Now's not the time for this discussion."

Leaning her head back, she closed her eyes. "I told you to stop coming. It wasn't fair to you to feel like you had to keep coming out."

Rafe glanced at her. "Not a damned thing about any of this was fair, Krystal, and we came to see you because we wanted to."

"It was my problem. There was no reason to drag you into it."

Linc gritted his teeth. "There was every reason. We belong together, Krystal. You're ours."

She shook her head lethargically from side to side. "Please. I just…can't."

Rafe sighed and shared a look with Linc. "Fair enough, baby. You're beat. Can you tell me where the funeral home is? We'll take care of that first, and then we can get you settled."

* * * *

By the time they finished at the funeral home, Krystal felt drained, numb, and so exhausted that she found it difficult just to put one foot in front of the other.

They left the funeral home in silence, and instead of being led to the front seat again, she found herself sitting in the back seat with Linc. Leaning her head back, she stared out the window, Linc's and Rafe's presences allowing her to relax in a way she hadn't in a very long time.

She would allow herself a few minutes to regroup but wouldn't allow herself to get used to depending on them.

She was just so tired.

She closed her eyes, letting herself drift off into a world halfway between sleep and wakefulness. She pushed aside thoughts of the funeral, her brother, and her future plans to just let her mind rest.

Instead, she couldn't stop thinking of Rafe and Linc and the pain of saying good-bye to them one last time.

She opened her eyes again, the ache in her heart made even more potent by the numbness surrounding it.

After several minutes, Linc spoke from beside her. "I didn't realize that the funeral was already paid for." He kept his voice low as if afraid of upsetting her again.

If he only knew how much she wanted to throw herself at him and beg him to take her with him.

Krystal blew out a breath in the hope of releasing some of the tension inside her. She continued to stare out the window, squinting against the bright sun, her eyes burning. "In order to get government assistance, I had to use her money from the sale of her house to pay for her care, but they allowed me to prepay for her funeral."

Her eyes had become gritty, making it difficult to keep them open, but she wanted to keep looking out, sad that her mother wouldn't see another beautiful day.

Sad that she had to face a life without Rafe and Linc.

Linc wrapped an arm around her and held her against his chest. "You've been through so much."

Consumed with her own thoughts, Krystal slumped against him, the feel of his hold both heaven and hell.

He felt so solid and warm, and in his arms, she found the strength she desperately needed to settle.

At the same time, she missed him already and looked toward a dark time when she knew she'd never see either one of them again.

She'd never again feel alive in the way she did in their arms.

When Rafe stopped and turned off the engine, she reluctantly sat up, surprised to see that he'd pulled into the parking lot of a restaurant known for serving breakfast all day.

When Rafe got out and opened her door, she took his outstretched hand automatically, not resisting when he helped her from the car and wrapped an arm around her, pulling her against his side.

They silently crossed the parking lot and went inside, Linc and Rafe on either side of her.

The air conditioning chilled her, and she pulled the sweater she wore more firmly around herself, not remembering putting it on.

The last time she'd seen it, it had been draped over one of her suitcases.

She slid into the booth the hostess led them to, moving over when Rafe slid in next to her. Ignoring the menu, she wrapped her hands around the cup of coffee Rafe poured from the insulated carafe.

Linc pushed her menu toward her. "What do you feel like eating, baby?"

The endearment sent a rush of warmth through her, followed almost immediately by a chill when she reminded herself that it meant nothing. "Nothing. I'm not hungry."

Staring out the window, she half listened to their conversation as they discussed the menu.

She turned to Rafe, touching his arm to get his attention, but he'd already turned to her. "Would you please order a large orange juice for me?"

"Of course."

The waitress appeared again, and after taking a huge order for food, including three large orange juices, she disappeared again.

Linc reached across the table to take her hand in his. "I'm sorry we didn't get here earlier. We came as soon as the doctor called."

"I can't believe he called you."

Rafe slid an arm around her shoulders. "We left our cell numbers with him so he could reach us at any time. We told him to let us know when there was any change. Do you want to talk about it?"

Krystal sighed as the waitress approached with their juices, waiting until she left again before speaking. "I knew as soon as she woke up this morning that something was wrong. She just seemed a little off. Maggie came in with her breakfast, and she saw it, too. I think she knew right away what it was, but she rushed to get the doctor."

Krystal took a sip of her juice to swallow the lump in her throat. "I thought they were going to send her back to the hospital, but the doctor said that there was nothing they could do for her at the hospital that he couldn't do there." Using her finger, she traced a bead of moisture down her glass, her stomach clenching at the memory. "He knew it was over. So did I, I guess. It scared me, but at the same time, I prayed for God to take her quickly. She'd suffered a long time."

Linc nodded, his eyes filled with sympathy. "Yes. She did. So did your father, and so did you. Now you need to take care of yourself and let us take care of you."

Shaking her head, she took another sip of juice, resisting the urge to gulp the entire glass. "No. I'm not about to be a burden to you or anyone else."

She laughed humorlessly, wrapping her hands around the coffee cup again to warm them. "There is no one else, is there?"

Rafe gathered her close. "*We're* here. Just lean on us for a while."

Inwardly cursing at herself for throwing a pity party, Krystal pulled away from him and sipped at her coffee. "You're right. You're here right now, and it's been a great help to me. All I have to do is get through the funeral, and then I can move on. I need a little sleep."

Sitting back when the waitress reappeared, Rafe nodded and ran a hand over her hair. "You need to rest. We'll be there to help you get through the funeral. In the meantime, you need to eat."

Krystal blinked when the waitress set a plate in front of her piled high with pancakes, scrambled eggs, bacon, and hash browns. "I didn't order this!"

Rafe picked up her fork and handed it to her. "I know, but drinking coffee and acidic juice isn't going to do your stomach any favors. You haven't eaten all day, have you?"

"I couldn't. With so much going on, I didn't even think of food."

"Exactly." Linc gestured toward her plate. "You don't have to eat all of it, but I expect you to make a decent dent in it."

Stabbing a bite of the scrambled eggs, she looked up to see Linc watching her, his eyes filled with concern. She felt as if she should say something and searched for the words. "I appreciate that you came, but—"

"Don't say anything that you're gonna regret. Just leave it alone."

Krystal swallowed heavily. "I see no reason to avoid the issue. I think—"

Linc's expression hardened. "Shut up and eat, Krystal."

"I'm just trying to say—"

"We know what you're trying to say, and it's pissing us off." Linc pushed the syrup closer. "We should leave and go back home and forget all about you."

Taken aback at his angry tone, Krystal glanced at Rafe to see that the anger that had been in his eyes since appearing at the nursing home had sharpened. "You should forget about me and be happy with someone who doesn't have so much baggage."

Rafe lifted her fork to her mouth. "We can't forget about you. Eat."

She tried to take the fork from him, but he wouldn't release it. "You're going to regret it. I'm not the same person I was before."

Rafe kept the fork held to her lips, raising a brow when she hesitated. "We can do this the easy way or the hard way. Your choice."

Not trusting his mood, she ate the bite he offered and took the fork from him.

Linc looked up from his plate. "We've all changed, Krystal. Being away from you has taken a toll on us, too."

"You deserve better."

Rafe frowned when she set the fork down, picking it up again and stabbing another bite of scrambled eggs. "We want the best. We can't settle for less than the woman we love."

"Don't say that!"

It would be hard enough saying good-bye to them without hearing them talk about love.

"That woman you cared about is gone." She shouldn't have been surprised when he slipped the fork into her mouth again.

Rafe gave her a warning glare before handing the fork over to her again. "No, she's not. She's just been through a lot and needs to recover. She needs to rest and be taken care of—"

"No." She dropped her fork and reached for her juice, her stomach in knots. "I don't need to be taken care of, and I'm sure as hell not going to have you in the position of being my caretaker. God, I never want to put anyone in that position."

Linc smiled. "And there she is."

Rafe stabbed a bite of his pancake, dredged it through a puddle of syrup, and held his fork to her mouth. "If you believe that you don't need someone to take care of you, you're sadly mistaken. Have you looked in a mirror lately?"

Krystal shoved his hand aside. "Thanks. I know how bad I look. Just leave me alone."

Life stirred in her, but it hurt so much she fought to push it back again, reaching for the numbness that had consumed her for so long. "Please."

Linc shook his head. "I'm afraid that's something we can't do. You begged us to leave you alone so that you could take care of your mother, and our presence upset her. We did. We checked up on you, but we left you alone. You cut us out of a very important part of your life, and we had no choice but to let you because we didn't want to upset you. I'm mad at myself for that, and I'm sure as hell not going to let it happen again, especially since there's no longer a reason for it."

Rafe tightened his hand around his thick mug of coffee until his knuckles turned white, his eyes narrowed and shooting sparks. "You didn't even tell us that you were living in a fucking chair next to your mother's bed."

Startled by his anger, Krystal blinked, her stomach knotting even more. "It was none of your business. It was my problem, and I handled it."

Staring down at her plate, she resented them for piercing the numbness around her. "You should have found someone else."

Rafe turned to her, a muscle working in his jaw. "Christ, you try my patience."

Setting her fork aside, she touched Rafe's arm. "Please understand. I'm empty inside. I can't be what you want."

She wished she had the words to make them understand, but their conversation had taken the last of her reserves—reserves she hadn't known existed.

Rafe covered her hand with his. "You're exactly what I want."

"What *we* want." Linc reached out and took her other hand in his. "We knew that you were the woman we wanted from the very beginning. We understood how difficult it was for you to accept loving both of us and we took it slow. Too slow, it turns out."

Rafe wrapped his hand around hers. "If we'd known what was about to play out, we would have done things differently. We hadn't really established what we wanted with you before you were pulled away from us. That won't happen again."

She found herself watching his mouth as he spoke, remembering the first time he'd kissed her.

It had been in the emergency room of the hospital where she'd met him.

After he'd been discharged, he'd come down to the emergency room where she worked to ask her out, and she'd breathlessly accepted.

Before she could blink, he'd backed her behind one of the privacy curtains and tenderly brushed her lips with his, seeming surprised when her breath caught.

Wrapping an arm around her, he'd pulled her close, his strength surprising, especially since he was recovering from a gunshot wound. "You're very sweet. I don't think one taste is gonna be enough."

He'd kissed her again, a deep kiss that made her head swim.

Dizzy, she'd clung to him, and when he'd lifted his head, she had to hold on to him in order to steady herself in a world suddenly tilted.

When she'd opened her eyes, he'd been staring down at her with the strangest look on his face.

His slow smile had made her heart beat faster. "No, I'm afraid a taste only makes me want more."

Feeling his gaze, she returned to the present, struck by his searching look.

His eyes narrowed, harder than she could ever remember seeing them. "Let's get one thing straight, Krystal Kane. You're coming back to Desire with us if we have to drag you kicking and screaming. We can do that the easy way or the hard way, as well."

She wished she could go back to that time and to feel the way they'd once made her feel. Her heart felt too heavy for that now. "I can't. Too much has changed. I think it's better if both of you go back now. Thank you for coming. It means so much to me."

Linc's eyes narrowed. "Your politeness is getting on my nerves. Eat. Then we'll go back to the hotel and you can take one of your nice long baths and go to sleep in a real bed instead of a fucking chair."

The thought of being able to have a long hot bath instead of the quick tepid showers she'd had to take over the last few months sounded like heaven.

She looked down, surprised to see that she'd eaten almost everything on her plate, and was suddenly exhausted.

Setting her fork aside, she reached for her juice again, surprised to find the glass full.

She glanced at Linc's empty glass and realized that he'd switched them at some point.

The conversation was cut short when the waitress appeared to ask if they wanted anything else.

With her stomach full and warmed by the sun coming in through the window, Krystal half listened to them speak to the waitress, suddenly finding it difficult to keep her eyes open.

She finished her juice, automatically putting her hand in Rafe's when he held out a hand to her to help her from the booth.

She found herself in the back seat once again and, when neither man spoke, started to doze.

She must have fallen into a deeper sleep than she'd meant to because the next thing she knew Rafe had stopped the car again.

She woke, blinking against the bright sunlight, so tired that her eyes burned with the effort to keep them open. "Where are we?"

Linc helped her out. "We're at the hotel." Linc held out a hand to her and helped her from the car. "We didn't take the time to check in, but we called ahead. As soon as we get you to the room, we'll get the luggage."

She sat with Linc in the lobby while Rafe checked them in, watching the people laughing and going about their business without a care in the world.

She'd been like that at one time in her life.

She knew it.

She remembered it.

But she couldn't remember what it felt like.

Faster than she'd expected, Rafe joined them again. "Let's go."

Focusing on putting one foot in front of the other, she walked between them to the bank of elevators. "This looks like a nice place."

Linc smiled and pulled her against his side. "It's a wonder you can see anything with your eyes closing the way they are. You're in desperate need of a nap."

Krystal willingly leaned back against Linc during their ride in the elevator, closing her eyes and dropping her head back against his chest. "Yeah. Maybe."

When Rafe took her hand in his, she opened her eyes and followed him out of the elevator, stumbling as they started down a hall.

She found herself suddenly swept off her feet.

Dropping her head against Rafe's shoulder, she sighed. "Thank you. I'm sorry. I'm so tired."

Pressing his lips against her hair, Rafe carried her down the hallway. "There's nothing to be sorry for."

Linc opened the door and stood aside. "Get her settled. I'll be back with the suitcases."

Krystal stirred, lifting her head. "Just bring the green one for me, please."

Linc ran a hand down her arm, smiling faintly. "Okay, baby."

Rafe carried her to the bathroom, seating her on the toilet before turning to start her bath water, worried at Krystal's extreme lethargy.

She looked around, frowning. "What are we doing in here?"

The fact that she hadn't even realized they'd come into the bathroom convinced him that he'd made the right decision. "You'll feel better once you soak for a while."

He hated that she looked so lost, and despite the warm weather, her hands still felt cold.

She sat there looking at the water, her expression blank.

Once he'd adjusted it to the right temperature, he bent to untie her sneakers, hoping a bath would warm her. "Let's get your clothes off so you can get in."

Nodding, she reached for the hem of her shirt. "I can do it." She paused as if waiting for him to leave the room.

If she thought for one minute that he would allow her to continue to put distance between them, she was very much mistaken.

He would do everything in his power to reestablish the intimacy that had been such a big part of their relationship. "I doubt it."

Her shoulders seemed too slender to carry all the burdens heaped on them, and he was determined now to take the load.

Giving her a small smile, he lifted her chin to look into her eyes. "I'm not gonna attack you, Krystal. I just want to help you. You've been tough for years. Enough. Just let go. I've got you. For God's sake, can't you just trust me?"

She smiled sadly, a slice to his heart. "I trust you, Rafe. It's just that I can do it myself."

Rafe sighed, holding on to his temper with a tenuous grip. "Krystal, I'm well aware that you've been doing everything for yourself for a long time. Now, Linc and I are taking over. Lift your arms." He tightened his grip on her chin. "We can do this the easy way or the hard way. Once again, your choice."

Krystal blinked, clearly shocked that he'd put his foot down, something neither he nor Linc had ever done with her before.

Lifting a brow in question, he waited until she nodded and lifted her arms.

He undressed her as he would a tired child, and once she was naked, he picked her up and gently lowered her into the tub, alarmed at how thin she'd become.

Smiling at her soft moan as the warm water enveloped her, he rose again and stripped out of his shirt before reaching for the washcloth and soap.

After he washed her face, she kept her eyes closed, so he rolled a towel and eased her back. "Here, baby. Just lie back and relax."

Her eyes popped open, and she looked slightly nervous at first, but Rafe lifted her arm and slowly washed it, taking his time as he slowly washed between each of her fingers.

He took his time washing her in the hopes of soothing her and getting her used to his touch again. "There's a shop in Desire where all the women go. They sell all kinds of scented lotions and bath stuff."

"Hmm."

He kept his tone low and soothing, telling her about some of the people and shops in Desire as he gently washed her, inwardly smiling when she closed her eyes again and slowly relaxed.

Her breathing evened out, the warm water, his light caress, and his boring monologue doing the trick.

Linc came in several minutes later and picked up the clothes Rafe had tossed aside. "How's she doing?"

Krystal gasped and sat up abruptly, splashing water, blinking as if coming out of a trance. She hurriedly covered her breasts with her hands, her eyes wide. "I'm naked."

Rafe smiled and reached out to grab the towel she'd used as a pillow, shaking it out as he rose. "That's usually how people take a bath." Offering a hand, he helped her to her feet. "Come on. Let's get you dried off before you get chilled again."

Linc cursed under his breath, his frustration at waking her evident in his voice. "I'll get her one of my T-shirts to sleep in."

Aware that Linc left the room, Rafe dried Krystal, ignoring her efforts to help him. "Just relax, baby. We'll have you bundled into bed in no time."

By the time he finished drying her, she swayed, holding on to his shoulders for support.

After slipping one of Linc's T-shirts over her head, Rafe carried her back into the bedroom where Linc waited, having already pulled the covers back.

Krystal's eyes closed as he pulled the covers around her, and he hoped that she would get some of the sleep she desperately needed.

Her long lashes fanned over the dark circles beneath her eyes, her too-pale features slightly flushed from her hot bath.

After slipping off his boots, Rafe slid into bed beside her, the need to hold her overwhelming.

After the rush of the last several hours, he finally had the chance to just hold her in his arms and come to terms with having her with them again.

Braced on an elbow, he watched her, surprised when her eyes opened again and she stared blankly at his chest.

He rubbed her back, sharing a look with Linc, both of them remaining silent in the hopes that she would fall asleep.

"I wouldn't blame you if you told me that you've met someone else."

Biting back frustration, Rafe continued to rub her back and arm. "Not even interested in anyone else. We waited for you. You're all we want."

She closed her eyes again, and he hoped she would sleep, but minutes later, they opened again.

"You don't even know me anymore."

"We know you, baby." Lowering himself to his side, he kept an arm around her and kissed her hair. "We know you better than you realize, and you know us. What's on the inside is what counts, and that very rarely changes. We know what we want, and it's you. Shut it down, Krystal."

It took several more minutes, but finally her eyes closed and stayed that way. Her breathing evened out again, but he kept rubbing her back, gradually slowing his strokes.

Rafe was too keyed up to sleep but remained beside her, loving the feel of her next to him in a way he hadn't experienced with her in years.

After checking to make sure the door was secured, Linc pulled the curtains closed and sat gingerly on the other side of the bed to pull off his own boots. "I can't wait to get her home."

"Yeah." Careful to keep his voice as low as Linc had, Rafe readjusted the covers over Krystal. "She's got a lot of healing to do, but at least we're with her now. Christ, she's gotta be beat."

Rafe lay next to her a long time, just listening to Krystal breathe and thinking about the days ahead.

Tomorrow he'd book a flight for the following day so they could leave right after the funeral.

There would be no reason to stick around, and he suspected a change in scenery would do Krystal a hell of a lot of good.

Once they got Krystal to her new home, they could finally start their lives together.

The worst was finally behind them, and things should run smoothly from there.

Chapter Four

Krystal woke to the smell of coffee, her first thought that Maggie had brought her a cup from the nurses' station.

She stretched, automatically stiffening and putting her hands out for the arm rests so that she didn't fall.

Not finding them, she jolted with a gasp, disoriented to find herself in a dark room.

"Easy, baby." Linc pulled the curtain open, flooding the room with bright morning sunlight. "We wanted you to sleep so we didn't open the curtain."

The sound of the shower running told her that Rafe was still there, and suddenly the memories of the previous day came back in a rush. "I'm not at the nursing home."

"No, baby." Linc sat on the bed next to her and pulled her into his arms. Wearing the familiar jeans and T-shirt, and smelling like male and fresh sunshine, he felt like home. "You're here with us. How do you feel?"

She lifted her head from a chest that felt more muscular and wider than she remembered and forced a smile. "I'm fine."

"Yes, I'm sure you are." Leaning back, he looked down at her with a scowl. "I don't know why I ask that question when I keep getting the same lie for an answer." He bent to brush his lips over hers, a tender kiss that stirred something warm inside her. "I got coffee from downstairs. As soon as you get ready, we'll go get something to eat."

Krystal touched her fingertips to her lips, the tingling sensation setting off a stream of memories, the memories that she'd clung to during the long quiet times she'd spent sitting next to her mother's bed. "No room service?"

He lifted her hand to his lips with a smile, kissing the fingertip she'd touched to her lips before brushing his lips over hers again. "Feels good, doesn't it?" Straightening to his full height of six feet two inches, just an inch shorter than Rafe, he braced his hands on his hips and smiled down at her. "I didn't order room service because I didn't want them knocking and waking you up."

Krystal slid out of bed, looking down at herself in surprise. "What am I wearing?"

Linc grinned and went to the small table by the window and poured her a cup from a thermal carafe. "My T-shirt. I have to say it never looked that good on me." Sipping at his own coffee, he dropped into one of the chairs.

Shaking her head, Krystal smiled, the warm feeling spreading as she approached him. "You always say that."

Lowering the cup, he regarded her steadily, the green in his hazel eyes prominent. "So you haven't forgotten. I'd begun to wonder."

Conscious of the fact that she wore nothing except an overlarge T-shirt that came almost to her knees, Krystal added cream and sugar to her own coffee, her hands shaking. "I remember everything. It was a wonderful time in my life."

Reaching out, Linc ran a fingertip down her arm, his gaze on her breasts making her nipples tingle. "For all of us. I can't wait to get back to it."

"Stop. It's been too long." Pulling away, she crossed her arms over her chest, trying to ignore his smug smile. "You and Rafe don't seem to be listening to me. I'm not that person anymore. I don't even know if I can be."

He picked up his cup again, his eyes sharp. "None of us are the same people we were three years ago, Krystal. You've had a hard time of it, and Rafe and I figured out just how much you mean to us. We'll give you time, but we're not letting you keep putting distance between us anymore."

"I'm sure you've dated other—"

"No. We haven't. We knew as soon as we left that you meant more to us than we'd suspected. There was no other woman for us."

"Things are different now."

"Of course they are. Drink your coffee."

She smiled and obeyed him, moaning in pleasure at the delicious brew. "This is so much better than hospital and nursing home coffee." She took another sip, and eyed him steadily, uncomfortably aware of how awful she looked while he'd grown more handsome. "Tell me the truth. Why are you here?"

Linc set his coffee aside, took hers from her, and set it on the table and pulled her onto his lap, all in one movement. "Because we love you, Krystal. More than we thought as it turns out."

Tears burned her eyes, the feel of being in his arms so good she couldn't resist leaning in. "You shouldn't have come. I need to get over you."

"Like hell." Leaning her back over his arm, he took her mouth with his, deepening his kiss almost immediately, the taste of him so familiar it brought a lump to her throat.

When he slid a hand under her borrowed T-shirt to caress her bottom, she moaned at the pleasure of having his touch and having him wrapped around her.

Her nipples burned against his chest, the warmth of his body against hers seeping deep into her soul—something she couldn't allow.

"No!" Overwhelmed, she broke free and jumped to her feet.

She'd always melted in their arms, but the sharp need from a kiss and a light caress sent her senses reeling.

Crossing her arms over her chest, she shook her head. "This isn't a good idea. It's stupid."

Linc reached for his coffee again, a faint smile tugging at his lips while his gaze sharpened. "There's something wrong with me kissing you?"

"Yes." She picked up her coffee, her hand shaking, and moved away, stopping abruptly when Rafe, naked except for a towel wrapped around his hips, emerged from the bathroom.

Running a towel over his wet hair, he glanced from her to Linc and back again, his gaze narrowing. "Problem?"

Lifting her chin, Krystal eyed his chest, finding it even wider and more muscular than it had been three years earlier.

Even then they'd been sexy as hell.

Now they were nothing short of breathtaking.

Stronger, more masculine, and even more intense than the men she'd remembered from three years earlier, Rafe and Linc reminded her just how hard they'd been to resist and why she'd kept them at a distance during their visits.

The slight changes in them only made them sexier—their bodies hardened as much as their masculine determination.

Wrapping her arms around herself, she eyed his chest again and let her gaze drift lower to his flat stomach, a thrill going through her when she saw that his six-pack had become more clearly delineated than she remembered.

When her gaze drifted even lower, she swallowed heavily at the tenting in the towel wrapped around his hips and hurriedly lifted her gaze to his again.

A dark brow went up, his eyes glimmering with a combination of amusement, concern, and desire. "What happened?"

Swallowing heavily, she lifted her chin and, aware of Linc's steady stare, retrieved her coffee. "Linc kissed me."

Dropping the ends of the towel he'd used to dry his hair around his neck, Rafe smiled faintly, his hands going to his hips. "So?"

She found her attention drawn to his hands and then, to her consternation, the tenting again. Stunned by the rush of warmth, she took a hurried sip of her coffee, burning her tongue. "It's not a good idea."

His slow smile did funny things to her stomach, making her body tingle with the awareness that had long been dormant. "It's a hell of an idea. I hope you don't think it's an isolated incident."

He slowly closed the distance between them as if afraid of frightening her and lifted a hand to grip her chin. Lifting her face to his, he studied her features with sharp eyes. "Of course, we want to make love to you, but you're worn out. We're not teenagers who can't control ourselves. We've waited three years for you. Another few days, or weeks, isn't going to matter. But we can't resist touching you every chance we get. We've missed you more than you would believe. What's important is that we're together now. Just rest, and we'll get through this together."

"I appreciate—"

Rafe's eyes hardened dangerously, a look sharper than she remembered. "Yes. We know that you appreciate us coming. We've got it, Krystal. You don't have to keep saying it. Now, why don't you get ready to go out to breakfast? I'm starving. At least that's one hunger I can satisfy now."

* * * *

They ate breakfast in the same restaurant where they'd eaten the night before, but with her stomach in knots, Krystal pushed her plate aside after only eating half of her food.

Beside her, Linc frowned, worried about her weight. "Baby, eat some more."

"I can't. I'm not used to eating so much." She reached for her second glass of orange juice and drained it. "This is delicious, though. I'll be so glad when tomorrow's over. It's a huge relief that they could arrange it so quickly."

Linc nodded, offering her a strip of bacon, irritated that she shook her head in refusal.

The realization that her stomach had probably shrunk due to not having enough to eat hit him hard, and he couldn't help but wonder how long it had been going on.

Or what else she'd been keeping from them.

He glanced at Rafe, unsurprised to see that he looked equally pissed off.

Not wanting to upset her, he cut into his pancakes. "I saw that you'd hung up a black dress to wear tomorrow. Are you sure you don't need anything else out of the other suitcases?"

Sipping coffee, she shook her head. "No. All of the clothes in there need to be washed. I used the laundromat in the shopping center next door, but I haven't had a chance to do any laundry for a while."

Linc pictured the area in his mind, the result pissing him off even more. "That shopping center might be what you would call *next door*, but it's about a half-mile away from the nursing home."

Rafe set his coffee mug on the table with more force than necessary. "And along a busy street. You fucking *walked* there dragging a suitcase?"

Krystal shrugged. "I never went during rush hour. I usually went when my mother was being bathed and settled for her afternoon nap. I only went a few times. I'm afraid that's why the wheels on my luggage are a little worn. That parking lot could use some work."

Linc bit back a curse. "They're more than a little worn, Krystal. They're destroyed. You would have had to carry them instead of pulling them." With a sigh, he reached for his own coffee mug, furious at the mental image of her trying to carry such heavy cases. "Don't worry about it. We can do laundry when we get home. Do you have enough to wear until then?"

"Yes. I have everything I need."

Linc shared another look with Rafe but said nothing. She had no toiletries at all and had been using the things offered by the hotel and the small amount of toiletries he and Rafe had brought with them.

When they got back to Desire, they'd get her the things she needed, and when she felt better, she could pick out things of her own.

Noticing that her eyes had begun to droop, they finished their breakfast and went back to the hotel.

Walking through the lobby, he kept his arm around her, furious that she'd already become pale and listless again. "You haven't mentioned your brother. Does he know that the funeral's tomorrow?"

Krystal sighed, leaning heavily against him. "I don't know where he is. Maggie, the nurse at the nursing facility, tried to call him, but the last number he gave me has been disconnected."

Neither Linc nor Rafe cared for her brother, and after they realized that Kevin had left Krystal to deal with her parents on her own, they outright disliked him.

They made their way up to the room, and it didn't surprise Linc that Krystal kicked off her shoes and stumbled to the bed. "My head hurts. I think I'll lie down for a little while."

Linc removed his boots and stretched out beside her, pulling the light blanket over her. "That's good, baby. You need to rest."

Although he'd never watched much television, he turned it on, keeping the volume on low in the hopes that the low sound of it and the hum of the air conditioner would lull her to sleep.

Rafe sat and removed his boots, running a hand over Krystal's arm as he stretched out on the other side of her.

Both of them sat propped up by pillows with their legs stretched out in front of them, watching an old western that Linc had seen at least a dozen times.

They both watched her more than they watched the movie, and Linc breathed a sigh of relief when Krystal fell asleep almost immediately.

Not used to being cooped up for so long, Linc started to get cabin fever, but making sure Krystal got the rest she needed took precedence over everything else.

He knew the funeral would be rough on her and couldn't wait until it was over and they could get her home where he and Rafe could watch over her, get her to rest, and spoil her the way they both desperately wanted to.

And they could finally begin their lives together.

He stared at the television screen without really seeing it, his mind on the days ahead.

Krystal's response to his kiss had been even more passionate than in the past and had a desperation to it that told him just how much she'd missed him.

The months of loneliness had taken a toll on her, and he vowed to himself that she would never feel that loneliness again.

He smiled to himself at the thought of her in Desire, the knowledge that she would have friends and people looking out for her even when he and Rafe weren't with her filling him with satisfaction.

They could build a good life together there—a life filled with love and laughter.

They could start a family and set down roots.

They could be happy and make her happy.

If she'd only give them the chance.

She'd only slept about an hour when she woke suddenly with a jolt and a gasp. "Mom."

He and Rafe both sat up abruptly, reaching for her.

Linc caught her to him, alarmed that her entire body shook. "Hey. You're okay."

Because he was holding her, he felt her shuddering breath, the sob accompanying it like a stab to his heart. Rubbing her back, he held her close, irritated to find that all of her muscles had tensed. "You're okay, baby."

She leaned into him as he worked at the tight muscles in her back, slumping against him for several minutes before straightening. "I'm sorry. I need to get up."

She spent the day restless, but sluggish, running a hand over her dress several times as if checking for wrinkles. She laid out a pair of black heels and pantyhose, along with a bra and panties that she folded and refolded several times during the day.

They ate lunch at the hotel restaurant, where she picked at a salad, moving it around more than eating it.

Linc and Rafe tried to get her involved in conversation several times, but she didn't seem to want to talk, not even when they talked about Desire and her new home.

She quietly stared at the wall or out the window of their hotel room, apparently lost in her own thoughts.

With the funeral scheduled for the next morning, they gave her space, irritated and worried about the small amount they could get her to eat but promising themselves that things would be different when they got back to Oklahoma.

* * * *

Afraid she would oversleep, Krystal lay awake, staring at the ceiling, not wanting to move so that she didn't wake Rafe or Linc, who lay on either side of her.

She'd forgotten what it felt like to feel warm and safe and had to keep reminding herself that she couldn't allow herself to get used to it.

Linc and Rafe wanted the woman she'd been in the past and wouldn't believe her when she said that woman no longer existed.

Despite their claims, Krystal knew Linc and Rafe wanted to resume the carefree and fun affair they'd had in the past, and she couldn't imagine ever being that woman again.

She couldn't remember the last time she'd laughed or cried or gotten excited about anything.

She felt numb, watched the world around her from a distance, and felt as if she was no longer a part of it.

Physically and mentally exhausted, she just wanted to sleep and forget everything, but Rafe and Linc's reappearance into her life made it impossible.

Memories of the good times they'd had in the past made her yearn for another chance with them, but she dreaded the inevitable end.

She couldn't relive the pain of saying good-bye to them.

She felt as if she was barely hanging on by a thread and just wanted to curl into a ball and sleep forever.

Their presence made her wish things could have been different.

They made her want more.

By the time the sun rose, her eyes had become gritty, but her mind wouldn't settle enough for her to sleep.

Today, she had to bury her mother.

And try again to get through to Rafe and Linc.

No matter how hard she tried, she didn't have the strength to fight her growing love for them, a love that had grown through the years and that held more substance and depth than it had in the past.

She was very much afraid that allowing herself to sink deeper would end in a heartache she might never survive.

* * * *

Aware that Rafe and Linc watched her closely, Krystal showered and dressed between sips of coffee they'd ordered from room service.

Rafe handed her a triangle of buttered toast. "Eat this. Your stomach must be churning. We'll get something to eat afterward."

She nibbled at the toast, more to ease her burning stomach and avoid an argument with him than because she wanted it. "I don't think going to Desire with you is a good idea."

"That's okay." Rafe slid a hand down her back, bending to kiss her hair, which she'd put up in a knot. "We do. You're coming with us, Krystal."

"I think we should talk about this."

Linc rose and handed her another triangle of toast. "We did it your way. Now we're going to do it our way."

Frustrated, with both alarm and excitement warring within her, Krystal took another bite of toast and washed it down with the glass of orange juice they'd ordered. "I think you're going to regret it."

"Where would you go if you didn't come with us?" Linc bit into another piece of toast, his gaze steady on hers as he chewed it.

Krystal shrugged and finished her toast before reaching for the orange juice. "I was going to get on a bus and head east. I'd planned to stop when I found a place I'd like." She gulped the juice, savoring the taste.

Closing the distance between them, Linc wrapped an arm around her. "So you didn't have any concrete plans?"

"I just want to get away."

"Then come with us." Rafe took her hand in his. "It's a good place for you to rest and recuperate. If you're not happy, we'll take you wherever you want to go." Rafe took her empty glass from her and slammed it on the table. "But I'll be damned if we're gonna let you push us away anymore."

Eyeing each of them, she sighed. "I don't remember the two of you being so hard-headed."

Linc smiled and took the paper cover from another glass of juice. Handing it to her, he touched his lips to hers. "We prefer to think of ourselves as *determined*."

After gulping down more of the cold, fresh juice, she wiped her mouth. "We're going to be late."

Rafe met her gaze in the mirror as he finished tying his tie, a muscle working in his jaw. "No, baby. We're not gonna be late."

"Do you know where the cemetery is?"

Turning, he faced her, the sharpness in his eyes softening slightly. "I've already put it in the GPS. Let us worry about things for a while. Okay?"

Nodding, Krystal slipped on her shoes and went back to the table to pick up her small black clutch, her hands shaking so badly that she immediately dropped it.

She started to bend to pick it up, her body stiff and protesting the movement, but Linc beat her to it. Accepting it from him, she nodded, unable to work up even a semblance of a smile. "Thank you."

"You're welcome." Lifting her chin, he searched her eyes. "Still have that headache, don't you?"

She nodded again, immediately regretting it. "A little."

It felt like a spike stabbed her head every time she moved it—the aspirin she'd taken for it barely touching it.

Knowing nerves had triggered it, Krystal resigned herself to the fact that she would have it for a while, hoping that it would go away after the funeral.

Both men looked handsome in their suits, their serious expressions and concern in their eyes reflecting the gravity of the situation.

She sighed, wishing she could just crawl back into bed. "You even brought suits. You knew you were going to stay for the funeral."

Rafe smiled faintly, but she had the feeling that he was angry about something. "Of course we were going to stay for your mother's funeral, Krystal. We wouldn't leave you to face it alone. Are you ready to go?"

* * * *

Rafe held on to his temper for Krystal's sake, but he desperately wanted to hit something.

Krystal had spent the entire night twisting and turning in her sleep, and she'd woken in the early morning darkness to stare up at the ceiling.

He hadn't spoken or even moved, willing her to go back to sleep, but she hadn't, and when he'd gotten up at sunrise, she'd scrambled out of bed right behind him and disappeared into the bathroom.

He wasn't at all surprised that she had a killer headache.

They stopped at the store in the lobby, and he bought her a pair of sunglasses, her silent acquiescence telling him just how badly her head hurt.

They drove to the cemetery in silence, with Krystal sitting absolutely still the entire drive. She'd dropped her head back to the headrest and kept her eyes closed the entire trip.

Krystal hadn't wanted a viewing because she said that no one would attend, but he hadn't quite believed it.

Now he did.

Only the minister stood at the graveside, and as they parked the car, he saw that the nurse who'd been with Krystal when they'd arrived pulled in behind them.

The three of them quietly greeted the minister and Maggie but then remained silent and stared at the coffin.

Rafe stood on one side of Krystal while Linc stood on the other, their dark glasses hiding their eyes.

When another car pulled up, Rafe stiffened, watching out of the corner of his eye as Krystal's brother, Kevin, got out.

Wearing torn jeans, muddy boots, and a dirty white T-shirt, Kevin approached, stilling briefly when he recognized Rafe and Linc before determinedly continuing toward Krystal.

Rafe shifted his stance slightly, his hated and mistrust of Krystal's brother putting him on guard.

The other man stood almost Linc's height, but he'd lost a lot of weight in the time since Rafe had last seen him.

He and Linc both strongly suspected that Kevin had lost the weight because of the drugs he took, and Rafe could see that even now they flowed through his system.

They both knew that Krystal's brother had always done whatever it took to get money for his habit and had moved frequently in an effort to stay one step ahead of the law.

He didn't care at all if he was her brother. He didn't want the other man anywhere near Krystal.

Hiding a smile when Kevin glared at him for not moving away from Krystal to let Kevin stand beside her, Rafe kept a sharp eye on him as the minister finished the brief service.

He glanced at Maggie, surprised to see that Kevin's appearance seemed to anger her and that she kept looking protectively at Krystal.

As soon as the minister finished, Kevin abruptly walked behind Rafe and approached his sister from behind. "Can we talk?"

Rafe had already turned to face her, as had Linc, both men hovering protectively over her.

Krystal gave her brother an emotionless look before turning back to thank the minister and Maggie.

Both Rafe and Linc also thanked them for coming, and Rafe took the time to thank Maggie for all she'd done for Krystal and her mother, all the while aware of Kevin's impatience.

Kevin didn't bother to even address the minister or Maggie, shifting restlessly behind Krystal until she turned away and started back toward the car, rubbing her forehead.

Rafe shared a look with Linc as they walked on either side and slightly behind her, staying close but reluctantly giving her a chance to talk to her brother.

Krystal glanced back at each of them as if comforted by their presence as she slowly walked toward the car. "I'm surprised to see you, Kevin."

Kevin scraped a hand through his overlong and dirty hair. "What are these guys doing here? I thought they moved to that town in Oklahoma where all those weirdos live."

Rafe raised a brow at that. "The town's called Desire, and we don't allow *weirdos* in our town."

Kevin stiffened, the warning in Rafe's tone apparently getting through to him.

Krystal sighed, her shoulders slumping. "We haven't seen you in months, Kevin, and the number you left was disconnected. How did you know Mom had died?"

Walking slightly in front of Rafe, Kevin glanced back at him over his shoulder, his nervous look filling Rafe with satisfaction. Focusing on Krystal again, Kevin shrugged. "I figured you'd used the same funeral home you used with dad. I just checked their website every day for obituaries."

Wrapping her arms around herself as if chilled despite the warm day, Krystal glanced at her brother. "Mom wanted to see you. She kept asking about you."

"Yeah, well, I've been a little busy. I have a life, you know."

Rafe lifted a brow when Krystal didn't respond to that but then saw how pale she'd become.

Krystal kept moving toward the car, her movements even more sluggish than earlier. "Why are you here, Kevin?"

"Now that Mom's gone, we need to split the money."

"There *is* no money, Kevin."

He stopped abruptly and turned toward her, grabbing her arm. "What do you mean there's no money? We have the house to sell."

Rafe gripped Kevin's wrist, squeezing and holding the other man's gaze until he released his grip on Krystal.

Krystal pulled her arm back and slumped against Linc when his stone-faced friend slid an arm around her waist from behind. "I had to sell the house, Kevin. How do you think I paid for the funeral? Mom had to use all of her assets to pay for the nursing home until the money ran out. That's when the government took over her bills."

Kevin's eyes went wide. "The money's gone? You stupid bitch!"

Because he was watching Kevin's body language, Rafe anticipated the other man's intention, whipping a hand out to grip Kevin's wrist before the other man could grab Krystal's arm again. "I wouldn't."

Kevin tried to pull away, but Rafe held firm. "This is none of your business!"

He watched Linc wrap a protective arm around Krystal and lead her to their rental car but kept his tone low so as not to upset her any further. "That's where you're mistaken. Anything that involves Krystal is very much our business."

"I need that fucking money!"

Rafe's earlier anger came back in full force, the threat to Krystal enraging him and bringing all of his protective instincts to the surface.

"It wasn't your money, and your mother needed it for her care. But you wouldn't care about that, would you?"

Releasing Kevin's wrist, he gripped him by the front of his T-shirt and lifted him to his toes, fully aware that the drugs in Kevin's system could make him stronger and very unpredictable. "Do you know that your sister was homeless? Do you know that she's been sleeping in a fucking chair in the nursing home next to your mother's bed?"

Kevin looked surprised, but not concerned at that piece of information. "What happened to her apartment?"

"She lost it when she gave up her job to be with your mother."

The other man shrugged, glancing toward the car. "That was her choice."

Rafe smiled coldly, not bothering to hide his hatred as he released Krystal's brother. "Yes, it was. And now she's coming home with us. If I were you, I wouldn't get within a hundred miles of Desire, Oklahoma. Are we clear?"

Kevin's eyes filled with rage. "You're not going to keep me from my sister."

Rafe pulled a card from his pocket. "Here's my number. If you want to see your sister, or talk to her, you have to go through me."

Kevin looked down at the card and paled. "It says here that you're a deputy. You're still a cop?"

"I am, and so is Linc. We both love your sister, and we're taking her home with us. She's been through enough, and we'll do everything in our power to keep her from getting hurt again."

Leaning close, he gripped the front of Kevin's T-shirt again. "Even from you. Keep your drugs and your problems away from her."

Kevin lifted his chin in a show of drug-induced bravado. "Or what?"

Rafe smiled coldly, wishing the other man would come at him so he could get rid of some of his pent-up anger. "Or you won't like the consequences. I'll very much enjoy beating the hell out of you."

Chapter Five

After leaving the cemetery, they stopped at the hotel only long enough to change into comfortable clothes, retrieve their luggage, and check out, with Krystal walking beside them as if in a daze.

She didn't speak and had drawn into herself again, frustrating Linc by closing them out.

At least she wasn't arguing with them anymore, and hopefully they could get her to Desire without incident.

They'd had to help her change her clothes when she stared down at the pile of comfortable clothing already laid out for her as if the process of dressing seemed too much for her.

They'd stopped at the hotel restaurant, where they'd gotten her to eat a bowl of soup and some crackers, hoping to settle her stomach.

"Gracie's chicken soup is much better, and the chicken and dumplings at the diner is to die for." Linc rubbed her back again, glancing at Rafe, who looked just as concerned as he felt.

Krystal nodded, giving him another distant smile.

Wrapping her hands around the cup of tea Rafe had poured for her, she sat quietly, staring across the table at Rafe's plate.

Watching her, Rafe lifted his cheeseburger to her lips, looking pleased when she took a small bite.

He managed to get three small bites into her before she turned away again, staring down into her cup of tea.

Ignoring his offer of a French fry, she sipped her tea and wrapped her hands around the small clutch she held on her lap.

When they got up to leave, she allowed Linc to take her hand and lead her outside while Rafe took care of the check.

She got in when he opened the front passenger door for her, staring out the window as he slid into the driver's seat.

He met Rafe's scowl in the rearview mirror before reaching out to cover the hands she kept clasped on her lap, irritated to find them cold again. "Are you sure you're okay? Are you comfortable?"

She nodded again, not speaking, and dropped her head back against the headrest.

Once at the airport, Rafe kept her hand in his while they turned in the rental car and made their way to the terminal.

She didn't show any interest in anything as they got onto the plane, putting her head back and closing her eyes almost immediately.

She walked when they led her and sat when they told her to, going through the motions with a blank look on her pale face, her eyes drooping.

Linc covered her with a sweater they'd taken from her suitcase, noting that she'd paled even more.

Sitting in the seat between them on the plane, she dozed briefly, only to wake with a start.

"Easy, baby." Wrapping an arm around her while reaching under the sweater to take one of her cold hands in his, Linc pulled her against him. "Go to sleep. Rafe and I are here. It's safe to sleep."

"I can't believe she's gone."

Relieved that she'd spoken, he met Rafe's gaze over her head. "I know, baby. Everything'll be all right. Once we get home and you get some rest, we can settle down."

"I knew she didn't have long. I thought I was ready. Why wasn't I ready?"

The confusion and lost little girl in her voice tightened Linc's gut. "You've had a lot to deal with. You're exhausted. Worn out and running on fumes. You need to recharge and get used to us again and your new home."

She sighed, her shoulders slumped as if the weight of the world rested on them. "I can't make any promises. Right now, I just feel so empty. I feel like I need to be doing something. The trouble is, right now, I'm too tired to figure out what I need to do."

"You don't need to do anything right now except come home with us where you belong. You need to rest. Eat. Get strong again. Learn your new home and make new friends. Good friends." He pressed his lips to her hair, lifting her hand slightly to play with her fingers.

Thinking about the changes she would want to make in her new home—the changes that would make their house feel like a real home—he smiled. "We need your help with a few things as soon as you feel up to it."

Lifting her head, she stared up at him, looking more alert than she had since that morning. "What do you need me to do?"

Unable to resist, he touched her lips with his and straightened again, pleased that she showed interest. "Rafe and I moved to Desire because we could live the way we want to with you there."

"People really have more than one lover there?"

Inclining his head, Linc smiled. "And more than one husband. You'll meet them. It's a small town where everyone looks out for everyone else."

Rafe took her other hand in his. "And the men look after *all* of the women."

Krystal frowned. "I don't understand."

Rafe lifted her hand to his lips and frowned before tucking her hand between both of his, probably to warm it. "It means that when Linc and I aren't around, the other men in town will know who you belong to and will watch over you. If you're ever scared or lost or whatever, you can go to someone else and they'll help you."

"Why would I be scared? Is it a big town?" Krystal frowned, trying to remember what they'd told her about their new home.

She couldn't remember anything other than that they'd taken jobs as deputies.

Shaking her head, she accepted the bottle of water from Linc. "I never expected to go to Desire with you, so I never listened when you talked about it. I didn't want to imagine myself there. I kept waiting for a month to go by when neither one of you showed up."

She took a deep breath and blew it out in a rush. "Every time one of you left, I assumed it was the last time I'd ever see you. Why didn't you find someone else?"

Linc smiled and bent to touch his lips to her forehead. "There is no one else. Just you. Now I know why you always looked so surprised when I went to see you."

Krystal turned to Rafe, unsurprised that he watched her, his expression unreadable. "How about you?"

Rafe blinked, one dark brow going up. "What about me?"

"Are you happy there?"

With a smile, he slid his hand to her thigh. "I will be now."

The warmth of his firm hand on her thigh sent heat all the way to her slit, and she found she had to fight not to shift in her seat. "I can't believe you found a place like that."

Rafe patted her thigh and dropped his head back. "Since neither one of us was willing to give you up, we looked online for a place where we could live openly in a ménage relationship—a place where you wouldn't feel embarrassed that you had two lovers. We found Desire and went to check it out. We were very impressed with the small-town atmosphere and the way men looked out for their women there. We liked the sheriff and his dedication."

Sitting up again, he smiled. "He was impressed with our records, but when we were interviewing for the job, he asked us point-blank what we felt about ménage relationships. When we told him that we were involved in one, he hired us on the spot. Told us he wouldn't hire anyone who had any prejudices against ménages or other sorts of relationships. He doesn't want any trouble in *his* town."

The combination of nerves and excitement made her head start hurting again. "I don't think you've thought this through. You can't move to another city—another *state*—and plan for a new life when you don't know what's going to happen."

Linc smiled. "We knew exactly what was gonna happen, Krystal. Within a week of leaving California, we knew that you were the woman for us, but we knew we had to wait for you. We knew how nervous you got every time we went out together and that you were worried about what people would think about you having two men in your life. We found a place where we could make a home and waited for you."

"I don't think we should rush into anything."

Rafe sighed. "We waited three years for you, Krystal. That's far from rushing. We've had plenty of time to think about what we want, and we know it's you."

Linc took the bottle of water from her when she finished drinking and recapped it. "Look, we're not gonna rush you into anything. Take your time. Rest. Heal. Get your bearings. In the meantime, we're going to prove to you that you love us, and that we belong together."

Wrapping her hands together in her sweater, Krystal dropped her head back, suddenly exhausted again, the lingering headache now throbbing. "After all you've done for me, the last thing I want to do is hurt you."

Linc reached into his pocket for the small tin of aspirin and offered her two and her water again. "You can stay with us while you figure out how you feel and what you want to do. We want you with us, and we're sure as hell not leaving you to your own devices. You're too vulnerable for that right now. We know you can't make any decisions about your future just yet, Krystal. Take the time you need to figure it out."

Grateful, Krystal accepted them and washed them down before handing the bottle of water back to him and once again dropping her head back. "Thanks." Remembering something he'd said, she lifted her head again. "You said that you needed my help with something."

Linc grinned and recapped her water. "When we realized that Desire was the kind of place we wanted to build a life, and a place where you could be happy, we applied for jobs there, and when we got them, we bought a house."

Blinking, Krystal glanced at Rafe, who nodded. "You bought a house? I pictured you living in an apartment or something."

Rafe shrugged and sat up to readjust her sweater over her shoulders. "No apartments in Desire. Anyway, there are three brothers, the Prestons, who design and make custom furniture. We bought a bed and other furniture for the master bedroom so it would be there when we finally got you home. Lookin' forward to using it."

Krystal tried to ignore the warm rush at the word *home*. "I don't understand. What do you need my help with?"

Linc slid a hand under the end of her sweater to take her hand in his. "The rest of the furniture. We have a card table and folding chairs for a kitchen table and two recliners and a television in the living room. Twin beds in each of our bedrooms—our *old* bedrooms—and dressers. Other than that, we didn't pick out any furniture because we wanted you to pick it out. The recliners can go along with the furniture in the bedrooms. We bought something cheap just to get by, and it's outlived its usefulness."

"I don't understand why you want *me* to pick stuff out."

"Because we want you to feel as if it's your home. We picked out the house, so the rest is up to you. That is, after you get some rest."

Just thinking about it exhausted her. "I can help you pick some things out in a day or two."

Rafe chuckled and dropped his head back again and closed his eyes. "There's no hurry. We've lived with it the way it is for a long time. Something tells me you'll be dying to go get stuff in a day or two."

Following his lead, she dropped her head back and let her eyes flutter closed, trying to picture buying furniture with them.

Her mind wandered to thoughts of her mother, and then to Kevin.

He'd looked tired and stressed.

And high again.

Not wanting to think about it, she let her mind drift, trying to imagine a town where women freely had more than one husband.

At Linc's urging, she laid her head on his shoulder and tried to imagine herself living in the town they'd described.

For the life of her, she couldn't quite imagine such a place.

Warmed by their presence, she relished the feeling of security of having both of them on either side of her and let herself fall asleep.

She woke suddenly to Linc pressing a kiss against her ear. "Wake up, baby. We're here."

They made their way through the airport with impressive speed, and before she knew it, she sat in the front passenger seat of a large SUV while Linc and Rafe stowed their luggage in the back.

When Rafe slid into the driver's seat, she turned to him with a smile, relieved that her headache was gone. "I can't believe it's dark, but this morning seems like a lifetime ago."

He smiled faintly and started the engine. "Yeah. It's been a long day. We'll stop and have dinner, and then we'll head home."

Home.

Her pulse tripped at the thought of it. "I am getting hungry."

Her stomach growled as if to emphasize her claim.

Rafe grinned as if she'd done something fantastic. "That's great. What kind of food do you have a taste for?"

Krystal smiled again. "I know you probably want something more substantial, but I'm dying for pizza. I can't even remember the last time I had a slice."

Rafe inclined his head and put the SUV in gear. "I know the perfect place."

Within ten minutes, he pulled into the parking lot of a small Italian restaurant, and once inside, she paused, closing her eyes and breathing in the delicious smells. "God, that's incredible." She flattened a hand over her stomach when it growled again. "I'm suddenly starving."

A jovial older man approached, not much taller than Krystal. "Linc! Rafe! I haven't seen you in—"

He stopped abruptly, his jaw dropping. "Well, hello."

Rafe slid an arm around Krystal's shoulder. "Tony, this is Krystal. She's dying for pizza."

Tony wiped his hands on the apron wrapped around his round belly and offered a hand with another grin. "Hello, Krystal. It's so nice to meet you. You've come to the right place. I make the best pizza in Oklahoma—really the best anywhere—but I don't want to brag."

Krystal smiled, enjoying his accent and amused by his claim. "I'm dying for some."

Rafe's hand slid to her back. "Since when do you not brag?"

Once they were seated in a booth, she looked around, unsurprised that the place was packed. "Is Desire far?"

Linc waited until the waitress finished delivering a pitcher of beer and three glasses and started to pour. "No. You'll learn Tulsa soon enough. People shop here for what they can't get in Desire."

Rafe smiled at the waitress in thanks for the breadsticks she brought and handed Krystal one of the menus. "Which is an increasingly short list. A lot of new stores keep opening in Desire. What kind of pizza do you want?"

"Just plain cheese." She handed the menu back to him and reached for her glass. "Do you know how long it's been since I had a beer?"

Linc grinned and took a sip of his own beer. "Three years?"

She took a sip, a moan escaping at her taste of the ice-cold brew. "So good. It's going to go perfectly with my pizza." She glanced at each of them, pleased to see they seemed a little more relaxed.

Dressed again in jeans and T-shirts, they seemed more comfortable than they had in California.

She took another sip and accepted the breadstick Rafe offered. "Tell me more about the town."

She listened, fascinated as they told her about several of the people who lived in Desire, people who were obviously their friends.

Frowning, she tried to remember the names of the people they mentioned. "So Clay and Rio are brothers who share a wife? Boone and Chase are brothers who share a wife? The Prestons who made the furniture are *three* brothers who share a wife?"

Rafe inclined his head and sat back as the waitress arrived with their food. "Yes."

"Good God. The poor woman."

Linc choked on his beer. "*Poor* woman? Jared, Duncan, and Reese worship the ground Erin walks on and spoil her rotten."

Rafe grinned. "I can't think of anyone in Desire that that doesn't apply to."

Krystal pulled a slice of pizza free from the tray, her mouth watering. "Are all the men who share wives brothers?"

Rafe picked up his fork and dug into his lasagna. "Of course not."

Krystal blew on her slice to cool it, glancing at Rafe. "Why—of course not? I've never heard of a town like this before. I have no idea what's normal there."

Linc shrugged and dug into his seafood dish. "Some are friends, like King and Royce, who are married to Brenna, and Dillon and Ryder, who are married to Alison."

Rafe met Linc's gaze. "Some not quite so friendly, like Jake and Hoyt."

Linc swallowed his bite of food and reached for his beer. "They're getting closer. It was rough for a while, though." He turned to Krystal. "Nat was already married to Jake but had a history with Hoyt. Jake and Hoyt were best friends. When Hoyt retired from the Navy, he wanted Nat back. Nat's the mother of Hoyt's son, and they were together years ago. Jake was in love with Nat but didn't want to intrude on Hoyt's relationship with her. When Hoyt joined the Navy, Nat didn't want to go with him because she'd learned that she was pregnant. She didn't want to leave home and wanted to stay close to her sister, Jesse."

Krystal frowned, searching her memory. "Clay and Rio's wife?"

"Yes." Linc smiled, clearly pleased that she'd remembered. "Hoyt had to leave, and Nat refused to, so Jake stepped in, married Nat, and they've been married for years."

Pleased that she'd been able to keep up, Krystal took another bite of the incredible pizza. "But Hoyt's back in the picture again?"

Rafe nodded and scooped another bite of lasagna. "Even though Nat loves Jake like crazy, she's never fallen out of love with Hoyt, who used to come home on leave to visit his son, Nat, and Jake. Hoyt remained friends with Jake, but he was still in love with Nat. When he retired, he told Jake he was coming to get her back."

Finding herself intrigued after months of numbness, she paused with the slice of pizza halfway to her mouth. "Jake was all right with that?"

Rafe swallowed and sat back with a sigh. "I think Jake always suspected that Hoyt would want Nat back one day, which was why he moved them to Desire in the first place. He also didn't want Nat to always wonder about another man. She loves him, but I think he was worried about putting her in a position to choose. Sharing her is a hell of a lot better than losing her. This way, everyone's happy."

Krystal couldn't help but wonder.

Linc set down his fork and reached for his beer again. "Lucas, Devlin, and Caleb are friends, and they just married Stormy."

Krystal picked at a piece of cheese. "So every woman in town has more than one husband?"

Stabbing another bite of seafood and pasta, Linc smiled. "No. Some have only one. The important thing is that no one judges. Here, have a bite."

Krystal leaned forward, her gaze caught in his. She opened her mouth, her pulse tripping when his eyes narrowed and darkened. Taking food into her mouth, she stared into his eyes, stunned by the fluttering in her stomach.

After slipping the fork free, he bent to touch his lips to hers. "You're right. You have changed."

Krystal swallowed the bite of shrimp and pasta, almost choking on it. Reaching for her beer, she blinked back tears. "I knew it. Look, I—"

Wrapping an arm around her waist, Linc yanked her closer. "You're even sweeter, something I hadn't thought possible, and there's a maturity to you now that wasn't there before. There's a passion inside you that makes me want to take a bite out of you."

Krystal sucked in a breath, a moan escaping when his other hand slid to her thigh. "Linc."

Lifting his hand, he gripped her chin and tilted her face to his. "Do you know how long I've waited to hear you say my name like that?" He touched his lips to hers and nibbled at her bottom lip, breaking away with a curse. "Christ. Not the time nor the place. Eat your pizza."

Krystal looked over to see Rafe sitting back in his seat, quietly sipping his beer and smiling. "What's so amusing?"

Rafe set his beer down and reached for her, pulling her closer to him. "I want one."

Their attention and the beer she'd had made her giddy. A giggle escaped before she could prevent it. "One what?"

Gripping her chin as Linc had, he stared into her eyes. "One of your kisses."

Laying a hand on his chest, Krystal smiled and leaned forward. "Just one. We're in public, you know. People are going to stare."

Rafe bent closer. "They're used to seeing people from Desire. I want your mouth."

She parted her lips in expectation. "And I want yours."

She barely got the words out before he took her mouth with his in a brief kiss that made her head swim.

Straightening abruptly, Rafe cursed under his breath, his heart pounding nearly out of his chest. "Christ, you're right. We can't do this here. I'm trying to be tender with you, and I want to shove these dishes aside and take you right here on this table."

With another soft giggle, a sound that made his chest swell, Krystal slumped against him, meeting Linc's smile. "I sure as hell hope you two aren't making a mistake."

Linc gestured toward the remaining pizza. "Finish your pizza so we can get you home. You're beat."

"I couldn't eat another bite."

Rafe smiled when Krystal finished her beer and yawned, pleased that she had a full stomach and the beer had relaxed her.

He wanted her to get a good night's sleep and willed his cock to behave.

She'd just buried her mother that morning and had been whisked out of that life and swept into a new one she would have to adjust to.

To his delight, she fell asleep less than five minutes after they got back into the SUV and started for home and was still asleep when they pulled into the driveway.

He carried her into the house, his chest swelling at the thought of finally having her home. He carried her straight to the master bedroom, a bedroom they'd furnished but never used, grateful that they'd taken the time to put fresh linens on the bed before they'd left the house.

She barely stirred as he stripped her out of her jeans, shirt, and sweater while Linc dealt with her shoes and socks.

After removing her bra, he tucked her into one of his T-shirts and settled her into the center of the bed, pulling the covers over her before straightening.

He and Linc stared down at her for several minutes, the sight of her bundled into the bed they'd bought to share with her bringing a lump to his throat.

Linc blew out a breath. "Christ, I thought this day would never come."

"Yeah, well, it's here, and I don't want to blow it. Let's get the luggage."

"I'll get it. Stay here with her. I don't want her to wake up and find herself alone."

The sound of a text coming in had Rafe digging his phone out of his pocket.

See you're home. Everything ok?

Rafe smiled at Ace's text, not at all surprised that Desire's sheriff was the first to know that they were home.

Yes. She's sleeping. Exhausted.

Let me know if you need something. Looking forward to meeting her.

Thanks. How are you doing?

FINE!!!!! Let me know when to schedule you again.

Rafe smiled, understanding his Ace's frustration at constantly being asked how he was after the accident.

Monday. It would give them several days with her together, and then they could slip into a routine.

Staggered?

Yes. Thanks.

He set the phone on his nightstand and slipped off his boots before going into the bathroom and turning on the light, partially closing the door so the light wouldn't wake Krystal. After putting out fresh towels, shampoo, and soap, he went back to her, closing the door almost all the way again, leaving just a small stream of light coming into the room in case Krystal woke during the night.

He smiled at the sight of Linc climbing into bed with her.

Wearing just his boxer briefs, Linc gingerly adjusted his pillow and turned toward her, bracing himself on an elbow and smiling like an idiot as he stared down at her.

Suspecting his smile looked just as ridiculous, Rafe undressed to his boxer briefs and climbed in on the side closest to the bathroom.

He and Linc both slept light, and both had learned how to sleep when they got the chance from their stints in the army.

A peace he hadn't felt in almost three years settled over him, and when she turned toward him, bending a knee and sliding her leg over his, Rafe smiled again in the semi-darkness.

Sliding a hand to her thigh, Rafe closed his eyes and let sleep overtake him.

Chapter Six

Krystal woke to the smell of bacon and sat up, surprised that she'd obviously slept through the night.

She'd been looking forward to seeing the house, but she'd apparently slept through her arrival.

She liked what she could see of it, immediately feeling right at home in the large room.

A stream of sunshine came through a small opening in the blinds at the window, illuminating the room in a warm glow.

Stretching, she looked around, taken in by the beauty of the gleaming furniture.

The huge bed that she slept in, made of the same light wood as the rest of the furniture, had an upholstered headboard that invited her to lean against it.

Smiling to find it even softer and more cushiony than she'd expected, she took a moment to admire the rest of the furniture.

They'd claimed that it was custom, and she believed it.

Two matching chests stood on opposite sides of the large window, while the dresser with the attached mirror had been placed right across from the bed, enabling her to see herself from where she sat.

Studying her reflection, she smiled at the picture she made in the white T-shirt. Not exactly sexy, but it was loose and comfortable.

She faintly remembered being undressed and bundled into the large T-shirt by Rafe, but she'd been so tired she hadn't cared about anything except getting back to sleep.

She couldn't remember when she'd slept so well.

She had more color than she'd had in a long while and felt more energetic than she had in months.

She smiled when her stomach growled.

She was also very hungry.

The open door allowed the delicious smells to reach her, as well as the comforting sounds of Rafe and Linc moving around in the kitchen.

She could hear them speaking in low tones but couldn't quite make out more than a few words—something about a diner and bacon burning.

Smiling at the sound of a deep voice cursing, she shoved the covers aside and got up, grimacing when her stiff body protested.

She'd spent months sitting beside a bed and gotten more out of shape than she would have liked to admit.

Deciding a shower would loosen her up, she looked around for her suitcases but didn't see them anywhere.

Looking back at the bed, she noticed that the pillow she'd slept on lay between two others, each with dents in them, telling her that Linc and Rafe had slept with her again.

She'd slept deeply, as she hadn't in a long time, proving just how much she trusted them.

Wrapping a hand around one of the bedposts at the foot of the bed, she leaned against it and stared at the bed, imagining herself in the middle of the huge, beautiful bed with the men who'd once been her lovers.

She'd missed them so much and had spent the time since her father's diagnosis doing her best to forget about them.

She knew she couldn't expect them to wait indefinitely for her.

But they'd waited three years for her to be free again.

She would forever cherish the time she'd spent with her mother and father when they'd needed her, but she'd lost so much time with Linc and Rafe.

For the first time in a long time, her future lay in front of her.

It excited her as much as it scared her.

Dropping onto the foot of the bed, she held on to the post and laid her head against it, her stomach clenching.

She hadn't even been able to take the time to mourn her father because her mother had needed her.

She'd tried to be strong for her mother, but between working and taking care of her father, she'd already been exhausted.

She didn't remember a time when she wasn't tired.

She hadn't even finished taking care of the paperwork dealing with her father's death when her mother had fallen ill.

Month after month of hospitals, paperwork, and all the work involved in selling her mother's things so she could put the house up for sale all blurred into each other.

Looking back at the enormity of what she'd done staggered her.

She didn't know how she did it, especially after Kevin disappeared.

Now her parents were both gone, and Kevin hadn't seemed to care.

He'd only come for the money.

No hug. No appreciation for what she'd sacrificed.

No apology for not being there to help.

He'd taken off as soon as her father had been diagnosed, which had pissed Rafe and Linc off and had made them hate Kevin even more.

After the incident at the cemetery, she doubted she'd ever see her brother again.

In such a short time, she'd lost her entire family.

She was alone.

Memories of her childhood, when she and Kevin had been close, came back in a rush.

Her parents laughing.

Kissing.

Holidays.

Vacations.

They'd been so happy until the day of her father's diagnosis and their entire world had changed.

Now everyone is gone.

She realized that she was feeling sorry for herself but couldn't help it.

Everything had changed, leaving her feeling bereft, confused, and guilty for feeling a small sense of relief.

Tears started streaming down her face, and once they started, she couldn't stop them.

Her hair draped like a curtain around her face, and she realized suddenly how long it had been since she'd worn her hair in anything other than a ponytail.

She didn't remember the last time she'd had a haircut.

Or painted her nails.

Or been able to cry and be held.

A sob escaped, and then another, the overwhelming sense of loss consuming her.

"What the hell? Hey!"

Rafe scooped her up and sat on the foot of the bed with her in his arms, pressing his lips to her hair as he began to rock her. "Oh, baby. I knew this was coming, but listening to you cry is breaking my heart."

"I'm s-sorry." She tried to push away from him, but Rafe wouldn't let her. "I don't know what happened."

Rafe pressed his chin against the top of her head and continued to rock her. "You haven't cried, baby. Linc and I have been waiting for it, but you've been so used to holding it in that we were getting a little worried. Seems like a good night's sleep and a chance to close down for a little bit is what you needed."

Lifting his head, he gripped her chin and tilted her face to his, wiping tears away with his thumb. "That's it. Let it all out."

She clung to him, burying her face against his chest, soaking his soft T-shirt. "Just leave me alone."

His lips touched the top of her head. "That's something I can't do. You can't go it alone anymore, Krystal, and there's no reason for you to even try. Besides, we won't let you."

Krystal gulped, another sob escaping. "They're all gone. Even Kevin. He didn't even hug me."

"I know." Rafe's voice remained soft but took on an edge. "It's his loss, baby. The drugs have taken over. Linc and I are here for you. We're not going away."

She couldn't stop sobbing, the feel of his warm strength surrounding her bringing on a fresh round of tears. "I know. I'm j-just f-feeling s-sorry for m-myself." She sucked in a shuddering breath and curled into him. "Please just hold me."

"Of course, baby." Hugging her closer, he continued to rock her. "For as long as you want. Just let it all out."

"She okay?" Linc's low voice came from the doorway.

Turning her head from where she rested it on Rafe's shoulder, she met Linc's gaze, sucking in a steadying breath. "I'm fine. J-just stupid."

His smile set off another succession of sobs. "Not stupid at all." Closing the distance between them, he crouched at her knee. "I'm just glad you're finally letting it go."

Sucking in several cleansing breaths, Krystal wiped her eyes. "I didn't cry at the funeral. I didn't cry when she died. I woke up feeling great, and then this happened."

"Do you want to talk about it?"

Shaking her head at Linc's question, she sat up straighter. "No. It just kind of hit me all at once. Can we talk about something else?"

"Of course." Rafe pushed her hair back, smiling as he wiped her tears. "You got a good night's sleep. I'm glad. And I'm glad you felt better when you woke up. It seems the pizza did the trick."

Linc rubbed her thigh. "We cooked breakfast. We thought we heard you moving around, so Rafe came to get you. Are you hungry?"

"I was." She appreciated that they allowed her to change the subject. "The smell of bacon woke me up."

Rafe slid a hand to her belly. "But now your stomach's churning. I'm sure it'll feel better once you start to eat. Nothing heavy. Just scrambled eggs, toast, and bacon." He smiled down at her and pushed her hair back. "I'm afraid that's the extent of our cooking skills."

She smiled as she knew he meant her to. "You must be getting pretty bored with it."

Linc rose, smiling down at her. "I went out to get the ingredients for breakfast this morning. We usually eat at the diner. You know that neither one of us likes to cook, and the diner makes great food."

"I don't mind cooking for you while I'm here."

Rafe and Linc exchanged a look, and she knew it had to do with the idea that she might be leaving, but she felt as if she had to be honest.

Rafe nodded once. "Fine. Maybe, after you eat and get dressed, we can go to the grocery store. We don't usually keep much here."

"Speaking of getting dressed, where are my suitcases?"

"I put all of our luggage in the laundry room when we got home last night. I've already started washing our clothes, but I didn't want to start yours until you got up. I'm not sure if you have things that have to be washed differently or that can't go in the dryer." Linc grinned and went into the bathroom, reappearing with a bag that had obviously come from a store. "I stopped and got this for you because I knew you didn't have a lot left to wear. I figured you'd find it when you got up to go to the bathroom."

Krystal climbed from Rafe's lap and accepted the bag. "You didn't have to buy me anything."

She reached into the bag and, to her surprised delight, felt something incredibly soft. "What is it? It's so soft."

She pulled out a pair of light pink cotton pants and sweater, along with a short-sleeved T-shirt that matched. Pink panties and pink bra of the softest cotton followed, along with a pair of thick pink socks in the same shade. "This is wonderful! Thank you. It's all in my size, too."

"I told Marissa the size of your dress, and she helped me. She said it's called loungewear and would be comfortable to lie around the house in, but that it was perfectly fine to wear out in public."

Nodding, Krystal forced a smile. "Who's Marissa?"

Rafe chuckled and got to his feet, running a hand down her back. "She's the manager of the lingerie store that Erin and Rachel own. You have no reason to be jealous. We don't want anyone except you."

Linc hugged her, kissing her forehead. "She already has three men interested in her, and she's fighting it all the way. Interesting to watch. We're all just waiting for her to cave."

Intrigued at how easily they seemed to accept ménage relationships, and how well they seemed to know everyone's business, Krystal smiled. "What makes you think she will?"

Rafe rose and ran a hand over her hair. "She loves them, and they love her and her little boy, Sammy. Do you want to take a shower and get dressed first, or do you want to eat?"

"I'll eat first. I don't want breakfast to get cold. Do you know where my sweater is?"

"Hanging on the back of one of the chairs in the kitchen. We thought you might need it. Will you be warm enough with it?"

"I'm fine."

Rafe scowled. "Hmm. Yes, I'm sure you are."

Linc crossed his arms over his chest and glanced at Rafe. "I don't know about you, but I'm getting a little frustrated with that answer."

"I know what you mean." Rafe wrapped an arm around her waist and pulled her onto his lap as he sat on the foot of the bed again. Bending her back over his arm, he took her mouth with his and slid a hand to her breast, lightly caressing her nipple with his palm over her borrowed shirt.

A moan escaped and then a soft cry, her head spinning with the stirring of desire that sent ripples of heat from her nipple to her clit.

Almost as quickly as it started, his kiss ended as he lifted his head to stare down at her with eyes that glittered. "You're so sweet. I've missed you. Missed this."

"I have, too." She reached up to stroke his short hair, glancing at Linc. "I don't want to lead you on, though, and I sure as hell don't want to make promises that I can't keep."

Rafe smiled and lifted her to her feet, running a hand over her bottom. "Don't worry about it. What you need to think about now is to rest and heal. We'll take things nice and slow. We've waited for you a long time, and we can wait a little more. Now that you're here, we can afford to be a little patient. Let's go eat, and after you've had your shower and get dressed, we can go walk around the town a little. We can go get some groceries and show you around a little." His gaze raked over her. "And get you a robe. I want you to have everything you need."

Although curious about her new home, however temporary, she would have preferred to spend the day on the sofa just relaxing.

The hopefulness in their eyes had her nodding with a smile. "Sure. I'd like that. Thank you."

Rafe's eyes flared. "You're welcome. Come on. Let's eat."

After putting on a pair of thick socks Linc gave her, Krystal went with them out to the kitchen, pausing when she saw the small card table and folding chairs. "You weren't kidding." She took her sweater from the back of one of the metal chairs and slipped it on.

Linc eyed the table and grimaced. "No, we weren't. I can't stand this table anymore. We should pick out a table today."

"If you couldn't stand it, why didn't you pick one out before?"

Linc retrieved a paper plate of bacon from the counter, holding the unsteady plate out with both hands. Once she took a slice, he set it on the center of the table. "We were waiting for you. Besides, we told you, we don't eat here."

"Oh." Biting into a strip of bacon, she looked around.

"The counters and cabinets are beautiful." She moved to the counter, sliding a hand over the cool white marble, a beautiful contrast to the dark wood of the gleaming cabinets.

Rafe turned from pouring her coffee and handed the mug to her, gesturing for her to sit at the table. "When we bought the house, we had the kitchen and bathrooms remodeled and had all the hardwood floors redone. We knew when you got here you wouldn't want a lot of construction mess and people in the house, but when you decide what you want to do, you just have to let us know."

Linc set a paper plate of scrambled eggs and toast in front of her. "Not now, though. Just take some time to get comfortable and rest. Orange juice?"

She picked up her plastic fork, her list of things to get for the house growing. "Absolutely."

Linc watched her eat, pleased that she'd cleaned her plate. Holding out the plate of remaining bacon, he smiled when she took another strip. "You have more color, at least. I know you're not up to meeting a lot of people, but it'll be nice to show you off. I think people were beginning to think that you're a figment of our imagination."

She smiled, her cheeks flushed. "I'm afraid I won't make it very far. I've been spending most of my time sitting in a chair."

Rafe sat back, watching her as he sipped his coffee from another mug, apparently the only glass dishes in the house. "A little exercise will do you good, but we won't push it."

After eating, she started a load of her laundry and took several pairs of shoes and a coat to the bedroom to put them away.

Leaning against the doorway, Linc watched her disappear into the walk-in closet. "What happened to all of your clothes?" He clearly remembered her having a hell of a lot more than the few he'd seen.

Her answer came from inside the closet. "A lot didn't fit me, and I could only pack what I had the room for."

Clenching his jaw, he raised his voice so she could hear him clearly. "You can buy some now. You've got plenty of room. That closet is yours, and the dresser. If you need more room, let us know."

She came out of the closet, blinking at the sight of Rafe coming into the room with a pile of T-shirts.

He opened an empty drawer in the dresser closest to the closet and stuck the piles of shirts inside. "You can use these to sleep in whenever you want."

Krystal moved closer to Rafe and peeked in the drawer, frowning. "It's empty. Where are your clothes?"

Rafe smiled. "In our rooms. Our *old* rooms."

Blinking, Krystal met Linc's gaze. "Oh."

Rafe gripped her chin, dropping a quick kiss on her lips before releasing her. "We'll share this room with you now, but Linc and I have our stuff in the other rooms."

"So last night was the first time you slept in here?"

Linc smiled, amused that it clearly pleased her to hear that. "Of course. Why would we sleep in the same bed without you in the middle? I'm gonna move some of my clothes to this room while you take your shower."

He turned away, smiling to himself.

Krystal's presence already made the house feel more like a home, and he couldn't wait for her to pick out things to complete it.

Most importantly, though, she'd finally begun to let down her guard with them—so much so that she'd finally shed the tears she must have been holding back for a long time.

More than anything she'd done in the last three years, it gave him hope for their future together.

Chapter Seven

Linc smiled to himself, filled with an inner peace more potent than he'd anticipated.

Standing with Rafe at the front of the lingerie shop, he watched over Krystal as Marissa helped her pick out more things.

Amused that her cheeks flushed when she picked out several new bras and panties of the same soft cotton as the ones she now wore, Linc glanced at Rafe, finding his friend staring at Krystal with hungry eyes.

When Erin Preston, one of the owners of the shop, appeared from the back again, she set the large bag she'd retrieved on the counter. "Here are the other colors. There's a light blue, light gray, and lavender. I included the cotton shirts and socks, as well. I also picked out the thick robe you wanted—in pink, just like you asked."

Linc smiled. "Thank you."

It pleased him immensely to know that he and Rafe could provide Krystal with comfort in some small way, and he hoped she would allow them to comfort her in others.

Linc paid for the purchase and glanced back at her. "You set up an account for her, didn't you?"

"Of course." Erin's smile held a hint of sadness. "I'm glad to finally meet the woman you've been waited for. I'm just so sorry to hear that she's lost her parents. Poor thing. I can't even imagine what she's been through."

The sadness in Erin's eyes reflected the memory of losing her own parents.

Linc sighed. "Yes. She's had a rough three years, and it's gonna take a while for her to recover. She's thin as a rail, but at least this morning she's got some color."

Erin smiled. "Love can heal a lot of hurt. My money's on the two of you."

"Thank you. How's the baby?"

Erin grinned, her eyes dancing. "Getting bigger every day and spoiled rotten. He's home with Reese today. I understand they're having *man* time."

Linc inclined his head, holding back a smile as he handed the bag to Rafe. "I'm sure they are. Man stuff is important. They have a lot of talking to do. There are some things that only another man would understand."

Erin eyed him dubiously. "Uh-huh. Well, their conversations must be pretty exhausting because, when I get home, they're both asleep on the sofa."

Krystal came up to the counter with several bras and panties, and more socks, still in a conversation with Marissa. "Most of mine got ruined by the old washers in the laundromat, and I couldn't hang anything to dry. It all had to go in the dryer."

Marissa smiled politely, and Linc couldn't help but notice that the dark circles under the other woman's eyes had gotten even worse. "That'll do it. I'm sure you'll love these. They're made for comfort, but they're so beautiful. Rachel and Erin only stock the best."

"I see that." Krystal turned to smile at Linc and Rafe, her smile falling when she saw the bag Rafe held. "What did you buy? You can't shop for me."

Erin snorted inelegantly. "I wish I had a nickel for every time I heard that."

Linc grinned, shaking his head. "I can imagine. Yes, Krystal, we *can* shop for you. It's more of the clothes you're wearing. They're comfortable so we bought other colors for you." He turned to Erin. "So, are Jared and Duncan at the store?"

"Yes, they're working in the workshop in the back. They're actually making a small table and chairs for the playhouse Boone and Chase are building for Theresa. You finally going to pick out some furniture for your house? Now that Krystal's here, I'm sure you all want something a little more substantial than that card table. Are you going over?"

"Yes. We want to pick out something from the showroom."

"In a hurry, are you?"

"I can't stand that card table any longer. One wrong move and everything on it is gonna end up on the floor." He hid a smile when Rafe moved to the other side of Krystal at the counter, reaching out to finger one of the bras she'd picked out.

Erin nodded. "They'll be relieved to see you. Ever since word got out that you left—and why—everyone's been thinking about you." She turned to smile at Krystal. "My sister, Rachel, will be sorry she missed you." She reached for one of the cards displayed on the counter and held it out. "Here, Krystal, take my number. If you need something, or just want to bitch about men in general, call me."

Rafe's eyes narrowed, his lips twitching. "Funny. I might just tell Jared and Duncan when I see them."

"Do you think it's a secret?" She patted Krystal's hand. "All the men here know that we bitch about them."

Rafe grinned. "If your men are so bad, why do you always have a glow? Why are you always smiling?"

Erin blushed, trying to hide a smile as she lifted her chin. "I never said they were *all* bad. The men in Desire do have their good points."

Krystal smiled and leaned toward her, smiling conspiratorially. "I'd like to hear more about this. I never knew there was a place where a woman could be with more than one man so openly."

Nodding, Erin sighed. "Neither did I until I got here. I came because my sister had fallen for two men and came here to drag her back to Texas."

Linc took the bag from Krystal. "And ended up with three husbands of your own."

"Yeah. I did. Damnedest thing."

* * * *

Krystal walked between Linc and Rafe toward a huge building that appeared relatively new. "Does everyone in Desire know everyone else's business?"

Rafe paused on the sidewalk in front of the building, looking up at it. "Pretty much. Place looks good, doesn't it?"

Following his gaze, Krystal frowned, studying the front of the brick building and wondering what she was looking for. "Is it new?"

Linc flattened a hand on her lower back, silently urging her forward. "The business isn't, but the building is—at least most of it. The other one was burned down. They lost a lot of merchandise and had to start over."

"And you want to buy from them because you all support each other."

Rafe opened the door for her. "And because they're friends and make the best furniture around. They make furniture that is not only beautiful but solid and meant to last. You like the bedroom furniture, don't you?"

Krystal smiled, touching his arm. "It's beautiful. You chose something you knew I would like, didn't you?"

Linc urged her forward with a hand at her back. "Of course."

They walked inside, and the man identifying himself as the manager greeted them with a smile, gesturing toward the back. "Jared and Duncan are working in the warehouse, but they said to tell you to go ahead back whenever you're ready."

Drawn to the gleaming displays of kitchen furniture, Krystal wandered in that direction. One in particular caught her eye, a dark wood that would look perfect with the kitchen cabinets and had seating for eight.

It was a table for company. For a family to gather around.

Imagining sitting at the table with Rafe, Linc, and children, she swallowed the lump in her throat and determinedly moved on to the next.

The smaller table that seated four seemed much more suitable.

If they had another couple over, they would be a chair short, but they could manage.

There wouldn't be enough room for serving dishes for a larger meal, but it would do.

The lighter wood wouldn't look as good in the kitchen, but it wouldn't look bad, either.

Of course, the lighter wood didn't really match the kitchen, but it would be just what they needed.

She looked at several others but surreptitiously kept eyeing the larger one, already picturing it in the kitchen with brightly colored placemats and real plates and flatware.

The larger one had padded seats and backs, the white and gray pattern a perfect match for the marble countertops.

Running her hand over the back of the chair of yet another set, she had to admit that all the furniture she saw was of a quality that even her untrained eye could appreciate.

She looked up to see that Linc and Rafe looked around, deep in conversation, and took the opportunity to glance at the set she liked from another angle.

Seeing the price tag, she gulped and looked away again, focusing on yet another table that had been made of the same dark wood as the first, but still only seated four.

* * * *

Rafe glanced at Krystal again, hiding a smile. "I wonder if she thinks she's fooling us."

Linc followed his gaze with a smile. "Adorable, isn't she? She likes the dark pecan one. Went to it right away and now is doing her best to avoid it. It actually matches the kitchen."

Shaking his head, Rafe crossed his arms over his chest, no longer hiding the fact that he watched her. "She keeps glancing at it, although she's trying hard not to. She wants it, but she's trying to hide it. That pisses me off. We need to establish intimacy with her again soon."

Linc nodded in agreement. "Agreed. And women think men are hard to understand. I'll go ahead back and tell Jared and Reese that that's the one we want no matter what she says. I'll wait for you and Krystal there."

* * * *

Once they finished at the furniture store, they walked back toward the center of town again, passing the lingerie store. When Krystal recognized their SUV, she started toward it, only to have Rafe take her hand in his and lead her farther down the sidewalk.

"We have another stop to make. You unpacked and didn't have all the stuff that the women around here swear you have to have."

"I don't need anything." She had enough of what she needed and hated the thought of spending the little money she had on something frivolous.

Rafe frowned. "Of course you don't. We're stopping in anyway."

Linc walked slightly ahead of her up the steps of a small store, holding the door open for her. "You need to pick out some things that we understand are absolutely necessary to women. Please don't make me go in there and pick stuff out."

Amused at that, Krystal shook her head as she climbed the stairs and walked inside, immediately pausing to breathe in the incredible scents.

After spending months sitting in hospitals and the nursing facility, and surrounded by antiseptic and not so pleasant smells, she closed her eyes and took another breath, surprised that tears burned her eyes.

When a hand flattened on her back, she opened her eyes and looked up at Rafe. "Sorry. It just smells so good in here."

Rafe smiled and bent to touch his lips to her forehead. "It does. Pick out whatever you need or want. If the scents in here make you happy enough to bring tears to your eyes, I want you to bring them home. I'm looking forward to our bedroom and bathroom smelling just as good. Maybe it'll help you relax."

Krystal smiled up at him, watching a dark-haired woman approach from the corner of her eye. "After months of hospital smells, this is like paradise."

Linc closed in on her other side and gestured toward the approaching woman with a warm smile. "Krystal, this is Brenna. I'm sure she can help you."

Brenna grinned. "Absolutely. Hi, Krystal. It's so nice to finally meet you. I'm so sorry about your mother."

"Thank you." Krystal's eyes went wide as she scanned the store. "This is incredible. I don't even know where to begin. Is it all right if I just look around?"

"Of course."

Before she could move away, another woman appeared from the back, her cheeks flushed. "Linc! Rafe! I'm so glad you're back." Smiling, she held her hand out. "I'm Jesse Erickson. You must be Krystal. I've been looking forward to meeting you. I'm so sorry to hear about your mother."

Liking the other women immediately, Krystal smiled, anxious to explore the store. "Thank you."

Jesse grinned at Rafe and Linc. "You two have never been in here before, have you? What do you think?"

Linc grinned and pulled Krystal closer. "It smells good in here, but I have no idea what any of this stuff is. Do us a favor, Jesse. Please help Krystal pick out …whatever and set up an account for us."

Jesse nodded and smiled again. "Absolutely. Clay and Rio are in the back if you want to go back and have a cup of coffee. There was some coffee cake when I was back there last, but with those two, I can't promise anything."

Rafe eyed the assortment of glass shelves and the rows of glass bottles and jars. "That sounds safer." Bending to kiss Krystal's forehead, he ran a hand down her back. "We'll be right behind that curtain, baby. Have fun and let us know when you're done."

Linc took her hand in his. "You're in good hands. Relax, look around, and get whatever you need." He lifted his gaze to Jesse's. "Don't let her skimp."

Shaking her head, Jesse smiled faintly. "I won't pressure her. We'll pick out something she likes, and she can come in and look at something else when she needs to get away from you two. Now shoo. Go keep Clay and Rio company."

As soon as Linc and Rafe walked away, Jesse took Krystal's arm and led her to a large display of beautiful glass jars and bottles. "I'm so glad you're here. I'm happy to finally get to meet the woman who Linc and Rafe have been waiting for. I'm just glad Rafe and Linc could be there for your mother's funeral. When they heard she'd passed, they couldn't get to you fast enough."

Krystal smiled, distracted by the beautiful displays but anxious to learn more about the women who lived in Desire. "They've been great. So you have two husbands, too? Clay and Rio, right?"

Beaming, Jesse nodded. "Yep. I know. It's a shock. I first came here to visit my sister, Nat, and she introduced me to Clay and Rio. The rest is history."

Immediately feeling comfortable in the other woman's presence, Krystal sighed, pleased that she'd already heard about Nat and her relationship with Jake and Hoyt. "It must be so nice to know what you want."

Jesse blinked. "Who the hell said that? Are you kidding? I knew no such thing and fought it with everything I had."

With a sigh, she glanced toward the curtain where Krystal knew the men had gathered. "I had just gotten out of a horrible marriage and swore I'd never love any man again. I was dead inside. I'd been hurt so many times that I just built all these walls between myself and the rest of the world. Nothing touched me. Nothing fazed me. When I came to visit Nat, she introduced me to Clay and Rio."

Intrigued by Jesse's flush and the glow of love in her eyes, Krystal picked up one of the bottles and breathed in the scent of lavender. "How did you know you could feel anything again? I have to admit that I'm feeling more than I thought, but I feel so empty inside. I can't believe they waited for me. I'm not the same person anymore. What if they're in love with a woman who no longer exists?"

Jesse smiled, her eyes welling with tears. "When I met Clay and Rio, I tried to keep them at a distance, positive that I had nothing to offer either one of them. They knocked down the walls I'd spent years building as if they weren't there. They accepted me for who I am, and I'm better with them than I've ever been. I've never known such love. Such a sense of security. Not just physical security, something I didn't even realize I never had with my husband, but emotional security. I can be myself. It still amazes me that I can argue with them and I still feel safe. I still feel loved. I can go to either one of them with anything. We can talk about everything. Now I can't imagine my life without them."

Krystal admitted to herself that she'd already begun to feel that way with Linc and Rafe but feared that it was far too soon. "I feel physically safe with them, but I'm afraid when they realize that I'm boring now, they'll get tired of me. They'll wish they'd listened to me, and by then, I'll be in so much in love with them that I won't survive the breakup. I don't want to hurt them either. I owe them so much."

Jesse's eyes went wide. "Dear God, please don't tell them that. Or tell them once and drop it. They'll wonder if you're with them just because you think you owe them. They're strong men, and if there's one thing I've learned about the men in this town it's that they *love* to be needed. They're preening like peacocks today. They bought you something, didn't they? They did something to make you smile."

"Yes. They bought this outfit and more like it from the lingerie shop. I also picked out some bras and panties, and they said to put it on their account. They fixed breakfast. They made me pick out a kitchen table."

Nodding, Jesse rearranged some of the jars, apparently more for something to do than because the display needed it. "Good. They loved that. Now, pick out some stuff in here and let them pay for it. I have your welcome basket in the back all ready, so I won't let you pick out duplicates."

Brenna came up beside them. "Do yourself one better. Pick out a couple of scents that you like and ask their opinions. The samples are all around. Put them on your neck and your wrist and have them smell them. That drives King and Royce crazy."

Krystal mentally rifled through what she'd heard about Brenna. "You have two husbands, too?"

Brenna grinned. "Better, I have two Dominants as husbands."

Krystal blinked, her smile falling. Not sure if she'd heard Brenna right, she glanced at Jesse for confirmation. "What?"

Brenna wiped the already immaculate glass with a small cloth. "Yep. They own the club with Blade, Kelly's husband."

Krystal nodded and swallowed the dozen questions that sprang up in her mind. "Oh. That's nice."

Throwing her head back, Brenna laughed. "Go ahead. You can ask. You're dying to know if they use whips and chains on me."

Krystal's face burned. "I…um."

Brenna shook her head and picked up a jar to wipe it clean of fingerprints. "It's not like it sounds. Chains are for restraints, not for hitting, and yes, both of my husbands are very good with the whip."

"And they use it on you?" The question slipped out before Krystal could swallow it, and mortified that she'd asked it, she shook her head. "I'm sorry. Forget I asked that. It's really none of my business."

Batting her lashes, Brenna smiled. "When I'm bad, they do, and believe me, I'm bad as often as possible."

Jesse giggled. "You should see her on days when she knows she's earned a spanking. She watches the clock all day and is giddy as a teenage girl going on her first date."

Brenna giggled again. "Stop. I'm not that bad."

Jesse gave her a friendly smile. "Like hell. Makes me jealous."

Krystal swallowed heavily, a memory from the past creeping in. "Are you saying that your husbands spank you?"

Jesse touched Krystal's arm. "There's no reason to look so scared. Believe me, if Linc or Rafe decide to spank you, you're probably going to like it a hell of a lot more than you'd be comfortable with. These men have a way of getting their point across, and somehow making it an erotic experience at the same time. They're so damned good at it that it's frustrating."

Intrigued, Krystal smiled. "How would you know that everyone else is as good at it as Clay and Rio?"

Jesse smiled again, glancing at Brenna. "Because we all talk. When you live in a town like this, where the men are determined to keep their women safely under wraps in any way possible, it helps to have other women to confide in. Hell, they all go to the club and think up ways to drive us crazy, and it's only fair that we do the same to them. Hope and Charity opened a woman's club for just that purpose."

Krystal stilled. "What do you mean *under wraps*?"

With a smile, Jesse glanced toward the back. "The men in Desire feel safer when they're in charge." Shaking her head, she smiled again. "But as anyone in Desire can tell you, the women are in charge most of the time because nothing makes these men happier than knowing that their women are happy. They're a mass of contradictions. The men in this town are old-fashioned as hell. They consider it their right to protect their women, which includes everything from making sure she doesn't put herself in danger to making sure she gets enough rest. They open doors, carry anything heavy, and are the most protective men I've ever met. On the other hand, they're very progressive. Clay and Rio support my need to work, and they're very proud of what I've done with this business. They don't expect me to be home to fix dinner every night and grab dinner more often than not with no complaints. But if they feel like I'm overworked, they'll charge in, throw me over a shoulder, and take me home without hesitation."

Brenna nodded thoughtfully. "And they don't judge a woman for being with more than one man and are completely comfortable with Domination and submission, but if any man treats his woman badly, he'll be run out of town in a heartbeat. None of the men in this town would allow their woman to leave the house dressed in suggestive clothing, which will probably earn a spanking, but don't see anything wrong with a woman living with three husbands."

Krystal frowned, the knowledge that Rafe and Linc had embraced such a town not as surprising as it should have been. "Lord, I don't know how I'll ever figure out the rules in this town."

And she couldn't help but wonder if Rafe and Linc had depths to them she hadn't yet had the chance to explore.

Jesse smiled and patted her arm. "You'll learn fast, and we're all here to help. Honey, we're all in the same boat, and I gotta tell you, I wouldn't give it up for the world. They'd never hurt you, but most of the men in this town spank their wives, kind of like the men did a hundred years ago. Sometimes playfully, but if you ever do something they see as putting yourself in danger, you're probably in for more than a playful spanking."

Krystal felt a rush of warmth, the memory of their playful spanking in the past stirring her in a way she hadn't been in a long time. "Wow."

Jesse smiled as another customer came in. "I wouldn't worry about it right now, if I were you. They're very careful around you because of all you've been through."

Picking up another tester, Krystal sighed. "Yes, I know. I appreciate the chance to get some rest and get my bearings back, but I want normal—whatever the hell that is."

Jesse patted her arm again. "Just take it one day at a time. Something still exists between the three of you, or you wouldn't be here now. You wouldn't be so worried."

Brenna eyed her appraisingly. "And you'd be planning your exit. Have you thought of what you would do if you left Desire?"

Krystal blew out a breath. "I was working on that before they showed up. I figured I'd start east by bus until I found a place that felt right."

Brenna glanced at Jesse before turning back to Krystal again. "Have you thought about where you'd go if you left here?"

"Well, no."

Brenna grinned, apparently pleased with herself. "There you go. Just relax. If it doesn't work out, at least you'll know that you tried. Can you imagine yourself being happy if you left now without ever knowing?"

"Let nature take its course." Jesse shrugged. "If it's supposed to happen, it will. If not, it won't. If the chemistry between the three of you is any indication, there'll be another wedding soon."

Krystal's stomach did a flip-flop, and with her heart pounding furiously, she lifted her hands and backed away. "Whoa. Nobody said anything about marriage."

Jesse laughed at that. "So you think they waited three years for you, bought a house to live in with you, and raced out to get you as soon as the doctor called them because they wanted an affair?"

"Holy hell." Krystal pressed a hand to her stomach, her knees rubbery. "They said they wouldn't rush me."

"Right. One day at a time." Brenna led her to the samples of body cream. "Pick some out that you like. Let's test them on your men."

After smelling all of them, Krystal fell in love with the apricot. "I just love this one. I have no idea why, but it makes me smile. And it sure as hell doesn't smell like hospitals and nursing facilities. It's fresh. God, I miss fresh."

"Can't say that I blame you. It's one of my favorites, too. Come here." Brenna rubbed some of the apricot scent on Krystal's neck and inside of her wrist on one side. "Okay, that's the apricot. Which other one is a contender?"

"I think the lavender. It's fresh, too, and I think I'd like to use it at night."

"Good choice. It's a relaxing scent, and it'll be good for you." Brenna applied lavender to the other side of her neck and her other wrist. "God, this brings back memories. I think I'm going to try a few new samples tonight. Go back and let your men get a whiff of you."

Jesse giggled. "Krystal, your basket has several different scents so you can continue this game at home."

Stunned at Jesse's generosity, Krystal gaped. "You don't have to do that. I don't need a gift basket."

"We give a gift basket to all new residents. It's a way to welcome them, and it's good for business." Jesse recapped the jars and winked. "Once you see how good our products are, you'll be back."

Bubbling with excitement, Krystal started toward the back, but Brenna caught her arm. "You look too excited. Take a few deep breaths. You have to look like you just don't know and are anxious to please them. They'll love it. It makes them feel all manly inside, and they'll be willing to give you whatever you want. That's one of the ways to make these men putty in your hands."

Krystal had never had friends who talked to her so bluntly and found herself laughing, relaxing. "I hope you don't mind if I come in here often. You're so blunt. I love it."

Brenna leaned closer, keeping her voice at a whisper. "You should come to the women's club. We love to talk about other ways to make our men putty in our hands."

As Jesse went to help another customer, Brenna walked with Krystal toward the back, keeping her voice low. "In this town, there are very few secrets. The women like it because we all get the chance to talk without being judged, and we've all learned how to handle such strong, ridiculously chauvinistic men. They'd be the first to admit it, but not to us, but the women are in charge here, no matter what anyone tells you. You just have to learn to play your men. Now. Serious face. Look hopeful as if you really want them to like it and ask if they'd rather you pick out something else. They'll be mush. Every damned man in town is an alpha male, and you gotta learn how to handle them.

They have no defense at all against their women. They'll meet tough with toughness, but femininity renders them helpless. Go get 'em."

Krystal nodded and made her way to the back, her mood lighter than it had been in a long time.

Taking a deep breath, she pushed the curtain aside.

As soon as she walked through the curtain, Rafe and Linc jumped to their feet, all conversation halting abruptly.

Rafe reached her first. "Krystal, this is Clay and Rio Erickson. Clay, Rio, this is Krystal."

Clay rose and offered a huge hand with a smile. "The woman we've all waited to meet. We'd begun to think that Rafe and Linc made you up."

Krystal smiled, easily imagining him with Jesse. "I'm very real." She glanced sideways at Linc and Rafe before meeting Clay's gaze again. "I just can't believe they waited."

Clay sighed and glanced toward the curtain, smiling at the sound of Jesse's tinkling laughter. "The right woman is hard to find and well worth waiting for." He smiled in sympathy. "We're very sorry about your mother."

"Thank you."

The other man stepped forward, his eyes twinkling. "We're just happy you're here now. Some rest will do you a world of good."

Wrapping an arm around her, Rafe frowned. "Are you done already? Didn't you pick anything out?"

Krystal smiled and shrugged, leaning into him. "I have a bit of a dilemma, and I hope you can help me."

"Of course, baby. What is it?"

"I like two and can't decide. I really like the apricot, but I wanted to know what you thought of it. I mean, if I wear something that you don't like…"

Rafe grinned. "Let me smell."

Krystal obediently lifted her wrist. "Breanna put some on my wrist and on my neck. She said that sometimes it'll smell differently."

"Well then, I think it's best if we check both." Bending, Rafe nuzzled her neck. "Christ, I want to take a bite out of you."

Krystal couldn't contain a giggle. "I also like the lavender. It's supposed to be soothing, and I thought I could wear the apricot during the day and the lavender at night. Brenna said the lavender is supposed to relax me. I don't know if you'll like it, though."

"Where is it?" Linc's voice had a gruffness to it as if he'd swallowed glass.

Rafe straightened, staring down at her with eyes that glittered as he waited for her to answer.

Tilting her neck, Krystal pointed to the other side. "Here." She lifted her wrist. "And here."

Linc bent to nibble at her neck while Rafe lifted her wrist to his nose and inhaled deeply.

With a groan, Linc kissed her neck, brushing his lips over the sensitive skin there. "I love it."

Rafe nibbled at her wrist. "Buy both."

When Linc straightened and slid an arm around her, she looked up at him with a smile.

"Are you sure? I mean if you're just saying that—"

Linc shook his head and cut her off. "Jesse!"

Jesse appeared far too quickly, her eyes dancing in a way that seemed to amuse Clay and Rio. "Yes?"

"Whatever you have in apricot and lavender, please."

"Of course."

Krystal sniffed her wrist with a smile, loving the scent. "Are you sure? I mean, I can choose something else."

Rafe sat back at the table and pulled her onto his lap. "Not a chance."

When Rio sat, Jesse allowed him to pull her onto his lap, their movements smooth and natural as if from long practice.

Leaning into Rio, Jesse laid a hand over the one he wrapped around her waist. "Krystal was really worried that you wouldn't like them. I'm glad. Her gift basket has several other scents to try. Some women like to change them for the seasons, some are stuck on the ones they've chosen, and others like a selection."

Rio sniffed Jesse's neck. "I'm addicted to peach. You'd better never change."

Clay dropped into his seat again and chuckled. "She's come home smelling like all of them, especially if she was helping Nat whip up a batch, and it didn't make a damned bit of difference."

"True." Rio hugged Jesse. "I can't resist you no matter what you smell like."

Krystal smiled, a little jealous at seeing how close Clay, Rio, and Jesse were.

When Jesse reached back a hand for Clay, he took it in his automatically.

They even moved together.

Patting Rio's arm, Jesse rose. "I'll go gather everything for you."

"Thank you." Krystal turned her head to look up at Rafe. "Are you sure you like them? I don't want a scent lingering in the bathroom that you don't like."

"Of course we like it. Baby, you can choose whatever you want. The house already feels like a house now that you live there, but now it'll really start to smell like a home."

Touched, Krystal smiled and rose. "I'm going to go pay for everything. I'll be right back."

"No." Rafe pulled her back onto his lap. "Jesse will take care of it."

Shaking her head, Krystal tried to get up again. "No. Stop with the accounts. I want to pay for my own things."

Clay shook his head, setting down his coffee. "That's not how things are done in this town."

Intrigued, but leery, Krystal allowed Rafe to pull her back down to his lap again. "What do you mean?"

Clay shrugged. "I mean that, in Desire, women shop and charge everything to their husbands."

Lifting her chin, Krystal stared at Clay, while well aware of Rafe's and Linc's attention. "I don't have a husband. Besides, I prefer to support myself. I don't want to depend on Rafe and Linc to pay for everything. I want to work."

Linc touched her arm. "You're not in any condition to work right now. If you decide to work later, then your money is yours. You can spend it however you like."

Rio grinned. "We take pride in spoiling our women. Hell, Jesse has no idea how much the bills cost in our house. She makes her own money and spends it on whatever she wants on her trips to Tulsa. If she needs more, we always have some put away that she can take whenever she wants."

"Yes, but you're married."

Rafe stiffened. "We're living together and have claimed you. You're ours."

Krystal stiffened and jumped to her feet, putting aside the word *claim* for another time. "Look, I appreciate—"

Rafe rose to his full height, his hands on his hips, his eyes narrowed. "Don't go there."

Aware of Clay's and Rio's amusement, and not wanting to argue in front of an audience, Krystal took several steps back. "You're even more chauvinistic than I thought."

"And we like it that way. We're not changing, Krystal."

"Neither am I." She glanced at Clay and Rio. "I think we should talk about this later."

Rafe inclined his head. "You got it. I'll go get your things."

"Damn it, Rafe."

"Enough." Linc wrapped an arm around her waist. "Thanks for the coffee. We've got to go."

Clay chuckled, and as Linc rushed her from the back room and through the curtain to the store, raising his voice, he called out. "Good luck."

Krystal glared up at Linc and turned to look back toward the kitchen. "I don't need luck."

Another chuckle came from the back, and Clay appeared at the curtain. "I was talking to Linc."

* * * *

Krystal hid a smile when Jesse winked at her as they left Indulgences and walked between Linc and Rafe to their SUV. "Can we go home now?"

Inwardly wincing that she'd called their house a home, she watched them stow her bag and gift basket in the back.

Her home.

Linc and Rafe glanced at each other as if placing more significance on the word than it warranted.

Linc shook his head. "Not yet. We have to go to the grocery store. After that we'll go home so you can take a nap." One dark brow went up as he opened the front passenger door for her. "You're a little grouchy."

"I'm not grouchy. I'm pissed." She opened the back door herself and crawled inside. "You're not going to take over my life."

She waited until they both got in and closed the doors behind them and both men turned in their seats to look at her. "My life was taken away from me before. I had no control at all. Now I'm free to do whatever I want. I need this freedom. I need to be able to breathe."

Linc blew out a breath and glanced at Rafe. "We don't want to take that away from you, Krystal, but you've been through a lot. You need to catch your breath, get your rest, and think about the future. There's no hurry, but Rafe and I have waited a long time for you. Now that we have you here, can you blame us for wanting to protect you? To take care of you? We've waited to be able to spoil you a little." He smiled and reached back for her hand. "Are you really gonna deny us the chance to make you more comfortable and give you some of the things you've been doing without?"

"I don't need to be spoiled."

Rafe lifted a brow at that. "You certainly do, and we're enjoying it. What did we ever do to you to make you feel we don't deserve the chance to enjoy ourselves a little?"

Amused, Krystal shook her head. "You think you're slick, don't you?"

Linc chuckled at that and brought her hand to his lips before releasing it. "I don't know. Did we win this little argument?"

Krystal sighed and looked out the window, admiring the flower boxes that lined the sidewalk. "I need to have normal, and I don't even know what that is. Shouldn't you go back to work?"

Rafe met her gaze in the rearview mirror as he backed out of the parking spot. "We took this week off to be with you. We both go back to work on Monday, but we'll work staggered shifts so one of us is with you."

Krystal sighed at yet another example of them treating her with kid gloves. "You don't have to do that. It's a small town, and I'm not going anywhere."

Linc turned in his seat to face her. "It's important to both of us to have some time alone with you. We both need that as much as we need the time with you together. It's important for you and me to have a relationship as well as you and Rafe."

Krystal dropped her head back with a sigh. "This is all so confusing. I can't believe the people in this town do this."

Rafe turned to smile at her as he pulled into another parking space. "Sharing women has been a way of life here for almost a hundred and fifty years."

Krystal blinked, sitting up abruptly. "You're kidding."

Linc grinned. "No. He's not. Women were in short supply back then, and it was a dangerous time. The men felt better knowing that if something happened to them, there would be someone else to take care of their wives. You'll meet Isabel Preston at the grocery store that she owns with her *three* husbands. Ben, Wade, and Cord."

"Good God." Krystal paused. "Wait. Preston? The furniture guys? Erin?"

Rafe shifted into park and cut the engine. "Yes. Jared, Duncan, and Reese are their sons."

Linc got out and opened her door. "Come here. Let me smell you again."

Pulling her from the seat, he held her several inches off the ground and against his chest, burying his face against her neck. "You smell delicious. I love the feel of you against me. I missed you so damned much."

Touched, she wrapped her arms around his neck and hugged him, her body humming with awareness and the stirring of arousal. "I missed you, too."

With a groan, he set her on her feet and abruptly released her. "That was a mistake."

Amused and filled with a sense of feminine power, Krystal flattened her hands on his chest and leaned into him, smiling at the unmistakable feel of his cock pressing against her belly. "Regret bringing me here already?"

His eyes darkened and narrowed. "Not a fucking chance. I like holding you too much, especially when out in public. If we were home, you'd already be naked."

The surge of need shocked her with its intensity. "Really?"

Linc used his fingertips to push back a tendril of hair the wind had blown over her face. "Really. I want you, Krystal, more than I'd even suspected. Being pulled apart the way we were makes our time together even more precious now."

She pressed her breasts against his chest, sucking in a breath at the friction. "Why don't you take me?"

His hands tightened on her waist, his eyes closing on another groan. "Don't tempt me. You've been through a lot. We don't want to pressure you."

Krystal couldn't help it. She burst out laughing. "So you moved me to a new town, have me picking out furniture for your house so that it feels like my home, and keep shopping for me because you don't want to pressure me?"

Linc's lips twitched. "Shut up, Krystal. We've waited a long time to make our house a home and to spoil you. We're enjoying the hell out of this." Taking her hand in his, he led her to the sidewalk where Rafe waited for them. "Let's go do some shopping. Pick out whatever you want. We have no idea what kind of things you want to cook or snack on, so don't be shy."

Krystal smiled at the memory. "If I remember right, every time I got a snack, you and Rafe ended up eating most of it."

Linc paused, drawing her close and bending to touch his lips to her ear. "Careful. This time I might very well snack on you."

Chapter Eight

Still distracted from the lingering effects of Linc's embrace, Krystal walked through the door he held open for her, hit almost immediately by the scent of fresh peaches. "Oh God. I want some."

Rafe closed in on her from behind, his muscular arm coming around her and pulling her back against him. He bent to touch his warm lips against her ear, sending a current of sensation straight to her nipples. "I was just thinking the same thing. It's been a long time since I used my mouth on your sweet pussy, and I'm desperately craving a taste."

Stiffening, Krystal swallowed heavily, the rush of heat intensifying. "Rafe!"

Releasing her, he turned her to face him, gripping her chin and giving her a quick kiss before straightening again. "None of us are gonna be able to hold off much longer, but it's only fair to make you suffer as much as I am."

Krystal's gaze dropped to his fly, the memories of how hot the passion had been between them igniting fires in her she'd thought long extinguished forever. "Rafe, I—"

Shaking his head, he retrieved one of the carts, a muscle working in his jaw. "Not now. Let's get the shopping done so we can get back home. You're too much of a temptation. Pick out your peaches."

Rafe stood by while she picked out peaches, letting his gaze rake over her as he added ingredients for a salad to the cart.

He'd missed her like hell, and the circumstances surrounding their reluctance to take her left him frustrated and irritable.

He'd loved her for years.

He'd waited for her for years.

But he hadn't realized how much that love had grown over that time.

Now that he and Linc finally had her home, he couldn't even imagine being parted from her again.

Just being around her heated his blood, and each time he thought about the circumstances that had kept them apart for so long, he had to tamp down another surge of anger.

So much wasted time.

He wanted her, and reestablishing the intimacy between them seemed to become more important by the minute.

He wanted there to be no misunderstanding about their intentions toward her, and reestablishing their sexual relationship would go a long way to reinforce the closeness they'd once shared.

He wanted forever, but he and Linc had promised not to rush her, adding to his frustration.

Linc groaned. "I'm gonna go pick out some steaks."

She took her time, seeming to savor the opportunity to choose strawberries and an assortment of fresh fruits and vegetables. "Do you know how long it's been since I had anything fresh? Canned peached. Canned oranges. Canned fruit cocktail." Holding an orange to her nose, she closed her eyes and breathed deeply. "Dear God. I'm in heaven."

Imagining that same look of bliss on her face as he pleasured her, Rafe tightened his hands on the handles of the cart, swallowing a groan. "Christ. Stop that." Yanking her against him, he buried his face against her neck and breathed in the scent of her. "If I come in my jeans in the middle of the grocery store, I'm not gonna be happy."

Krystal gasped in shock and then giggled, the sound making his cock pound even harder. "I think it's the apricot."

"This is the lavender side. No, baby. It's all you." Rafe almost swallowed his tongue when she turned and pressed her breasts against his chest. "Careful. It's been a long time, and I have a short fuse."

Krystal blinked. "You haven't been with another woman in all this time? No. I mean I have no right to ask, and I—"

Rafe bent to touch his lips to hers. "No. Neither Linc nor I have any interest in anyone but you. You're ours. We don't want anyone else. And you're damned sure not going to anyone else."

She flattened her hands on his chest and looked up at him through her lashes, a small smile tugging at her lips. "You're awfully arrogant."

Rafe smiled. "The word you're looking for is ruthless. You can fight it all you want, but you're not getting away from us again."

She blinked once, her eyes widening. "But what if I can't?"

Linc returned, eyeing them as he dropped the steaks into the cart. "Can't what?"

Krystal whipped around to face him. "What if I can't do this? What if you realize I'm not the person you remember? We didn't date that long."

"It was long enough for all three of us to know what we wanted." Linc smiled. "Rafe and I can make you happy, but we're giving you the time to figure that out for yourself, and in a place that you can feel comfortable while you do."

When Krystal blushed and snuck a glance at Rafe, he ran a hand over her bottom.

"Keep looking at me like that and I'll take you right here on top of the oranges."

Krystal's giggle brought his cock to full attention, uncomfortable under the circumstances. "I think that's something that might get you arrested."

Loving that they'd managed to draw out her playful side, a side he hadn't seen in far too long, Rafe dropped another kiss on her lips. "Well worth it."

Linc wanted to taste her himself. Pulling her to his side, he led her down the aisle. "Come on. Let's finish shopping so we can go home."

Each time Krystal paused to look at something, Linc and Rafe took the opportunity to touch her.

When she picked out cereal, Linc slid an arm around her waist, eyeing the box she held while sliding his hand higher to caress the outer curve of her breast. Smiling when her breath caught, he grabbed a box of another cereal, one that he preferred, and tossed it into the cart. "Take your time, sweetheart."

Krystal found herself leaning into his touch, her nipple aching for attention. Glancing up at him, she met his glittering gaze and, remembering the things Jesse and Brenna had said, decided that two could play his game.

Turning, she ran a hand over his chest and placed the box of cereal in the cart. "Thank you. It's been so long since I had the chance to grocery shop. Everything looks so good."

Rafe frowned and walked beside her as she started down the aisle again. "Nursing home food can't be all that appealing."

"It wasn't." She stopped at the meats. "You bought steaks for tonight, but I'd like to get some things to make for dinner."

Linc cursed. "Shit. I forgot the potatoes."

Rafe held up a hand. "I got them and picked out stuff for the salad." He shot Krystal a sharp look. "Krystal was driving me crazy sniffing at the fruits and vegetables. I thought she was gonna have an orgasm right there in the produce section."

"Oh, yeah?" Linc winked at her. "Sorry I missed it."

Placing his hands outside of hers on the handle of the shopping cart, Rafe pressed his body against hers from behind and started down the aisle again. "Let's pick out stuff for other meals when we need it. Tomorrow, Linc and I want to take you out to dinner."

Linc nodded. "Yeah. Get your snacks, drinks, and whatever you think we need. We'll go shopping tomorrow for plates and stuff to go on our new kitchen table."

Surprised, and excited at the changes they wanted her to make, Krystal stopped abruptly. "Do you really think the kitchen table will be there tomorrow?"

Rafe leaned forward, nuzzling her neck. "It'll be there tonight. Jared's just waiting for us to call and tell him we're home."

Krystal pushed back against him, wiggling her bottom against his cock. "We'd better hurry then."

Rafe's arm came around her. "No hurry. Get the things you want. I'm sick of looking at empty cupboards."

Krystal spotted popcorn and moved away from the cart, rubbing against Linc as she reached for it. "I used to love when you made popcorn and we watched a movie together."

Linc's hands closed on her waist, and with a chuckle, he pulled her back against him. "I remember the cuddling and the butter."

Her nipples beaded tightly at the reminder. "So do I. We'd better get extra butter."

In the frozen food section, Linc eyed her beaded nipples. "Your nipples are poking at the front of your shirt and making my mouth water."

She glanced at Rafe to see him staring at them as well. Smiling and filled with feminine power, she placed the cartons of ice cream in the cart and straightened, not bothering to pull her sweater closed. "I thought we were here to shop."

Linc's jaw clenched. "No. You're here to shop. We're here to watch you and carry groceries. You like teasing us, don't you?"

Lifting her chin, Krystal smiled. "Why yes. I think I do. What are you going to do about it?"

Linc grinned. "Tease you back, of course."

Her heart skipped a beat, and she found herself looking at each of them, some part of her feeling as if she was looking at them—*really* looking at them—in a way she hadn't in almost three years.

Rafe stared at her, the combination of concern, need, and hesitancy in his dark chocolate eyes, so different from the hungry playfulness from the past, a sharp reminder of just how much things had changed between them.

She met Linc's gaze, struck by the same hesitant watchfulness in his eyes, which added layers to the hunger darkening them. "It is different now, isn't it? It's sharper."

Linc smiled. "I want you."

Krystal nodded, her pulse tripping. "I know. I want you, too. It's time, isn't it?"

Linc smiled slowly. "Yes. I think it is."

Krystal placed her hand in his outstretched one, her body responding immediately to being held against his.

Silently, but with hurried steps, they made their way to the checkout counter, immediately greeted by a smiling older woman.

"Well, hello, deputies. This must be Krystal."

Linc all but threw items on the counter. "Yes, ma'am. Krystal, this is Isabel Preston. Isabel, would you please set up an account for her here?"

The older woman grinned, her eyes glowing. "Absolutely." Her smile dimmed, the sympathy in it bringing a lump to Krystal's throat. "I'm so sorry about your parents and what you've been through."

Krystal returned the other woman's smile, marveling at the older woman's calm beauty. "Thank you. Everyone's been so nice."

Isabel's smile widened again. "Desire's a small town, and we all look out for each other--something I'm sure you've heard a dozen times already. You're one of us now. It's nice to finally meet the woman these two handsome devils have been waiting for. I was starting to believe they just made you up."

Linc placed the last of the items on the counter and pushed the cart aside. "She's real, Isabel, and you'll be seeing more of her."

Rafe began carrying bags out to the SUV while Linc dug out his wallet.

"She's gonna start cooking for us."

Isabel watched Rafe go out the door with his arms laden with groceries. "What's the rush?"

Krystal hid a smile when Linc slid a sideways glance in her direction and patted her bottom. "Jared and Duncan are waiting for us to call them so they can deliver the kitchen table we just bought from them."

Isabel smiled and shook her head. "Good. You can finally get rid of that horrible card table."

Rafe came in and grabbed more bags before heading outside again. "We've been running around all morning, and Krystal needs to lie down. She's been sitting in a chair next to her mother's bed for months and isn't used to walking so much."

Isabel's smile became sympathetic again, but her eyes danced with amusement as she glanced at Linc before looking at Krystal. "You're right, dear. She does look a little flushed."

* * * *

As soon as they made their way outside, Krystal could no longer hold back a giggle. "I think she knew you were patting my butt when you pretended to have your arm around me."

Linc opened the back passenger door and all but shoved her inside, quickly following behind her and pulling her against him. "I'm sure she did." He was kissing her before Rafe could even start the engine.

The taste and feel of him brought back memories and ignited a passion inside her that quickly roared out of control.

With a groan, he flattened her on the back seat, covering her body with his, pressing her legs apart to make a place for himself between them. "This back seat isn't big enough for me to get as close to you as I need to."

Sliding a hand beneath her bottom, he lifted her against him, breaking off his kiss only long enough to stare down at her. "You make me crazy."

Wrapping her legs around him, she lifted into him, sucking in a breath at the feel of his cock pressing against her slit. "Good."

She didn't remember the hunger being so sharp. So intense.

His kiss had a possessiveness that she didn't remember, the kiss of a man who wanted to brand a woman as his.

Breathless when he lifted his head again with a curse, she gripped his hair and tried to pull him back down. "Please."

His hand slid from her bottom to her breast. "Hell. I didn't want to rush you."

Arching into his caress, she fought to get closer, hating the clothing that kept her from feeling his body against hers. "I need this. I need you. Both of you. I've been dead inside. Make me feel alive again."

Rafe pulled into the driveway and slammed on the brakes. "If you don't give in to that, you take care of the fucking groceries and I will."

"Like hell." Linc sat up and opened the door. "You get the groceries. I'll take care of Krystal."

Wrapping his hands around her calves, he slid her toward him and gathered her against him with a speed that made her giggle. "Linc!"

Flipping her over his shoulder, he patted her ass and strode toward the house. "Stop wiggling."

Rafe paused to open the door, running a hand down her leg as she passed. "Have fun."

Linc strode through the living room and started down the hall. "I think it's gonna be a little more than *fun*."

The way she fought to keep distance between them had heightened his sense of possessiveness, and her passion provided the opportunity for him to imprint himself on her in a way she wouldn't soon forget.

He planned to take full advantage of it.

He removed her shoes and socks and tossed them aside before lowering her to the bed and following to cover her body with his.

The slightly shocked, hungry look in her eyes made his cock throb with need for her, but he had no desire to rush their lovemaking.

He'd waited too long and planned to savor her, needing to create an intimacy between them that would make it even harder for her to walk away.

He stripped her out of her sweater, shirt, and bra, knowing that having her breasts exposed while the rest of her remained covered would heighten her awareness there.

With the intention of driving her wild, he reached for the box of condoms he'd bought that morning and took her mouth with his again.

* * * *

Dizzy from his kisses, Krystal clung to his broad shoulders, wrapping her legs around his hips and lifting herself to press against him.

Being naked from the waist up heightened her awareness in her breasts, filling her with a feminine sexuality that ripped through barriers she'd feared would stand in their way.

Needing more, she struggled to get closer.

Her nipples burned from the heat of his chest, but it wasn't enough.

She needed to feel his bare skin against hers—something she hadn't felt for far too long.

A whimper escaped when he softened his kisses to sip at her lips, the intimacy between them growing with a speed that swept past defenses before she could even think about shoring them up.

Frustrated when he lifted his head, she watched him retrieve a condom from the box he'd tossed on the bed. "You're so damned sweet. God, I missed you. Missed this."

"So did I." Frustrated when he gripped her wrists and pressed her hands against the pillow on either side of her head, she struggled to be free. "Linc! I want to touch you."

Lifting his head, he stared down at her, his narrowed eyes sparkling with green flecks. "Not now. I want to learn you all over again. Be still so I can explore."

Be still?

Krystal ached everywhere and fought to get closer. "Linc! Please!"

Linc nipped her bottom lip and gathered both of her wrists in one large hand, lifting them above her head. "No, Krystal. I've waited a long time for this, and I'm not gonna be rushed."

Stilling in shock at his cool steely tone, Krystal swallowed heavily and stared up at him, stunned by the determination in his masculine features.

"I've always been incredibly gentle with you because I didn't want to scare you, but as you said, things are different now. Sharper. You're mine, Krystal, and before we're done here, you'll know just how determined I am to keep you."

With her arms above her head, she felt even more exposed and even more feminine under the stark masculinity in Linc's hungry look.

The feel of his lips on her nipple drove her wild, the sensitivity there much more intense than she remembered. "Oh God! Linc, please."

Linc lifted his head to stare down at her, his hooded gaze mesmerizing. "I've barely begun. I told you that I'm not rushing this, Krystal. I want you to feel the same hunger that I do."

He lowered his head again, using his tongue to flick one nipple and then the other before brushing his lips over the sensitive underside of her breasts.

He used his mouth on every inch of her breasts, and writhing beneath him, she fought to get the attention to her nipples that she desperately needed.

Whimpering in frustration, she kicked at him. "I do! Take me, damn it!"

"Not even close, baby." Scraping his teeth over the outer curve of her breast, he slid his hand to her waist. "I could eat you alive."

"Take me." She ached for him, but despite the hunger in his touch and his hard cock pressing against her thigh, he seemed determined to make her wait.

Lifting his head, he held her gaze while slowly stroking her nipple, his eyes flaring at her cry of pleasure. "Oh, I'm gonna take you, darlin', but not yet."

Releasing her wrists, he slid his hands under her, lifting and arching her slightly as he lowered his head again to nuzzle her breasts. "You're even more beautiful now. Sweeter. I've missed those soft cries of pleasure."

Lowering her hands to grip his shoulders, Krystal cried out at the feel of his lips closing over her nipple, lifting up to him. "Linc!"

His hands moved lower, slipping inside the waistband of her pants and panties to close on her bottom cheeks. "I love the way you say my name." With a harsh groan, he straightened to his knees and stripped her pants and panties off. "I need to taste you. I need more of those cries."

Parting her thighs wider, he lowered his head, sliding his tongue through her slit.

Unprepared for the sudden onslaught, Krystal cried out and stiffened in shocked pleasure.

Stunned at the sharp pleasure, she instinctively tried to close her legs, crying out again when Linc firmed his hands on her thighs and lifted her higher.

He jabbed his tongue into her, chuckling softly as he lifted his head. "Think you're gonna get away from me, do you? Not a chance, baby. I've waited too fucking long."

Krystal gulped and sucked in another breath, given only enough time to call his name before he lowered his head again.

The heat and friction of his tongue against her clit made it tingle hotly with incredible pleasure, her excitement heightened by his unrelenting hold.

The fact that he forced her to accept the pleasure added to it, his obvious enjoyment in her filling her with a sense of feminine power and vulnerability that brought tears to her eyes.

It was even more intense than she remembered.

She came hard, the tingling heat rippling from her clit in all directions, bathing her in a shimmering warmth that had her body arching of its own volition as she reached for him. "Linc!"

Lifting to his knees, he loomed over her, bending to touch his lips to hers while using his fingers on her clit to keep the pleasure rolling through her. "There's my girl. Do you remember how it was between us?"

Lifting her hips into his touch, she gripped his forearm. "It wasn't like this."

Tears blurred the vision of his beloved face moving closer to hers, and with a smile, she slid her hands into his hair. "It's better."

Linc groaned and gathered her closer. "It's more mature now, and we've all had time to think about what we want. We all know what it's like to be apart." He stripped out of his clothes, his gaze raking over her as he rolled on a condom. "And we're sure as hell not gonna be parted again, if I have to tie you to the bed to keep you here."

Covering her body with his, he gathered her closer, a hand beneath her head tilting her face to his as he slowly entered her. "You're mine. Ours."

Wrapping her legs around his waist, Krystal let her eyes flutter closed, sucking in a breath when the head of his cock began to fill her.

"No. Open those eyes. I want to see them while I enter you."

Krystal forced her eyes open again. "Oh God!"

Staring into his eyes, she moaned as he eased into her, the full, stretched feeling even more intense than she remembered. "Linc. It's been so long. Oh God. Hold me closer."

Linc brushed her lips with his, his hold firming. "Easy. I've got you, baby. Christ, you're tight."

Krystal instinctively closed her legs on his hips and gripped his shoulders, the pleasure so intense she trembled with it. "Linc!"

Linc slid a hand under her bottom and lifted her slightly. "I know." His gravelly voice and the way his body shuddered against hers a testament to his own passion. "Nice and slow. You're killing me. You know that, don't you?"

The loving teasing in his tone eased some of her nervousness, and when he began to withdraw, she cried out in frustration and tightened her legs around him. "Don't go."

"I'm not going anywhere, baby. Nothing on earth could make me leave you now." With another groan, Linc stared into her eyes and slid deeper. "You feel so good, but I'm gonna take this slow if it kills me. I want it to last."

His shallow strokes pressed at a spot inside her that had need coming back in full force. His body surrounded hers, the heat and strength of it like coming home.

A sob escaped before she could prevent it, and she couldn't help but smile when Linc stilled, his eyes widening. "It feels so good to be with you like this. I can't believe how long it's been since I felt so warm."

Linc's muscles relaxed, his slow grin making her heart beat faster. "Then hang on, baby, because it's gonna get hotter."

Gathering her wrists in one hand, he raised them over her head, his eyes narrowed again. "Your pussy's milking me already. Take more."

"Yes." Lifting up to him, she took him deeper, crying out at the full, stretched sensation.

"Easy, baby."

"No." The feel of his hot, bare chest against her nipples had her writhing beneath him for more. "Take me. I need to feel this. I need to feel alive."

Linc cursed under his breath, his body stiffening again. "Stop wiggling. It's hard enough to go slow."

"Good." Pressing her heels into the backs of his thighs, she rocked her hips. "I'm not a virgin, Linc. You've taken me before."

"It's been a long time." His voice had deepened, becoming ragged. "I don't want to hurt you."

"You're killing me. Take me like you mean it, damn it!"

Linc abruptly withdrew, releasing her wrists. "No." Rising to his knees, he gripped the back of hers, parting them wide and lifting them high. "You're gonna take what I give you."

Stunned by the change in him, Krystal gulped as she took in his hardened features. "Linc?"

He thrust into her again, a little deeper than before and started to move, his thrusts coming faster, but not going any deeper.

"I missed this. I missed your tight pussy gripping me like this. You're even more passionate now."

"Oh God!" Krystal tried to rock her hips in time to his thrusts, but his hold didn't allow for much movement at all.

"I can only imagine how tight that ass is gonna be."

Her bottom clenched at the memory of their play there as they got her used to having her bottom breached and the one time they'd taken her together.

Thrusting deeper, Linc slowed. "I see you remember. I was the one to take your virginity there. Rafe and I can't wait to take you together again."

Just the thought of being taken in both openings quickened her pulse and had her clenching on him again. "Please."

Each slow thrust took him deeper. "Your pussy and ass remember who you belong to." He began to thrust faster, the friction and press of his cock against her inner walls sending her senses soaring. "Now we just have to remind the rest of you. Look at me."

Krystal's eyes snapped open at his sharp demand, the possessiveness in his hard look arousing her even more.

"Keep those eyes open and on me."

His demanding tone sent a thrill through her, the possessiveness and hunger in his eyes filling her with a sense of feminine power that heightened her arousal even more.

He thrust faster, his gaze holding hers. "Yeah. You can take more, can't you?" He stopped thrusting briefly, watching her eyes as he slowly slid deep. "Take it all, baby. God, you feel so good."

Krystal gasped, a whimper of shock and incredible need escaping as he withdrew slightly and thrust again. "Linc! It's so deep. Oh God!"

"Fuck! Christ, you're incredible." His eyes narrowed even more as he slightly withdrew again. "Do you like knowing what you do to me?"

Some instinct had her lifting her arms above her head, and she couldn't help but smile when his gaze narrowed and his cock jumped inside her. "What do I do to you?"

Her nipples tingled hotly under his gaze, the pure male hunger in his eyes heightening her sense of feminine power.

Sliding a hand to her breast, he tugged her nipple, his eyes flaring at her gasp of pleasure, narrowing when she lowered her hands to her breasts. "You make me crazy. I want you even more than I did before, and that was enough to make me wait three years for you to be free. You're not going anywhere. Put your hands above your head and keep them there. Next time I'm going to restrain you."

Bracing a hand on either side of her head, he waited until she obeyed him before moving again. He withdrew almost all the way and thrust deep, his thrusts coming harder and faster. "Come again for me. I want to hear those cries of pleasure again."

Caught up in the pleasure, Krystal cried out his name, gripping the edges of the pillow to keep from reaching for him. "Oh God! Linc." Overwhelmed, she let her eyes close as the tension built, the awareness in her nipples intensifying the pleasure. "Ohhhh!"

She went over in another rush of pleasure, stiffening as her orgasm crested. She reached for Linc, her sense of vulnerability leaving her with the need to hold on to him.

With a harsh groan, he thrust deep, the feel of his cock pulsing inside her sending more ripples through her.

His deep groan of pleasure reverberated through her when he covered her body with his again and gathered her close, as if knowing she needed it. "Christ, I love you."

A sob escaped, coming unexpectedly from somewhere deep inside her. "Oh, Linc! I love you, too. I've missed you so much."

Lifting his head, he smiled down at her, wiping away a tear. "And I've missed you. I'll fight for you, Krystal." Withdrawing slowly, he rolled to his side and gathered her against him. He kissed her hair and pulled the light blanket over her, holding her close. "You've been holding everything in for so long. It used to drive me crazy when I came to visit you, but I didn't want to push you when I knew you were dealing with so much. Now you can just relax and let Rafe and me take care of you."

Warm and replete, Krystal snuggled against him, finding it harder and harder to keep her eyes open. "I told you that I need to take care of myself."

His lips touched the top of her head again. "Look at it this way. We'll take care of each other."

Krystal smiled at that. "I have an idea of how you want me to take care of you."

He took the hand she held against his chest in his and toyed with her fingers. "I'm sure you do. But it's more than just sex, Krystal."

He lifted her hand to his lips. "Don't get me wrong. Sex is important. It creates, deepens, and enhances intimacy, but just having you here is a relief to us. You need to start to get comfortable here."

"So I can start to feel as if this is my home."

"I want you to think of this as your home, Krystal." He hugged her closer and blew out a breath. "Even if you don't like the town, I'd like very much for you to think of Rafe and me as your home."

Krystal's eyes popped open, and she jolted upright. "You would leave Desire if I don't like it here?"

Sitting up, Linc braced himself on an elbow and eased her back down again. "We would. Our home is with you, Krystal. We made this town our home with you in mind. But if we have to choose between you and living here, we'll quit our jobs, leave here, and find another place to live. We want you to be happy, baby."

Stunned and unnerved by his offer, Krystal sighed. "More pressure, Linc. Please don't do this to me."

Linc took her hand in his. "Just laying my cards on the table, baby. I'm not about to make it easy for you to leave."

Meeting his gaze, she closed her hand on his. "I'm scared."

"I know." Linc bent to touch his lips to hers. "There's something I want you to think about. For the last few years, your world has been spinning out of control. Rafe and I know that, and we've worked hard to make sure you have what you need to be grounded again. You're safe in Desire, and you're safe with us. We want to know that you trust us enough to let us be your rock."

Krystal remembered her conversation with Brenna and Jesse and the claim that it meant a great deal to the men to be needed.

Taking her hand from his, she cupped his jaw. "Linc, I want to, but I realized when you came for me just how much I needed you. It scared me. I knew if I'd called you, you would have come."

"In a heartbeat."

"Just knowing that gave me strength."

Linc smiled. "I'm glad."

Krystal sighed and leaned against his chest. "Everything's changed so fast. I just need the time to know that I'm not with you just because I need a crutch. I have to know that I can stand on my own two feet."

"Baby, you've already proven that. You had more heaped on your shoulders than most people deal with in a lifetime. Nobody could have handled it better."

Leaning over her again, he gripped her chin. "And you insisted on doing it alone. We only let you because our presence upset your mother. We're not leaving you alone again."

Dropping back, he pulled her close. "Take the time to recharge your batteries and figure out what you want to do. But you're not doing it alone."

Chapter Nine

Krystal woke slowly, smiling at the delicious warmth and lingering awareness in her pussy, clit, and nipples. A hard arm closed around her from behind, and from the opposite side of the bed where Linc had been when she fell asleep. "Hmm. Rafe." Without opening her eyes, she smiled and placed her hand over his.

Pressing his lips against her neck, he caressed her belly. "You slept through lunch."

Krystal smiled, moaning softly when his hand slid over her hip. "It was worth it."

Chuckling, he pressed his lips to her shoulder. "I'm glad. How do you feel?"

She rolled toward him, loving the feel of his hands moving over her, more soothing than arousing. "Looser. Happy." She drew a deep breath and let it out slowly. "Scared."

Sliding his hand higher, he gripped her chin and lifted her face to his. "Hmm. Linc told me. You tell me. What are you scared of?"

Warmed even more by his low, calm tone and the concern in his eyes, Krystal flattened a hand on his chest, disappointed that he wore a T-shirt. "Getting hurt. Hurting you and Linc. Depending on you too much. We've been apart for so long, and I still needed you."

Rafe bent to brush his lips over her, not releasing her chin. "You need to stop worrying and just let it happen. We need you just as much."

Blowing out a breath, she tucked her head under his chin, pressing her face against his chest. "I guess I've gotten used to worrying. It's ingrained now."

"I'm glad you told me." He pressed his lips to her hair. "We have to have honesty between us, or we can never trust."

She pressed her face against his chest and breathed in his fresh masculine scent. "How's this for honesty? I've changed so much that I don't even remember the person I used to be. God, Rafe. I was so stupid before. So sheltered. I never worried about having a place to live. I never worried about being alone. I never worried about where to wash my laundry."

"You don't have to worry about any of that anymore." Linc's voice came from somewhere behind her, the bed dipping as he ran a hand over her thigh and sat on the bed near her legs. "Rafe's right. We need honesty."

"Speaking of honesty…" Rafe tilted her face to his again. "When Linc and I found out that you didn't have a place to live and had been sleeping in the chair next to your mother's bed, we were furious at you."

His grip in her hair tightened, tilting her head back even more. "Still are. You shouldn't have kept that from us, Krystal, and it infuriates me that you did. It also hurts. You're not alone. You haven't been alone since we met you. We stayed away because our presence upset your mother and, therefore, you. She never understood how Linc and I could both love you, and we respected that. But it cost us dearly."

Krystal sighed, knowing that she owed them the same honesty. "I'm sorry."

Rafe kissed her hair. "When you could no longer afford your cell phone, you wouldn't accept the new one we got for you so that we could stay in touch with you."

Krystal's face burned. "I was afraid."

"Of what, Krystal? We just needed to hear that you were all right."

Remembering the long, sleepless nights sitting alone in the nursing home, Krystal shook her head and smiled sadly. "I was afraid of needing you too much—using you as a crutch. You didn't need me to call you in the middle of the night because I was overtired and feeling sorry for myself."

Rafe lifted her chin again, a muscle working in his jaw. "We would have come."

Cupping his cheek, she nodded and smiled faintly. "I know. I know you would have come, which would have made it harder to resist calling you."

Over the covers, Linc smoothed a hand over her thigh again. "You should have called."

Running a finger lightly over the neckline of Rafe's T-shirt, Krystal sighed. "How many times could I have done that before you and Linc got sick of my neediness?" Shaking her head, she let her hand fall. "No. I couldn't do that to you. It wouldn't have been fair to you to call you when I needed you and push you away the rest of the time. I decided that I couldn't be half-assed about it, so I chose to keep you at a distance. I was going to leave after the funeral and call you to let you know I was okay. It was for the best."

"Best for whom?" Rafe's eyes narrowed. "We would have tracked you down and dragged you back here."

Krystal smiled and shook her head, still overwhelmed that two such compelling men would wait so long for her. "I really expected you to find someone else. I'm still on edge waiting for you to tell me that you brought me here because you felt sorry for me but you've fallen in love with another woman."

Linc sighed. "You know, turning you over my knee sounds more appealing all the time."

Rafe lifted her chin, studying her features with narrowed eyes, dark with anger. "Your distance gave us more than a few bad moments."

Smiling in apology, she glanced back at Linc. "I couldn't afford to be anything else. I had to be distant for my own sanity. When you held me, it was so hard not to cry and beg you to stay. You talked most of the time about your new jobs here and how great the town was. I couldn't ask you to walk away from the new life you'd made just to sit there and hold my hand."

Linc bent to kiss her shoulder. "We would have. We would have been very happy to have you ask us for help—to need us."

Krystal gave him another small smile, fighting to push back memories of the loneliness she'd felt then. "I know. I *did* need you, but I couldn't put you in that position. Sometimes I thought I would go crazy. I wanted to beat my head against the wall, and other times, I wanted to walk out the door and just keep going. Other times I just wanted to curl in a ball and cry. I couldn't do any of those things, and it would have just frustrated both of you because I know how much you like to help. The reality was that there was nothing you could do."

Linc leaned partially over her, running a hand over her hair. "We wanted to be there for you. We wanted you to have someone to talk to and to be able to give you whatever you needed."

Nodding, she waved a hand. "I know. Anyway, it's over now. I just don't want to be pressured. Honestly, right now I don't think I can take it."

Rafe rolled her to her back and cupped her cheek, his eyes dark and narrowed dangerously. "Understood, but if you do anything like that again, or need something you don't tell us about, you're going over my knee. Are we clear?"

The conversation with Jesse and Brenna played in her mind again. She looked from Rafe to Linc and back again. "Jesse and Brenna said something about spanking, and you keep threatening it. I mean, we played before, but—"

Rafe ran his thumb over her bottom lip. "We've been very gentle with you because of all you've been through, but if you put yourself or us through any more of that, I'll spank your sweet ass in a heartbeat. Don't push me on this. You've worn out my patience on the subject."

Linc rose, standing next to the bed with his hands on his hips. "We'll get you a new cell phone, and you'll keep it with you, especially when you're not with one of us. If you need something, we expect to know about it. If you have a problem or concern, talk to us. We won't tolerate secrets from you anymore. You won't push us away again, Krystal."

Sitting up, Krystal pulled the light blanket higher to cover her breasts. "You know, I used to think you were old-fashioned—except for wanting to share me, of course. I understood—at least I thought I did—that you shared me because neither one of you were serious about me. I accepted that. All the rules are changing, and it's very confusing."

Linc sighed. "We were trying to ease you into it, but life interrupted. By coming to see you all the time, we'd hoped that you would realize how much you mean to us."

Krystal leaned back against the padded headboard. "I assumed you just didn't want to dump me while I was dealing with Dad and then Mom." Smiling, she eyed each of them. "You have to understand that I'd never met men like you before. Your chauvinism is coming really close to arrogance."

"Too bad." Rafe sat up, as well, bracing himself on a hand next to her hips and leaning close enough for her to see the glitter of anger in his dark eyes. "I think a little arrogance is in order in dealing with you. You seem hell-bent on suffering alone, and Linc and I have had enough of it."

Leaning closer, he kissed her, a gentle kiss that ended with a nip to her bottom lip, the combination of tenderness and arrogant male in his kiss much like the man himself. "You must be hungry. Let's go eat, and you can see how the kitchen table looks."

Determined to hide her disappointment that she'd chosen the smaller set, she plastered on a smile. "Sounds good. I'll get dressed and be out in a minute."

Rafe lowered the covers and bent to kiss her nipple, lifting his head with a smile when she gasped. "Why don't you just slip into your new robe? I'm gonna go start the grill and the potatoes, and we'll make a salad. We'll stay in tonight, and we can all relax and talk."

Krystal glanced at Linc to see his reaction, and as he had in the past, he smiled, his eyes flaring with heat. "Rafe's jealous as hell that I made love to you and is dying to have you again."

Crossing her arms over her chest, she eyed both of them. "And neither one of you minds when the other makes love to me?"

Rafe smiled and rose, tossing the covers aside. "Like Linc just said, I'm jealous, but since I plan to take you tonight, I can live with it. We both want you, Krystal, and plan to share you. My jealousy or Linc's is not your problem." He bent to touch his lips to her belly, raising his head with a smile. "And yes, we do plenty of talking about you behind your back. We have to be on the same page with you, or this won't work. If you try to pit one of us against the other, you'll get that spanking that intrigues you so much."

Lifting her chin, she covered herself again. "It doesn't intrigue me."

Rafe tossed the covers back again, exposing her to his gaze. "Liar." He moved the covers out of her reach. "And lying will get you a trip over my knee." He tossed her new robe to her. "Put on your robe. I'm gonna go start the grill."

Bundled in her new robe and wearing a pair of her new soft socks, Krystal walked down the hallway toward the kitchen with Linc's hand warm on her back. "I can't believe they delivered it so fast. I didn't hear a thing."

"We told them that you were sleeping. Rafe and I helped them bring it all in, and we were all very quiet. Everyone knows that you need your rest."

She slowed, glancing up at him over her shoulder. "Good Lord. I'm a big girl, Linc. I'm not going to throw a fit if someone wakes me from my nap. I don't even remember falling asleep. I was lying there with you and—oh my God!"

She stopped abruptly at the doorway, her hand flying to her mouth. "You bought the other table!"

Rafe turned from seasoning the steaks. "That's the one you wanted, isn't it?"

Krystal moved forward, reverently reaching out a hand to smooth it over the tabletop.

She couldn't believe they'd bought the one she wanted. "This one goes better in the kitchen. It's beautiful, isn't it? It looks even better than I imagined."

She pulled out a chair and lowered herself onto the leather cushion and glanced up at Linc, who'd followed her. "It's even more comfortable than I thought it would be."

She narrowed her eyes at both of them but couldn't stop smiling. "How did you know I liked this one? I didn't even look at it."

Rafe smiled, and both men looked inordinately pleased with themselves. "We're observant. How do you feel about making a salad?"

Krystal had more fun than she would have imagined, especially with paper dishes, and found trying to cut tomatoes and steak with plastic silverware an adventure with Rafe and Linc.

They broke several forks and knives while trying to cut their steaks, and Krystal found herself laughing out loud at their frustration, which she suspected they exaggerated to amuse her.

"You have to be gentle with it. You're a brute." She spoke between giggles, laughing even harder when Rafe gave up and picked his steak up and started eating it with his bare hands.

Unable to stop laughing, Krystal shook her head. "I suspected there was a little caveman inside you. Now I know it's true."

Rafe set his steak aside and wiped his hands, the gleam in his eyes her only warning as he rose to his feet. "Caveman, am I?"

His devious smile had Krystal jumping to her feet and holding out a hand in an ineffective effort to hold him off, a giggle escaping when he kept coming toward her. "Now, Rafe."

She took a step back and then another, laughing as she turned and took off. "Stop, you caveman!" Aware of Linc's amusement, she started to run, but her fuzzy socks got no traction on the hardwood floor in the hallway.

Laughing harder, she turned the corner to head down the hallway, her speed and the slick surface sending her flailing toward the opposite wall.

Rafe caught her before she could hit it, lifting her over his shoulder with a speed that left her dizzy. Sliding a hand up the back of her thigh, he slapped her ass. "I'll show you caveman."

Giggling, she kicked her legs, her bottom stinging slightly from his slap. "Rafe! What are you doing?"

He slapped her ass again and started down the hall to their bedroom. "Being a caveman, of course."

He bent and eased her down to the mattress. "I want you." He made quick work of the belt of her robe, unfastening it and parting the sides to reveal her nakedness to his heated gaze. "I want to learn every inch of you all over again."

He lowered his head, taking her mouth with a kiss filled with a passion and hunger that ignited her own.

Playfulness turned to heat in a heartbeat.

Wrapping her legs round him, she moaned in delight and slid her fingers into his hair to hold him closer.

His kiss, filled with heat, consumed her, the feel of his denim-covered cock pressing against her thigh thrilling her.

He tasted like pure male, the demand in his kiss sharper than ever and drawing an answering passion from her to meet it.

His tongue swept her mouth, the hand at her nape holding her in place for a kiss more possessive and domineering than she'd ever experienced.

It stole her breath, and she suddenly understood how much he and Linc had held back from her.

Sucking in a breath when his other hand slid to her breast, Krystal lifted into him, tightening her legs around him and tugging at his T-shirt with the need to get closer.

Swallowing her moan, Rafe broke off his kiss just long enough to strip off his shirt before reaching for her again. "Damn, you're delicious. I want you so fucking bad."

Scrambling to her knees, she reached for the fastening of his jeans with hands that shook with the need raging inside her. "Then take me." She rained kisses on his chest, loving the way his body stiffened when she freed his cock and closed her hand around it. "It was always good, but not like this."

Slipping her robe from her shoulders, he ran his hands down her back. "Love has a way of doing that." Gripping her wrist, he pulled her hand from his cock and slipped her robe the rest of the way off. "Another time. It's been too long, and I want you too much."

Closing his hands on her waist, he tossed her to the bed, wrapping his hands around her and lifting her slightly, arching her back and lowering his mouth to her nipple. "I wanted to take my time with you, damn it!"

Fisting her hands in his hair, Krystal pressed her heels against the backs of his thighs and lifted to him, his attention to her nipples creating an answering tug to her clit. "Don't you dare! Oh!"

Using his lips, he tugged at her nipple before raising himself to his knees and ripping the condom open with his teeth. "I want you too fucking much, but the next time I take you, I'm gonna make you suffer for all the time you made me suffer."

Spreading her thighs to watch him roll on the condom, Krystal moaned and reached for him. "Looking forward to it. In the meantime—oh!" She wrapped her arms around his neck, crying out in surprise when he didn't cover her body with his as she'd expected and, instead, gripped her bottom and lifted her to him.

Sitting back on his heels he positioned her over the head of his cock and lowered her, impaling her on its thick length. "In the meantime, I'm gonna sink my cock inside you."

Surprising her further, he closed his hand on her hips, keeping her still when she tried to move. "No." He brushed his lips over hers. "Be still. I've waited a long time to be inside you again, and I want to enjoy it for as long as I can."

Gripping his shoulders, Krystal lifted her face for his kiss, grateful when he immediately obliged her.

With a hand on her bottom and the other at her nape, he held her close, taking her mouth with his, the erotic dance of his tongue against hers thrilling her senses.

Struggling to move on him, she moaned in frustration, the friction of his chest against her nipples heightening the hunger even more.

Breaking off his kiss, Rafe stared down at her, his dark gaze filled with possessiveness. Using his powerful thighs and the hand at her bottom, he began to slowly thrust, his eyes narrowing even more at her cry of pleasure.

Aware that her position gave her no leverage to increase or limit his thrusts at all, Krystal hung on to him, grateful for his strength and support when the pleasure mounted.

He kept his thrusts slow but filled her completely with each stroke while each small movement provided a delicious friction to her nipples.

Filled with incredible heat, Krystal pulled his head back down for another kiss, needing the taste of him.

Rafe groaned and sipped at her lips, teasing her relentlessly. "I've waited a long time for this. Do you know how many times I wondered if I'd ever be inside you again?"

Krystal kissed him back, pouring her love and passion for him in every kiss. "I can't believe you waited for me. I was afraid to believe you would, and I knew I had no right to ask."

Tightening the hand at her nape, he tilted her head back, brushing his lips over her jaw. "Of course we waited. We had no choice. You were already in our blood." Lifting his head, he began to thrust faster. "You're ours, Krystal."

The hand on her bottom shifted slightly, a finger stroking the tender area around where his cock stretched her. "All of you."

He gathered her juices on his fingertip and slid it to her puckered opening. "Linc had the pleasure of taking this tight ass before circumstances parted us."

The realization that she sat spread wide on his lap with no way to close against him had her fidgeting. "Rafe!"

"Yeah, say my name. You didn't really think I would ignore your ass, did you?"

Shaking with sensation, Krystal sucked in a breath when he gathered more moisture and pressed his fingertip against her bottom hole. "I can't believe how you touch me."

The memory of Linc working his cock into her one erotic night had her bottom clenching with awareness.

Firming his hold on her bottom, he leaned forward to ease her back, the tip of his finger breaching her puckered opening and sending chills of awareness racing through her. "I can't wait to take this tight ass. I want to make sure that everything is mine. Ours. I'm greedy. I want every fucking thing about you."

"Oh God." Her toes curled when each thrust moved his finger, the slight burning sensation adding to her pleasure.

He began to move faster, taking her mouth again as he took her hard and fast, the pressure of his fingertip just inside her puckered opening overwhelming her with sensation.

The heat of his body surrounded her, the strength of his hold guiding her with a firm strength that both excited and reassured her.

His need for her resonated with every thrust.

Every groan.

Every kiss.

Lifting his head, he broke off another mind-numbing kiss to nuzzle her neck. "Now that I'm inside you again, I never want to leave."

Krystal moaned at the pleasure, tilting her head to give him better access. "It's so good. It feels so good to be with you like this."

His teeth scraped over her jaw, sending a shiver of erotic delight through her. "Christ, the way your pussy clenches on me."

Lifting his head, he moved the finger in her bottom, his eyes flaring at her cry. "Your ass is clenching on my finger, too. No more shyness between us. There's no room for that now."

"No. It's so real." Krystal clung to him as his thrusts came faster, the awareness in her bottom and the feel of his thick cock stretching her pussy, the friction against her inner walls overwhelming her.

His husky words of praise and need poured over her as she came, his hold tightening as the wave of bliss crested.

"That's it, baby. I've got you. It's damned real." He continued to thrust steadily, sipping at her lips while keeping the pleasure rolling through her.

Surging deep with a groan of completion, he withdrew his finger from her bottom, the sensation sending another rush of pleasure to layer over the first. "Oh!"

Lowering her to her back, he kept a hand on her bottom and slid the other over her hair and groaned again, dropping his head to the pillow beside hers with another groan. "Hmm."

Smiling, she struggled to catch her breath, running her heels over the backs of his thighs and her hands over his powerful biceps. Warmed by his body, she savored the lingering ripples of pleasure.

"Hmm? Is that it?"

She opened her eyes when he lifted his head, her smile widening when she saw that he stared down at her, his grin rueful.

A giggle escaped, the teasing glint in his eyes warming her even more. "Kinda hard to come up with real words right now."

Lowering his head, he kissed her deeply, a slow kiss of possessive tenderness that made her heart clench. Lifting his head again, he smiled down at her, his confident smile and the masculine satisfaction in his dark eyes telling her that he knew just how much pleasure he'd given her. "That's better. I'd hate to think that you just suffered through it."

Krystal smiled and clenched on him, giggling again when he groaned. "I liked it a little. You seemed to suffer through it pretty well, too."

Easing his weight from her, Rafe withdrew and rolled to his side, gathering her close. "It's even better than I remembered." Pressing his lips to her hair, he held on tight, knowing it would be some time before he got over his fear of losing her again.

"Being away from you was hell."

"I'm sorry. I had to."

Pulling the sheet over her, he turned her more fully toward him and rubbed her back, savoring the feel and warmth of her softness against him. "I know. Linc and I both understood what you had to do, but it didn't make it any less frustrating, especially when you started putting distance between us."

Tracing a pattern on his chest with a fingertip, Krystal lifted her face to his, her blue eyes dark with the remnants of desire. "I'm sorry for that, too. But I told you why I did it."

He kissed her hair again, loving the feel of the silky softness against his lips and the intimacy of her touch. "I know. I understood. I didn't like it, but I understood."

He pressed her face against his chest and caressed her hair with his fingertips. "It's over now, and you're with us. That's all that matters."

Lifting herself to her elbow, Krystal shook her head. "Rafe, I love you. I love Linc, but I don't know yet if this can work. Everything's happened so fast. I feel like I don't even know myself anymore. I've spent the last three years on a schedule and at the mercy of others. When my dad got sick, I worked. After work, I went to my parents' house to help my mother with my father and made dinner for both of them to give her a break. Appointments, treatments, scans, grocery shopping, and a hundred other things. My mother didn't understand the insurance and counted on me to help her. I didn't even have the time to clean my own apartment. I had to take time from work to take my father to all the appointments because my mother didn't want to go alone."

Aching for her, he idly ran his fingers through her hair. "We could see you were run ragged. I wish you'd let us help you."

Krystal sighed and pleased him by snuggling closer. "I know. I couldn't. I felt like if I let go for one minute, I would lose control. I was scared to let up. Eventually, I was cut to part time and couldn't afford my apartment anymore. I was barely there anyway. I had a little saved, and when the lease ran out, it was just easier to live with Mom and Dad, especially when the appointments became more frequent and he stayed in the hospital for extended periods. When he died and Mom had her first stroke, it started all over again."

Rolling to her back, she stared at the ceiling and blew out a breath. "Now I can do what I want, and it's more than a little disconcerting. I don't have to get up at any special time. I don't have to rush anywhere. It just feels…weird."

"And we took you out today. Shit."

Sitting up again, she leaned toward him, her blonde hair a curtain of silk around her face, gleaming with the light when she shook her head. "No. I have to admit that I really didn't feel like going out, but I'm glad I did. I loved meeting everyone. I loved seeing the town, and I really loved shopping. Thank you." She touched her lips to his, the feel of her hand against his chest easing some of the tension still remaining inside him—a tension that he knew wouldn't go away until things had been settled between them. "I haven't shopped in so long, and I really love my new things."

"You're welcome." Rafe smiled and covered her hand with his. "I enjoy seeing you smile. You have so little, and there's a possessive streak in me that gets a hell of a lot of satisfaction in seeing you wear something we bought for you. To see your pleasure in a table. To buy something that'll pamper you. God knows you deserve it."

Lifting her chin, Krystal smiled. "If you spoil me, I'll become such a brat that you won't want me anymore."

"Not a chance, baby." He leaned back, pleased to see that her features were flushed from their lovemaking and she seemed much more relaxed. "If you get out of hand, I'll just turn you over my knee."

Giggling, she tried to slap at him, but he caught her hand in his and kissed her fingertips before releasing it. "Brute." Cuddling closer, she sighed. "I feel like I'm dreaming all of this and I'm going to wake up sitting next to my mother's bed."

Rafe chuckled and kissed her as he rose with the intention of getting rid of his condom. "Not a dream, darlin'. This is the real thing."

His cell phone rang, and with a curse, he tossed the sheet aside. Bending, he reached into the pocket of his jeans and glanced at the display, frowning to see a number he didn't recognize.

Stiffening, he answered, hoping it wasn't an emergency. "Delgatto."

"I want to talk to my sister."

Krystal jerked upright, having obviously heard her brother's terse demand. "Kevin?"

"What do you want?" Rafe rose and went into the bathroom, ridding himself of the condom.

"I need to talk to Krystal. Put her on the phone."

Rafe raised a brow, turning again to see that Krystal had shrugged into her robe and followed him, standing at the doorway. Irritated that she'd paled and her features had become tight with tension again, he shook his head. "Now isn't a good time."

Clenching his jaw, he spoke through gritted teeth, reaching for her and gathering her close. "She's been through enough without having to deal with you."

Krystal shook her head and stepped back, holding out her hand. "Let me talk to him."

Irritated that her brother had managed to dispel her relaxed mood, Rafe wanted to hang up but knew that it wouldn't solve anything.

He reluctantly handed his phone to her, gathering her close again to reinforce the fact that she was no longer alone.

Rubbing her stiff shoulders, he listened to her part of the conversation.

"I don't have the money, Kevin."

A pause followed, one in which her brother spoke in a quiet tone that Rafe couldn't hear.

Krystal ran a hand over her hair, clearly agitated. "I told you what happened to the money, Kevin." Moving away from Rafe, she headed back into the bedroom and began to pace. "No, I didn't steal it, Kevin. It was Mom's money, and she needed it for her care."

Another pause.

"Because I couldn't handle her anymore! She was too heavy for me to lift, and there were times when I didn't have enough hands to change her and the bed when she had an accident! What the hell do you want from me, Kevin? She had to be watched twenty-four-seven. I couldn't sleep when she did because I had to do laundry, clean, and fix meals. I couldn't even get out to go to the grocery store, and there were times when I went an entire week without a shower! Where were you?"

Rafe's hands clenched into fists at his sides, and he found himself fighting to contain his fury at the thought of everything she'd been through.

He doubted that he'd ever hear the entire story, but each piece of the puzzle he got added to the picture of a miserable time in her life.

He and Linc should never have left her.

Out of the corner of his eye, he saw something move and turned to see that Linc stood in the doorway, his eyes narrowed and glittering with the same fury making Rafe's blood boil.

Krystal continued to pace, ignoring both of them. "Yeah, well, I lost my job because she needed me. I didn't put her in a home and just leave her, Kevin. I stayed with her. I had to sell the house and all of the furniture alone. Every cent had to be accounted for because she had to be broke in order to get financial help from the government. I didn't see you giving up your precious time to help me. It was my home, too, and I didn't have a place to live, either."

Linc came further into the room, stopping next to Rafe. "Her brother?"

"Yeah." Rafe blew out a breath, but his body continued to vibrate with rage as he stepped into his jeans again.

Linc braced his hands on his hips, his eyes following Krystal. "She hid a hell of a lot from us. I hate that she went through all of that alone. Every time I visited, she acted like she had it all under control. She didn't show a fucking thing."

Krystal paused next to the bed, her cheeks once again flushed, but this time with anger. Dropping to the bed, she closed her eyes, fisting her free hand on her thigh. "I don't care if you believe me or not. I'm not a liar, Kevin."

Linc kept his voice low. "How did he sound?"

"Desperate." Fighting not to rip the phone from her hand, Rafe crossed his arms over his chest. "Pissed. Stoned."

Krystal jumped up and began pacing again. "Well, that's what happens when you judge other people by your standards. You're used to hanging out with lowlifes. Don't talk to me like I'm one of them."

Rafe had had enough. "I'm gonna put an end to this."

Linc touched his arm. "I really don't like this. I'm going to the station and pull up a picture of him. I want to post it so everyone can be on the lookout for him. I want to know if he comes to Desire."

"What do you need the money so badly for?"

Listening to Krystal, Rafe, too, had a bad feeling about the whole situation and tried to console himself with the fact that he and Linc could now keep a close eye on her.

Krystal spun again, glancing at Linc as he left the room. "That's not my problem, Kevin."

Snaking an arm out, Rafe caught her around the waist, yanking her against him and taking the cell phone from her.

"Hey!"

Ignoring her outraged cry, Rafe held her close to his side and the phone out of her reach. "Enough!"

She blinked at his tone but quieted almost immediately, blowing out a breath and pressing her cheek against his chest.

Kevin's words slurred. "But I need it!"

Putting the phone to his ear, Rafe cut him off. "I don't give a shit what you need or what you think you're entitled to, but you're not to call and upset your sister again. Are we clear?"

"This is none of your fucking business!"

"I already told you how wrong you were about that. Don't call her again until you get your life in order, and don't call her to ask for money. Don't forget that you have to get through me to get to her. If you need to talk to me, feel free to call, but I won't have you upsetting your sister again."

Rafe disconnected, tossing the phone on the bed and wrapping both arms around her to gather her close, his anger growing when he realized that she trembled. "You okay, baby?"

"I'm fine."

Frustrated that even so soon after he'd made love to her, she kept an emotional distance between them, Rafe tilted her face to his in order to see her eyes. "You keep saying that to me and I really am gonna turn you over my knee. You're upset. Why would you try to hide that from me? Do you really think I don't know you well enough to see it?"

Krystal sighed and flattened a hand on his chest. "It's not your problem."

Rafe tightened his grip on her chin when she would have turned away. "Your problems *are* our problems, Krystal. That's how this works. You're not alone anymore. You're gonna have to learn to accept that."

"You've done enough, Rafe. I—"

"Woman, you try my patience." Partly to make her understand how seriously he took the situation, and partly because he wanted to distract her from her brother's call, Rafe lifted her from her feet with an arm around her waist and carried her to the bed.

Sitting on the edge, he hauled her facedown over her lap, smiling at her squeal of outrage.

Kicking her feet, she tried to get up. "Rafe! What the hell are you doing?"

Rafe watched her closely, prepared to release her if she appeared scared or nervous, but her small smile urged him on.

He'd do anything to distract her from the sadness that her conversation with her brother had caused.

Flipping the hem of her robe up over her shoulders, Rafe pressed a hand to her upper back to hold her in place while running the other over her ass. "I'm about to show you what's gonna happen to you each time you try to cut me out of parts of your life."

Gripping his calf for leverage, she turned her upper body to look up at him, the shock in her expression tinged with curiosity and a daring that had his cock stirring to life again. "You can't spank me!"

Smoothing a hand over the soft skin of her bottom and upper thighs, Rafe smiled, lifting a brow. "You sure about that, darlin'?"

Her toes curled, a telltale sign of excitement that Rafe planned to use to his advantage. Writhing on his lap, she pressed her thighs together. "I just don't want to involve you in my problems." Her tone held a pleading note as if begging him to understand.

Rafe understood very well, but he kept his own tone firm to let her know that he wouldn't allow her to get away with it. "You've made that abundantly clear."

Uncomfortably aware that her bottom was on display, Krystal fought the surge of excitement at the threat of a spanking, part of her wondering why such a thing would intrigue—and arouse—her so much. "I've been taking care of my own problems, Rafe."

"Because you cut us out. You wouldn't let us know when things were bad. I already made it very clear that neither one of us will ever allow you to get away with it again."

She cried out at the sharp slap to her bottom, more out of shock than pain. "Rafe!" She sucked in a breath when he caressed the spot he'd slapped, spreading the warmth in a way that made her clit tingle. "You have to understand."

"Oh, I understand you very well, darlin'." Another slap landed on her other ass cheek. "Now *you're* gonna have to understand something. Maybe a warm ass will get your attention."

Krystal arched into him when he leaned over her, taking advantage of the hand at her back moving away as he opened the nightstand drawer and reached into it. "I understand that you and Linc don't like my brother, but I can't just desert him."

"That doesn't mean that you have to deal with him on your own." The drawer closed again, and Rafe straightened, his forearm pressed against her back. "The drugs make him unpredictable, Krystal, and cloud his judgment. I won't allow you to deal with him on your own."

Krystal tried to lift herself again but couldn't budge, disconcerted when he lifted and parted her ass cheeks. "Listen, Rafe. I can handle my brother, and I don't need—oh!"

She jolted, overwhelmed at the feel of a finger, coated with cold lube, surging into her ass. "Rafe!"

Her bottom clenched on his finger, the vulnerability of being in such a position with a devious lover exciting her both physically and mentally.

Emotionally, he already had her.

"You have no idea what it does to me to hear you say my name like that." Holding her down and her ass cheeks lifted and parted, Rafe eased his finger slightly from her bottom before thrusting it into her again.

"Do I have your attention, baby?"

Gripping his leg, Krystal sucked in a breath, her entire body trembling with sexual awareness. "Jesus, Rafe! Of course you have my attention."

"Good." He moved his finger in a circular motion, pressing against her inner walls and making her puckered opening burn. "It's like this, Krystal. You're ours, and it's our duty to protect you. I know it's not something that you're used to, and not something you're entirely comfortable with, but this is the way it is and will always be. You're going to have to accept that nothing is more important to Linc and me than protecting you, caring for you, and making you happy."

Chills raced up and down her spine, and Krystal found herself fighting her growing arousal and attempting to keep her voice steady. "I don't n-need protection from my brother."

She tried to stop clenching on his finger, but sensation and awareness there made it impossible.

Withdrawing his finger abruptly, Rafe slapped her bottom again, a light slap that brought another rush of warmth. "I disagree. He's desperate for some reason, and that makes him dangerous."

Disconcerted that her bottom clenched at emptiness, Krystal tried to close her legs against the heightened awareness in her clit and pussy, mortified that her inner thighs had become wet with her juices. "I'm not afraid of him. Let me up."

Not wanting him to discover that she'd become aroused, Krystal tried to get up again, sucking in a breath when he eased his finger, coated with more lube, into her bottom. Her position and the slick lube made tightening against him useless, which somehow increased her level of excitement even more. "Rafe!"

"I don't want him upsetting you."

"He doesn't upset me."

Another slap landed on her bottom, just enough to warm her ass cheeks without causing any pain. "Liar." He withdrew his finger and patted the spot he'd just slapped. "Be still."

Krystal tried to turn again, stiffening with a gasp when something cold and hard pressed against her puckered opening. "What are you doing?" Squeezing her eyes closed, she struggled to keep her breathing steady.

"Inserting a small butt plug. It'll feel a little strange, but it's been awhile since Linc took this beautiful ass, and I want to get you used to loosening these muscles for when I take you."

He slowly pushed it inside her, and the lube and the way he held her ass cheeks spread made it impossible for her to stop him. "It also has the benefit of making sure I have your full attention."

Moaning in desperation when it widened slightly, she braced herself for more, but it narrowed again almost immediately.

"There. Damn, that's beautiful." He pressed against it, letting her feel that part of it remained outside of her.

Caressing her ass cheek, he leaned close again. "This should make your spanking a little more effective."

Krystal twisted around again toward Rafe, sucking in a breath when her movement shifted the plug in her ass. "Why are you doing this?"

Lifting his arm from her back, he cupped her cheek. "Look at me."

She lifted her gaze to his, her face burning.

Rafe's smile held a tenderness that brought a lump to her throat while the erotic intent in his eyes made her nervous as hell. "I need to protect you. I need you to look to me for protection and for guidance. For advice. For help. For support. I'll have that from you, Krystal. I won't settle for less."

The last several years had shown her the strength she possessed, and she couldn't imagine going back to the insecure and naïve woman she's once been. "I'm not helpless."

"I know that very well." Rafe's gaze sharpened as he slid a finger over her swollen and throbbing clit. "I don't expect you to be helpless, but I don't expect—nor will I allow—you to try to handle everything on your own. I need you to trust me enough to confide in me, and neither one of us wants your stubbornness to get in the way of asking for help when you need it."

Krystal clenched her hands into fists, involuntarily opening her thighs wider to get a more direct touch on her clit. Finding it hard to focus on the conversation, she bit back a moan when need had her clenching on the plug. "I'm n-not trying t-to hide anything from you, b-but I'm not dumping my problems on you."

"It's not dumping, and your problems are our problems." He continued to caress her clit, his eyes sharp on hers. "Spread your legs wider."

She obeyed him without hesitation, grateful when he removed his hand from her face to press at her back again so that she could look away. "He's my brother."

Lifting her ass in invitation, Krystal cried out when Rafe slapped her ass again.

He smoothed the heat in as he had before, his finger slowing on her clit. "He's dangerous, Krystal, and I won't have you dealing with him on your own, and I sure as hell won't let him upset you."

Several more slaps landed in rapid succession, and Krystal found herself lifting into them instead of trying to avoid them.

The heat and slight sting heightened the awareness in her bottom and clit and had her lifting and spreading her legs wider, desperate to ease the incredible ache.

"Rafe, please!"

Rubbing her bottom, he pressed against the plug, shifting it inside her. "Please, what, baby?"

"I need to come!" She couldn't believe that she'd actually said the words out loud, but the need he'd created made it impossible to think about anything else.

"And I need to finish your spanking."

Wiggling on his lap, she fought to get the friction she needed on her clit. "How do you know when you're finished?"

Frustrated at the slow strokes to her clit, she rocked her hips, crying out when he spanked her several times in rapid succession.

With a hand on her bottom, Rafe held the warmth in, using his other hand to stroke her clit and press against the plug in a way that kept it shifting inside her. "When you agree to stop keeping things from us. When you agree to lean on us when you need to. By the way, I won't let you come until you do."

"What?" Gripping the covers for leverage, she lifted herself, only to let herself fall again when another slap landed. "Damn it, Rafe. Let me up."

To her surprise, and disappointment, he lifted from his lap and to her feet, holding her by the waist until she steadied herself.

Releasing her, he raised a brow, a small smile tugging at his lips. "Happy?"

Stunned, Krystal gaped at him. "You let me up!"

Rafe lifted a brow. "You told me to, didn't you?" Gripping each side of the belt to her robe, he pulled her closer, each small step moving the plug in her ass. "It has to be consensual, darlin'. If you don't want to be spanked, then I won't spank you." Reaching inside her robe, he ran the back of his finger over her nipple. "I'll just have to find another way to get you to agree to let us protect you."

She wanted badly to rub her still warm bottom but didn't want to give him the satisfaction. "So if I never want a spanking, you won't give me one?"

"I didn't say that. You enjoyed it just now as foreplay, but there will be times when you'll deserve being over my knee."

"I will?"

Rafe inclined his head. "In order to keep you safe and to keep you from closing us out of your problems, we have to establish rules. Living in this town, we've learned just how important those rules are in order to protect you and take care of you the way we need to. When you break those rules, you'll have to accept those consequences."

"I don't like the sound of that."

The sense of security of knowing that she wasn't alone meant more to her than she would have imagined.

Still, she couldn't imagine herself rushing to them with every little problem, and after what she'd been through, every issue—even that of her brother—felt small.

"Liar. Your spanking aroused you. You're soaking wet." Rafe kissed her forehead and started out of the room, pausing when she called his name. Turning, he raised a brow. "Yes, baby?"

Hurriedly retying her robe, she folded her arms in front of her, trying not to stare at the top button of his jeans that he'd left unfastened. "You left that thing inside me!"

"That *thing* is called a butt plug—the smallest I could find—and it's in your ass where a butt plug belongs. It'll help those muscles loosen, and hopefully remind you of what I expect from you." He reached for his T-shirt and slipped it over his head, disappointing her by covering his rock-hard abs.

Krystal gulped, shifting restlessly and biting back a moan when it moved the plug inside her. "You can't leave me like this."

His brow went up again, and although he didn't smile, his eyes twinkled with mischief and desire as he buttoned his jeans. "You wanted me to let you up. Besides, there will be times when *this* is much more effective than a spanking. There are many forms of punishment."

Krystal gulped, not liking the turn getting her freedom had taken. "But I'm aroused."

Rafe inclined his head. "Delightfully so."

Krystal blinked, realizing that she'd greatly underestimated his stark sexuality and possessiveness. "And you're just going to leave me like this?"

His eyes narrowed. "I thought that was what you wanted."

So did I.

Swallowing heavily, she shifted restlessly again. "Do I have to be spanked?"

Eyeing her thoughtfully, Rafe rubbed his chin. "I'm afraid so. You won't obey me, and there's no way I can protect you if you won't. That's not something I can tolerate, Krystal. I can't have a woman in my life that I can't protect. There are no half-measures here, baby."

She glanced at the doorway, expecting Linc to appear. "Does Linc feel the same way?"

Rafe's eyes hardened. "He does, so don't think he's gonna go any easier on you. Neither one of us will put up with you trying to play one of us off of the other."

"So what if I promise to try to be more open?"

Shaking his head, he lowered his hands to his hips. "One more *I'm fine* from you is gonna put me over the edge."

Krystal pressed her thighs together, inwardly wincing that they'd become even wetter. "I'll do better. I promise to try to tell you and Linc everything when you ask." Not wanting him to look into her promise too closely, she stepped closer. "I'm sorry. Are we okay now?"

Rafe smiled, easing some of the knots in her stomach. "We were never anything but, Krystal, but I won't tolerate being lied to. Hiding things from me is the same as lying. You've dealt with problems long enough on your own. That won't happen anymore. Are we clear?"

"Yes." Moving closer, she laid a hand on his chest, her face on fire. "Rafe?" She wanted him to take out the plug and make her come, but embarrassment kept her from asking for it.

Thankfully, Rafe took pity on her.

Gripping her arm, he led her back to the bed and, to her delight, positioned her over his lap again. "The plug stays."

"What?"

Rafe used a strong hand to part her thighs again, using the heel of his hand to press against the plug while sliding his fingers firmly over her clit. "You're gonna be taken in the ass by both Linc and me, and we're gonna take you together. You'll never completely get used to having something in your ass, but having a plug inside you will help relax those muscles."

Krystal wondered if she should have said something in reply to that, but with the pleasure mounting and the burning in her clit becoming a raw, tingling heat, she found herself rendered speechless.

Bending close, Rafe slid a hand under her and caressed her breast before lightly closing his thumb and forefinger over her nipple and rolling it, the combination of pleasure and slight pain, the plug, and the expertise of the finger sliding over her clit proving more than her bombarded senses could handle.

She cried out and stiffened as she went over, once more stunned by the intense pleasure.

Caught up in it, she became dimly aware that Rafe crooned to her in a soft, loving tone, caressing her breasts and clit with slow strokes and dragging the pleasure out longer than she would have thought possible.

When the attention to her clit became too sharp, she whimpered.

Immediately, he lifted her, turning her in his arms to hold her against his chest. "You are so sweet."

Pressing her face against his chest, Krystal closed her eyes, smiling when he tucked her robe more firmly around her. "Rafe?"

"Hmm?" The arm around her tightened, the hand at her thigh caressing her through her robe.

Smiling against his chest, she laid a hand on his chest. "About the plug…"

Pressing his lips to her hair, Rafe chuckled softly. "I want you to keep it in for a bit. No more secrets."

Opening her eyes, she let her head fall back to rest against his arm. "I never said that." Smiling, she reached up to caress his cheek. "I think I'm going to become friends with some of the women I've met, and I have it on good authority that they all talk about their men. You know, I'll bet there are issues that come from having two lovers that I haven't even considered."

Rafe smiled slowly, bending to touch his lips to hers. "I'll bet."

Sliding her hand into his hair, Krystal smiled against his lips. "And if I can get inside information about how to handle two lovers, I'm certainly not telling you and Linc."

Delighted that she spoke of her future in Desire, Rafe slid a hand under the hem of her robe to caress her ass. "You can keep those secrets, darlin', but not the secrets that could be dangerous."

Krystal's smile tugged at his heart. "Kevin's made some mistakes, but he's not dangerous."

Determined to watch out for her despite her claim, Rafe forced a smile. "Let's agree to disagree on this one, Krystal. What did he say?"

With a sigh, she sat up, looking up at him. "He was counting on the money from the sale of Mom's house, and he's going nuts because it's gone. I asked him what he needed it for, but he told me that it's none of my business. He doesn't tell me much of anything. He won't even admit to me that he's using drugs."

Trying to ignore the knotting of his stomach, Rafe sighed. "He is, Krystal. Every time I've seen him, he's high on something. He's got all the symptoms of a meth user."

Krystal stiffened. "Meth?" She hurriedly scrambled from his lap. "No." Shaking her head, she took several steps back. "He wouldn't do something like that. It's got to be something like marijuana."

Watching her closely, he could see that the thought upset her, but he needed her to understand the seriousness of the situation. "Why did he leave your mother's house when your father was sick?"

Waiting expectantly for an answer to the question she'd avoided in the past, Rafe watched her closely for any sign of deception.

Krystal blew out a breath and wrapped her arms around herself, her face flushed. "My mom kicked him out when he started stealing my father's pain medicine. I don't know what to do for him. When we tried to get him into rehab, he disappeared."

Rafe clenched his jaw, furious at the thought of Kevin stealing pain medicine from Krystal's father while he dealt with cancer. "Is that why he wasn't at your father's funeral?"

Krystal shrugged, the sadness in her eyes and embarrassment reddening her cheeks tugging at him. "He didn't know my father had died. He was surprised when he came back and found out. By then, my mother had already had her first stroke. Can I take this out?"

Smiling, Rafe nodded, wanting to get her back in a good mood. "Come here. I'll take it out while you answer a few more questions."

He wanted to learn all he could but realized he could distract her from the anguish his questions brought her.

Getting to his feet, he gestured toward the bed. "On your belly."

He met her quizzical look with a raised brow, holding her gaze until she climbed onto the bed and lay on her belly.

Out of her line of vision, he slid the nightstand drawer open and retrieved the slightly larger plug that he'd already prepared. Easing onto the bed next to her hip, he lifted her hips and slid a pillow under them. "Did your brother come to see you and your mother while she was in the nursing home?"

He lubed the larger butt plug, holding it by the base between two fingers of the hand he pressed at her lower back.

Krystal shifted restlessly on the pillow. "Once. He never came back."

Gripping the base of the plug inside her with his right hand, he eased it slightly out of her. "Why not?"

Her bottom lifted as he partially withdrew the plug until the widest part stretched her bottom hole, the sight of it arousing him again.

Her small whimper and moan of pleasure delighted him even more. "Because...oh God...he tried to steal d-drugs from the c-cart."

Enjoying himself and her passionate response, he slid the plug back into her again. "What happened?"

A shudder went through her, and Rafe couldn't hold back a smile when she lifted up again, her toes curling. "He t-took off before the police could get there. Rafe!"

Smiling when she parted her thighs and rocked her hips, he eased the plug completely out of her. "You never told me that."

Exchanging the plugs, he watched in fascination when her glistening bottom hole winked at him, the sign of her ass clenching making his cock throb.

Krystal sucked in a breath when he pressed the larger plug lightly against her puckered opening, lifting into it in a way that he'd watched for. "I know you already hated him. I didn't want to make it worse, and there was nothing you could do about it."

Her words came out in a breathless rush, and delighted with her, he bent closer, nuzzling her neck. "There is now."

* * * *

Krystal fisted her hands in front of her, parting her thighs as the ache in her bottom became unbearable. "What do you mean?"

She forced herself to focus on the conversation, squeezing her eyes closed on a moan as he applied pressure, forcing her muscles to give way for the plug again.

"I don't trust your brother, Krystal, and I absolutely don't trust him with you."

Chills raced up and down her spine as the plug began to enter her again. "He's my brother, Rafe."

"And I'm your lover. So is Linc, and it's our job to protect you."

Parting her thighs wider, she lifted higher, taking the widest part of the plug and knowing it would narrow sharply again. "That doesn't g-give you the right to keep my brother from m-me."

Rafe pushed the plug deeper, but instead of narrowing as it entered her, it widened even more, and it hit her suddenly that it was a different plug. "It gives me the right to keep you safe. Are you forgetting how he tried to grab you at the cemetery?"

"He wouldn't h-have hurt me." She curled her toes as he kept pushing the plug into her, trembling with the effort it cost her not to clench.

Each time she did, it made the burning sensation more intense and sharpened the awareness there that made her hungry for more.

Rafe bent to nuzzle her ear, moving the plug in a circular motion as he pushed it deeper. "I saw the look in his eyes, Krystal. He's desperate and so strung out on drugs he's not acting normal. He was so high at the cemetery I'm surprised he could walk. You'll stay away from him."

A shiver went through her at the cold steel in his tone. "Rafe, you're overreacting."

He bent to kiss her shoulder. "That, too, is my right."

Krystal tilted her neck, inviting his touch, needing it more as the plug continued to push in small increments into her. "I think living in this town has made you even more arrogant. Oh God! It burns. You changed plugs, didn't you? This one feels even bigger!"

Rafe groaned and accepted her invitation, nuzzling her neck. "Because it *is* bigger."

Krystal cried out when the plug sank deeper, sucking in breath after breath at the full, stretched feeling. "Dear God."

The feel of warm lips on her bottom stunned her. Her eyes flew open, and meeting Rafe's amused gaze, she realized that Linc had rejoined them.

Chuckling softly, Linc scraped his teeth over her ass cheek. "What a delightful sight." Slipping a hand between her thighs, he parted them wider and began to caress her clit. "Can I ask what's going on?"

Rafe eased the plug back slightly and pushed it deeper, slowly fucking her ass with it, each slow thrust pushing it deeper. "Easy. Her clit's sensitive."

Lifting her head, she fisted her hands in the bedding, a moan escaping at the feel of his hands moving on her thighs. "Linc, tell Rafe that you don't have to protect me from my own brother."

Linc slid a finger into her pussy and began fucking her with it while Rafe did the same with the plug in her ass. "I disagree."

Fire raced through her, the attention to her pussy, ass, and clit driving her relentlessly toward the edge. "You can't do this to me."

The pleasure became almost unbearable, and she found herself fighting it with every bit of willpower she could muster. "I won't let you do this to me."

Rafe rubbed her back. "Do what to you, baby? Protect you? Possess you? Love you."

Krystal couldn't stand it anymore. Lifting to her knees, she made it easier for both of them to touch her. "Dear God. I didn't expect you to be this way."

She sucked in a breath when Rafe reached under her to tug at her nipple, the sharp pleasure travelling straight to her clit, pussy, and ass, heightening the pleasure of their attention.

Kissing her shoulder, Rafe chuckled softly. "Do you want us to stop?"

Linc's fingers on her clit and pussy moved faster, the expertise in his touch making her jealous as hell.

Throwing her head back, she rocked in time to Linc's movement, taking even more of the plug into her ass. "I hate both of you."

Rafe bent close, running his lips over her temple as he slid the plug completely inside her. "You love us. It makes you feel vulnerable, especially when your world has already changed so much. We're keeping you." He switched his attention her other nipple, rolling it between his thumb and forefinger. "Come again, while we're both giving you pleasure."

Linc pressed at a spot inside her pussy, his lips warm on her bottom cheek as he stroked her slick clit. "Now, baby."

Crying out at the pleasure, she bucked, her sensitized clit unable to take any more friction. "Oh dear God!"

Easing the strokes to her clit, Linc scraped his teeth over her ass cheek. "God, I love hearing you come."

After her orgasm crested and released her from its grip, Linc took pity on her and eased his fingers free, rubbing her bottom as he stretched out beside her. "That's our girl."

He kissed her tenderly, his gaze possessive. "Rafe's right, baby. You're ours." He gathered her close with a firm hand on her lower back. "We protect what's ours."

Moaning against the ripples of pleasure still vibrating through her, she let her eyes close again, suddenly finding it impossible to keep them open. "He won't hurt me."

Rafe kissed her hair and slowly eased the plug free, kissing her bottom when she moaned. "I'm not willing to take that chance. You'll do what I said and stay away from him."

Chapter Ten

When Krystal woke again, she found herself alone, but she smiled to herself at the knowledge that Linc, Rafe, or both would be close by.

The sun had started to set, casting long shadows across the bedroom, and she realized that she'd fallen into a deep sleep again and felt even more refreshed.

Hearing the deep voices of her lovers coming from the back patio, she stretched and rose from the bed, her clit still sensitive from her recent orgasms.

With renewed energy, she headed for the bathroom, anxious to use some of her new body products.

She had the huge shower to herself, and as she washed her hair, she smiled to herself at the thought that had gone into making the bathroom perfect for three.

Feeling refreshed and energized, she left the shower, wrapping the large bath sheet around herself and making her way to the counter on the left, one that apparently would belong to her.

The sink had been positioned off-center, leaving plenty of counter space for the basket that Jesse had given her.

She'd used the lavender body wash, shampoo, and conditioner, leaving them in the shower alongside the apricot scent of the same items.

Wondering how Rafe and Linc would react to her taking up most of the shelf, Krystal searched through the basket for the lavender body cream and smoothed it all over her.

Afterward, she left the bathroom in a cloud of lavender-scented steam and went back into the bedroom. She dressed in another of her comfortable lounge outfits, knowing that she would soon have to buy some other clothes but didn't want to spend the small amount of money she had until she found a job.

It was a subject she'd have to bring up again with Rafe and Linc as soon as possible.

Combing the tangles from her hair, she realized she also needed to buy a blow dryer.

And she desperately needed a haircut.

After braiding her hair, she secured it with a scrunchie, turning just as Rafe and Linc strode into the room.

Rafe reached her first, gathering her against him with a smile. "You look and smell delicious. How do you feel?"

Smiling when Linc moved in behind her and bent to nuzzle her neck, Krystal leaned back against him. "I feel great. I can't believe I fell asleep again."

Linc straightened and ran a hand over her braid. "You obviously needed it, and I'm sure a lot more. Do you feel like going into Tulsa tonight?"

"Sure. Do I need to change?"

Pleased that she had more color and seemed to move with more energy, Linc smiled. "No. You're fine. We want to go do some more shopping. I can't eat another meal from a paper plates. We started a list, but I'm sure there are things we didn't think of."

* * * *

As they drove out of town toward Tulsa, Krystal stayed silent, but Linc could almost hear her brain working.

Sitting in the back seat behind Rafe so he could watch her, Linc met Rafe's glance in the rearview mirror before turning his attention back to her. "Something on your mind, baby, or are you just thinking about what else we need to buy?"

Stopping at a stop sign, Rafe smiled in her direction. "We need a sofa."

Linc continued to watch Krystal, noting her preoccupied smile. "I don't know. I like the thought of her sitting in my lap in one of the recliners."

Rafe made the left turn and glanced at him in the mirror again. "Let's see if you feel that way when she's on my lap and you're sitting there alone."

Krystal turned slightly in her seat and looked from Rafe to Linc and back again. "Do the two of you ever go to the men's club?"

Rafe scowled and whipped his head around. "What do you know about the men's club?"

Sitting back, Krystal met Rafe's scowl with an impish smile. "I talked to Breanna while I was in Indulgences. She said that she's married to King and Royce and that they own the club with…I forget his name."

Rafe's eyes narrowed, and he glanced briefly at Linc. "Blade. Blade Royal. What about the club?"

Krystal shrugged, blushing adorably. "Brenna said that it's a club for Dominants."

Rafe glanced at her as he drove, clearly suspicious. "We've been in there, but we've never participated in the activities. Is that what you wanted to know?"

Krystal shrugged again, and even in the low light, Linc could see that her blush deepened. "You spanked me."

Rafe inclined his head. "I did."

She turned to Linc. "Did you know he spanked me?"

Hiding a smile, Linc met her gaze. "Yes. I also know you had the small butt plug inside you when he did it. Rafe and I have no secrets, especially when it concerns you."

"Oh." She looked out the window in silence for a minute or two before turning back to Rafe. "Is there something I should know about?"

Rafe chuckled at that, taking her hand in his and lifting it to his lips. "We need to be in charge, but you already knew that. We've always been this way, but moving to Desire and seeing how protected the women are, we've become even more so. We're not into some of what you would think of as extreme things."

"Like the whips and chains?"

Rafe chuckled. "Like the whips and chains. That doesn't mean I won't paddle your ass when I think you need it."

Krystal gulped audibly and looked away again. "You used to threaten to tie me up, but you never did it."

Linc smiled at the petulance in her tone. "You were a virgin when we met you. We didn't want to scare you by going too fast."

She turned to look at him, shrugging again. "That's why Rafe didn't spank me like he did this time. I guess we never really got to anything else."

Linc reached up to touch her shoulder. "No. we didn't, but we will. You need time to settle, but we won't put up with you hiding things from us."

Grimacing, she glanced at Rafe. "Rafe told you?"

Rafe answered before Linc could. "Of course I told him. We've already told you that there are no secrets between us, especially concerning you."

"Are the other men in Desire the same way?"

"Of course." Linc shared another look with Rafe in the mirror. "We all have to be on the same page, make sure you adhere to the same rules, and don't try to play one of us off against the other."

Krystal whipped around, glaring at him. "That sounds like something a mother and father would do with their child."

Rafe chuckled. "It does at that. Same rules apply. It's our job to protect you and make sure you're happy. We can't do that without keeping a sharp eye on you and making sure we agree on things regarding your rules and your care. But don't think for one minute that either one of us thinks of you as a child."

Linc smiled and touched her shoulder again. "It sounds more complicated than it is. Rafe and I naturally talk about you and ways to handle you and things we can do to make you happy. We both worry about you. We've waited a long time to have you to ourselves, and we're enjoying it very much."

"I'm glad, but I don't see how. You've been doing so much for me, and I feel like I'm not contributing at all."

Linc hated the sadness and insecurity in her tone. "Baby, you just buried your mother and you're exhausted. Give it time."

"Everything is happening so fast." Krystal turned to face the front again. "It's a lot to get used to. This is a very strange town. I mean, people are so friendly, but it's weird that they seem so open about their sexuality. Brenna wasn't at all embarrassed and willingly admitted to me that her husbands dominated her."

Rafe shrugged. "It's not something she would tell just anyone, but you're one of us, and she knows it." He paused as if waiting for her to say something, and when she didn't, he continued. "Besides, what's there to be embarrassed about? It's pretty common in this town, at least to some degree. King and Royce love Brenna very much. They spoil her rotten and are both very devoted to her. As Dominants who train other Dominants, they're very conscious of safety and watch Brenna closely. Whatever happens between them is consensual, and if she decided that she didn't like something, they would both respect that."

Turning in her seat, she faced Linc, including both of them in her question. "Would you respect my wishes if I said I don't want to be spanked any more?"

Taking her question seriously, Linc nodded. "Of course, but it's an effective punishment." Smiling at the memory of how she'd looked earlier, Linc chuckled softly. "I have a feeling that you would be one of the women in town who misbehave in order to earn a trip over their husband's knee."

She blinked at the word husband, and Linc didn't push it, knowing she would need time to get used to the idea.

Rafe turned to her with a raised brow. "It would also help your claim not to want to be spanked if you didn't get aroused when your ass is warmed."

A giggle escaped, and Krystal pressed her hand to her mouth in an obvious attempt to hold back another. "Damn it, Rafe. You're not supposed to say that."

"It's the truth, and I see no reason for shyness or lies." Rafe turned to give her another smile. "I didn't hurt you. Just warmed your bottom and played with you while I did it. Got your attention, didn't I?"

Crossing her arms over her chest, Krystal failed to hide a smile. "I still don't know if I like being spanked."

Linc hid a smile, wondering if she realized that she'd gone from not wanting to be spanked to not being sure in a matter of minutes. "You come when you don't like something, darlin'?"

Waving a hand dismissively, she turned in her seat again. "Nobody in town even blinked when they saw us together. I mean, they accepted that I have two lovers the same way they would as if I only had one. It seems almost normal. I was a little nervous when we went out to dinner last night, but in Desire, I actually *felt* normal."

Linc smiled at that, remembering his first impression of the town and how he'd looked for signs that ménage relationships were respected. "In Desire, it *is* normal."

"I'm beginning to see that." Krystal smiled again, a distracted smile that told Linc she still had more on her mind. "I was comfortable there. Happy."

She stared out the windshield again and, after another lengthy pause, turned back. "I guess I just haven't quite figured out how this works."

Rafe met Linc's gaze briefly in the rearview mirror and glanced at Krystal. "What do you mean? How does it work in what respect, baby?"

Krystal sighed and dropped her head back against the headrest. "We weren't together very long before my father was diagnosed."

"Forty-seven days." Linc stiffened, remembering when everything had fallen apart.

Krystal blinked and spun to him. "I can't believe you remember that."

"I remember everything."

Including how hard it was to stay away from you and the look in your eyes the night we took your virginity.

It didn't matter how many miles were between them. She'd belonged to them ever since.

Linc smiled in encouragement, reaching out to touch her silky hair. "Talk to us, Krystal. What's bothering you?"

She glanced at Rafe, biting her lower lip. "Our…affair was fun, but—"

Linc interrupted. "It wasn't just an affair, Krystal."

Krystal chewed her bottom lip again, something he ached to do. "But I was always under the impression that it was temporary."

Rafe sent her a dark look. "We knew that, but each time we tried to convince you otherwise, it seemed to upset you. So we backed off. If we'd known what was about to happen, we wouldn't have."

Linc fisted a hand against his thigh, remembering his frustration. "We knew we wanted you to be ours almost from the beginning."

Shrugging, she sat up again. "I didn't realize that."

Linc smiled. "Now you do. Krystal, we moved here because we discovered a place where we could live the way we wanted to with you. It wasn't a decision we took lightly. We had to leave San Diego to establish ourselves in a place we could set down roots. It was a hell of a gamble, but we had no idea we'd be parted for so long. We were furious with ourselves for a long time and wished we'd done things differently."

Rafe sighed and took her hand in his again. "We understood how much our relationship upset your mother and, therefore, upset you. We didn't want that, and so we concentrated on getting ready for the future. It was the only thing that kept us sane while we waited for you."

"We tried to tell you about the town, but you didn't seem to want to hear it." Linc met her look squarely, still remembering how her disinterest had chilled him. "It upset you, and you were already dealing with so much that we stopped talking about it. We didn't want to push you. But that cost us, too."

Krystal sighed and dropped her head back again. "I didn't want to hear about the town because I never really believed I would come here. I didn't want to imagine something that I didn't believe would ever happen. I'd planned to lose you. I kept waiting for you to get tired of waiting for me and find someone else. Forty-seven days isn't a very long time to know someone."

"It was long enough—more than long enough for Rafe and me to know what we wanted." Linc frowned. "That explains why you tried your best to keep us at a distance."

Krystal's hesitant smile swelled Linc's chest. "I fell in love with both of you. I know that you said that you loved me, too, but I never believed you."

It was Rafe's turn to frown. "You didn't believe that we really loved you? I've never told any other woman that I love her."

"Neither have I." Linc sighed. "You *did* seem to take it a little too lightly for a woman who was a virgin."

Krystal's sigh held a pain that stabbed at his heart. "It was like a fantasy. I thought about it a lot when I was sitting next to my mother's bed. I used to imagine getting home from work and coming home to you."

Rafe kissed her hand again and released it before making the turn into Tulsa. "Our hours will be staggered here. That way one of us should always be able to be with you. You ready to pick out a sofa?"

Linc hadn't expected to have so much fun.

After the incident with the kitchen table, he and Rafe knew what to expect.

Because of it, he and Rafe made sure they kept the prices hidden from her and walked with her through the displays of furniture, amused at her attempts to get them to voice their opinions.

Finally, she slowed her steps, eyeing one in a light blue color. "Look at this one. It has a chaise on each end. You two could stretch out on either side. There's plenty of room for me to stretch out in the middle."

Linc smiled, already picturing cuddling with Krystal on the large sofa and taking advantage of the room afforded by the chaises. "Or be on the chaise part with one—or both—of us."

He smiled when she moved to sit on it. "Do you like this one?"

He exchanged a glance with Rafe, already knowing that she did. He sat on the sofa next to her, impressed to find the sofa even more comfortable than it looked. "There's plenty of room."

Krystal ran her hand over the material, scooting closer to him. "Do you think it's too big for the room?"

"Not at all." Out of the corner of his eye, Linc saw Rafe gesturing for the salesman to come over. "We planned to throw out the recliners anyway. They've seen better days, and we only got them to have a place to sit and watch TV until you picked out something more permanent."

Krystal smiled. "I really like it, even the color. It's a very soothing color, and the material is so soft."

Linc smiled and put an arm around her. "Sold."

After Rafe ordered and paid for the sofa, they made their way to a kitchen store, which sold everything from dishes and glasses to silverware and items used for cooking, and Linc had to admit a hell of a lot of things that were a mystery to him.

Krystal began hesitantly at first, clearly not wanting to spend their money, but once she got started, her delight in picking out items for her new home gave Linc a satisfaction he hadn't anticipated.

Rafe set another pot into one of the three carts, along with a set of what Krystal referred to as bakeware. "Did you get the one you need to make the brownies?"

"As a matter of fact, I did." Giggling when Rafe pulled her close, Krystal grinned up at him. "It's the least I can do for all the money you're spending."

Rafe gripped her chin and bent to touch his lips to hers. "Are you having fun?"

She grinned, her eyes twinkling. "A little too much."

Rafe's hands settled on her waist. "Fun is good for you, and we're happy that we're finally making that place a home. Don't forget that all of this stuff is gonna benefit us, too. I'm sick and tired of eating off of paper plates."

By the time they finished and headed outside, Linc felt something settle inside him to see that Krystal seemed more relaxed with them than she had since her mother's death.

She practically glowed and had more energy than she had in days.

She was also more playful, something he planned to take advantage of on the ride home.

Pushing her own cart, Krystal glanced at Rafe with a giggle. "I just hope you like my cooking. I'm definitely out of practice."

Rafe smiled back and winked at her. "Even if you're a bad cook, I'll keep you. I'm sure I can find another use for you."

Linc smiled when Krystal gasped and slapped at Rafe, her enjoyment at his teasing like a fist around his heart.

Whether she realized it or not, Krystal had become more confident about the future of their relationship.

Once she set the house up the way she liked it, she would be even more comfortable.

Having her at ease would go a long way in making her see that she could have a good life with them.

On the other side of her, Linc pushed his own cart and breathed a sigh of relief that, after years of waiting, everything finally seemed to be coming together.

Chapter Eleven

Walking across the well-lit parking lot with Rafe and Linc, Krystal sobered as she looked up at each of them.

Walking protectively on either side of her, they scanned the parking lot as they made their way to their SUV, both men playfully teasing her.

Rafe turned to her with a devious grin. "I can't wait to christen that sofa. It's big enough to be able to get you in all sorts of interesting positions." He searched her features, her smile falling. "What's wrong?" He looked around, scanning their surroundings, and, apparently not seeing anything, turned to her again. "What is it?"

Feeling more lighthearted than she had in ages, she grinned up at him. "Little things that mean more than I expected."

Reaching the back of the SUV, Linc ran a hand over her back while Rafe unlocked it, still watching her as he pulled one of the carts closer in order to unload it. "What are you talking about, baby?"

Watching Linc and Rafe load the SUV with their purchases, Krystal smiled. "A little thing like crossing a parking lot at night."

Both men glanced around again as if searching for trouble. "What about it?"

Smiling, she glanced at each of them. "Being in a parking lot at night usually makes me nervous."

Rafe frowned and placed the last of the packages in the back before closing the lid. "It's good if it keeps you vigilant. You should be aware of your surroundings. I'll have to get you some pepper spray to carry in your purse."

She took the hand Linc held out to her. "I still have the one you gave me before. It's just so strange to walk across a dark parking lot without worrying."

Linc opened the back door of the SUV and gestured for her to get in. "I'm glad you feel safe with us."

"Why am I sitting in the back seat?" She climbed in, smiling when he ran a hand over her bottom, and moved her aside to climb in after her.

"Because it's lonely back here, and I want to play."

Rafe finished putting the carts in the rack and climbed into the front seat, turning in his seat to see that Linc had already covered her breast with his hand, having waited until the interior light went off. "I can see this is gonna be a long ride home."

Linc lifted her shirt and unfastened her bra, sliding it out of the way to caress her breast beneath her shirt. Brushing his lips over hers, he ran his thumb gently back and forth over her nipple. "Then I suggest you drive fast."

Sucking in a breath at the friction against her nipple, Krystal lifted her hands to sink them into his hair. "Too bad you don't have your police car. You could use the lights and siren."

She didn't get a chance to say more because Linc covered her mouth with his, pressing her lips open to delve inside.

He slid his tongue along hers, the gesture as erotically possessive as the way he cupped her breast and slid his thumb over her nipple.

Needing to touch him, she reached for his T-shirt, sliding it up and slipping her hands under it to touch him.

Loving the feel of hot muscle against her palms, she moaned and leaned into him.

Fire raced through her, his attention to her nipples heating her blood with a speed that staggered her.

Breaking off their kiss, Krystal shook her head and pushed him back and reached for the fastenings of his jeans. "No way. You're not doing that to me again. This time I want to touch you."

"Fuck." Linc lifted slightly when she got his jeans unfastened, lifting up with a groan when she started to yank them down. "Easy, baby."

"Fuck easy." Krystal bent over him to take his cock into her mouth, inwardly smiling at Rafe's low chuckle.

"Havin' a little trouble back there, Linc?"

Loving the feel of his hard, hot cock, Krystal flattened her tongue and ran it up the length of it before closing her mouth over the thick head again. Kneeling on the floor in front of him, she slid his jeans lower and gripped his powerful upper thighs.

"Son of a bitch!" Linc's pleasure-filled groan vibrated over her. "Christ, Krystal! Slow down. Goddamn it!"

His hands fisted in her hair, another groan escaping. "She took this from zero to fifty in seconds. Damn it, Krystal!"

Rafe chuckled again. "Sounds like you're havin' a little trouble handling her."

"I was just gonna play a little—son of a bitch!"

Krystal sucked his cock gently, using her tongue against the sensitive underside, her excitement growing when his cock jumped in her mouth and the muscles in his thighs tightened.

"Sounds like she got the better of you."

Krystal took the opportunity of dealing with only Linc to drive him as crazy as he made her.

The darkness surrounding them gave her a confidence she wouldn't normally have had

Afraid that if she lifted her head Linc would pull her from his cock, Krystal continued to use her mouth on him, thrilling at his groans and the way his body and hands tightened.

"Krystal? Baby?" Linc groaned when she took him as deep as she could and began to suck harder. Wrapping his hands around her upper arms, he tugged lightly. "Baby, come here. I want to make you feel good, too."

Lifting her head, Krystal continued to stroke his cock. "No. As soon as you touch me, I can't even think anymore. I want to please you. Am I doing this right?"

Lowering her head again, Krystal used her tongue on his cock, smiling at his groan. "Am I?"

Rafe laughed out loud. "Sure as hell sound like it to me."

"Fuck! Krystal. Enough!" Tightening his hands on her upper arms, he yanked her to his lap, laying her across it, his hands rough as he shoved her pants and panties to her ankles and then off, removing her sneakers in the process.

Giggling, she reached for him. "Don't you dare rip my new clothes!"

Linc avoided her hands and set her on the seat next to him. "I'll buy you as many as you want." Cursing, he pushed her hand aside when she tried to close her hand around his cock again. "No. Damn it! I'm already on edge. Let me get this fucking thing on."

He pulled a condom from his pocket and ripped it open with his teeth, rolling it on in the almost complete darkness while glaring at Rafe, who laughed even harder. "Shut up, Rafe."

"We're almost at the turnoff. Do you want me to pull over so you can drive and I'll take care of Krystal?"

"Fuck you. Keep driving."

Giggling, Krystal felt Rafe's gaze and turned to meet it in the rearview mirror.

Illuminated by the faint light from the dashboard, Rafe's eyes danced with amusement and a tenderness that warmed her even more.

Struck to see him look happier and more relaxed than he'd looked in the last three years, Krystal couldn't help but smile, laughing again when Linc reached for her.

She wrapped her arms and legs around him as he lowered her to her back, a cry of shock and pleasure escaping when he slid a hand under her back and bent to touch his lips to her nipple.

Nuzzling it, he groaned and slid lower, kissing and nuzzling his way down her body. "You know I have to get even."

He lifted her thighs and draped them over his shoulders, sliding his hands under her bottom and lifting her higher. "And I'm going to enjoy every second of it."

Krystal sucked in a breath at the slide of his tongue through her slit, crying out and digging her heels into his muscular back.

With a curse, Rafe turned the wheel, his speed slowing. "Let's see if you can make her come before I get into town."

Linc lifted his head slightly, scraping his teeth over the inside of her upper thigh. "A challenge I'll gladly accept."

Krystal cried out when Linc lowered his head to her slit again, the feel of his warm mouth closing over her clit and the quick flicks of his tongue so intense it stole her breath.

His determination and expertise with his tongue sent her over in a rush of heat, her body bowing at the intensity of it.

"There she is." From the front seat, Rafe chuckled. "God, I love listening to her come. My cock's hard as a fucking rock."

Linc lifted his head, moving up her body and gathering her close. "Yeah, and it feels even better." He thrust into her with a groan, taking her mouth with his and swallowing her moan of pleasure.

Some part of her realized that the SUV had stopped, but wrapped around Linc, she didn't pay attention.

Sliding her hands through his hair, she kissed him back, crying out when he broke off his kiss.

"Damn it!" Linc held her against him as he sat back on the seat, his hands going to her waist as he began thrusting again. "There's no damned room in here!"

Krystal's giggle ended on a moan when he thrust deep again. "We never had sex in a car before."

Rafe chuckled, turning in his seat to run a hand over her hair. "There's a reason for that."

Linc slid a hand to her back, the other closing on her hip. "There's a lot of things we didn't get a chance to do."

Moving her on him, Linc pressed his thumb against her clit and slid lower in the seat, adjusting her over his cock in a way that allowed it to go deeper. "Just make sure no one sees her."

"Not a chance. You two have already fogged up the windows."

Krystal moaned when Linc moved her on his cock and thrust deep, gripping his shoulders and throwing her head back.

Every deep thrust sent her higher and higher while each thrust moved his thumb over her swollen clit.

She searched his features in the darkness, the glimmer in his eyes reflected by the light from the dashboard.

Bending her back even more, he lowered his head, taking a nipple into his mouth and thrusting into her with deep, rapid thrusts. "You feel so good, baby. I've missed you so damned much."

Sensation shot from her nipple to her clit and pussy, and wrapping her arms around his neck, she used her knees to move on him in time with his thrusts. "Linc. Oh God."

Linc groaned and switched his attention to her other breast, his hands tightening on her. "That's it, baby. Come for me."

The knowledge that Rafe listened and watched in the rearview mirror made their lovemaking even more exciting and added to the intimacy.

Crying out when her orgasm hit her, she gripped him tighter, holding on as he thrust into her several more times in rapid succession before sinking deep with a harsh groan.

Slumping against him with her head on his shoulder, Krystal took several heavy breaths, smiling at the feel of his hands moving up and down her back. "Well, that was fun."

Chuckling, Linc bent to touch his lips to her hair while fastening her bra. "Yeah, it was." Tilting her head back, he touched his lips to hers and pulled her shirt down. "Sometimes I still can't believe you're here with us."

Rafe shifted the car into drive and pulled back onto the road. "I know what you mean. She okay?"

Lifting herself from Linc's cock, she dropped onto the seat next to him. "She will be as soon as she finds her panties and pants."

Linc got rid of the condom and righted his own clothing, fastening his jeans just as she slipped on her panties. "I'll help you."

He helped her work her pant legs over her ankles, kissing and sliding his hands over her thighs and making her laugh again. "Linc! Stop helping me!"

"Come on, baby. I *am* helping you." Slipping a fingertip into the leg of her panties, he caressed her folds. "I just want to make sure everything's in the right place."

Krystal's giggle turned into a gasp when he slid his fingertip over her clit. "Linc!"

Linc stroked her clit lightly before slipping his finger free again. "Hmm." After pulling her pants the rest of the way up, he wrapped an arm around her and pulled her onto his lap again. "I can't resist those little cries." He kissed her again, taking his time to nuzzle her lips as Rafe pulled into their driveway and cut the engine.

Cupping Linc's jaw, Krystal blinked when Rafe opened the door and the bright interior light came on. "I need my shoes."

Linc opened his door and slid his hands under her, holding her against his chest as he got out. "No. You don't."

Rafe smiled and tickled her foot as Linc carried her past him. "I'll get them and start carrying stuff in."

Laughing, Krystal jerked her foot away. "I can help carry stuff in."

Pausing next to her, Rafe bent to brush his lips over hers. "Now you have us to do things like that for you. I'm sure you'll be bossing us around in no time."

Krystal searched his features, looking for any sign of sarcasm, but found none.

Remembering her conversation with Jesse and Brenna, she smiled. "You don't seem too worried about it."

Rafe smiled again, his eyes narrowing slightly. "I'm not. We'll enjoy it, and if you get out of hand, we'll enjoy dealing with that, too."

Linc chuckled and carried her to the house. "It's a win-win for us either way." After unlocking the door and pausing on the threshold, he bent to touch his lips to her forehead and stare down at her. "Just having you here is a win for us."

* * * *

Even with both Rafe and Linc helping her, it took nearly two hours for Krystal to have everything washed, dried, and put away to her satisfaction.

Breaking down the last box for the recycling, Linc watched her, filled with satisfaction at her obvious happiness.

Despite her obvious fatigue, she practically glowed as she gathered the dishtowels and took them to the adjoining laundry room before coming back to scan the kitchen. "It looks so good. I can't wait to start cooking. It's been a long time since I had the chance to cook a meal or do any baking."

She went to the cookie jar she'd insisted they buy and adjusted its position slightly before stepping back again. "I remember how much you both liked my cookies. I could never keep my cookie jar filled."

Rafe wrapped an arm around her shoulders. "I'm looking forward to more cookies, but not tonight. You're done. Time for bed."

"Did you put the pillows for the sofa and the throw in the living room?"

Rafe kept walking, urging her down the hall when she tried to turn toward the living room. "They're fine where they are. There isn't anything you can do until the sofa gets here anyway. Time for bed."

"What are you going to do with the recliners?"

As they disappeared down the hall, Linc paused and looked around the kitchen.

Every surface gleamed from Krystal's cleaning binge, but instead of it looking sterile, it had a welcoming look that brought a lump to his throat.

She'd arranged colorful place mats on the table and other little touches around the kitchen, including a bright blue cookie jar that gave the kitchen a more cheerful look.

They even had a breadbox, although he had no idea why.

She'd picked out several cookbooks and had them stacked on the counter next to the refrigerator, her desire to learn recipes adorable.

He didn't care if she could cook or not and would gladly eat peanut butter sandwiches if she stayed with them.

He took a deep breath and let it out slowly in an effort to relieve the tightness in his chest.

He loved Krystal even more than he had before and hadn't realized how much until they brought her home with them.

Every day his love for her intensified as she slowly came out of her shell again.

He couldn't imagine a life without her now, which made getting her commitment to stay even more important.

He wouldn't be able to relax completely until everything was settled between them.

Chapter Twelve

Rafe sat back and sipped his coffee, enjoying the sight of Krystal moving around the kitchen. He and Linc had just finished their breakfast, and he found he couldn't tear his gaze away from her glowing features. "We need to get you a cell phone."

Krystal wiped her hands and poured herself another glass of orange juice. "I don't really think I need a cell phone."

Rafe rose and poured himself another cup of coffee. "I disagree. We want you to have a way to contact us."

Krystal shrugged. "You said that your schedules will be staggered, so it sounds like I'm always going to be with one of you."

Linc shook his head with a chuckle. "Baby, we're not gonna suffocate you. You might want to explore the town on your own, especially if one of us is sleeping. You'll also want to go to Tulsa with the new friends you'll make. We'd feel safer knowing you're only a call or text away."

Nodding, she turned back to them, sipping her juice before setting her glass aside. "I'd like to explore the town and learn my way around, but I'd also like to find a job."

Rafe turned and sipped from his mug, eyeing her as he leaned back against the counter, conscious of the fact that he had to tread carefully or risk pissing her off. "Baby, Linc and I aren't rich by any means, but we make good money here. We have no problem supporting you."

Her eyes flashed with something that looked slightly like panic. "I can't just sit around all day without doing anything. Besides, I already told you that I'm not going to be a burden."

Linc sat back, glancing at Rafe. "We don't mind that you want to get a job, but we both think you need to rest and get settled first."

Krystal reached for her glass again, but instead of picking it up, she pushed it aside. "I need to get my life back to normal. I've already had too many changes and working is a part of normal to me. I'll go crazy sitting around all day with nothing to do."

Rafe set his coffee aside and straightened, irritated that she didn't seem to trust them to take care of her. "You need to rest and just let yourself breathe for a bit for God's sake. You can trust us to take care of you, Krystal."

Krystal blinked as if shocked at his outburst. "Rafe, I never doubted that you and Linc could—or would—take care of me, but it's not your responsibility to do so."

Rafe had had enough. "Like hell!" Closing the distance between them, he gripped her upper arms, lifting her to her toes. "You're ours, Krystal, and I'm sick and tired of walking on eggshells around the issue. We want to marry you. Have children with you, damn it!"

Krystal's eyes went wide. "Children?"

Rafe sighed and bent to touch his forehead to hers, his anger dissipating. "Yes, baby." Lifting his head, he stared into her eyes, his chest tightening at the glimmer of happiness in hers. "We're in this for the long haul, Krystal. We're not ready to have children yet. You need to recover, and we need to spend time getting to know each other and getting used to being together again."

Linc closed in on her from behind, meeting Rafe's gaze over her head. "Rafe's right. We love you, Krystal. I know that it's hard for you to believe, but it's true. It's only grown stronger while we've been apart, and not having you with us has made us appreciate just how fragile and precious that love is. We have no intention of rushing anything, but it's important for you to accept that we want forever with you."

Krystal gulped audibly. "We never discussed marriage. Children."

Rafe could see she was nervous, but the fact that she reached out to flatten a hand on his chest while leaning into Linc spoke volumes. "We don't want to push you into something you're not ready for, especially after all you've been through. Just relax and get used to being the love of our lives."

Smiling up at him, she blushed. "How do you know that?"

"Because I'm smart. Ready to go get your new cell phone?"

"Okay. Would it be okay if I look online for refresher courses? I might need to take a few before I can get another job."

Rafe smiled and gathered her close. "You can look at whatever you want. The laptop is in my room."

A knock at the door interrupted them.

Straightening, Rafe kissed Krystal's hair. "Something tells me that's for you. I'll get it."

He still couldn't shake the uneasy feeling that Kevin would appear at their doorstep and was glad that he and Linc would work staggered hours so that one of them could be with her.

He opened the door, smiling when he saw that Hope Tyler, Ace's wife, and her sister, Charity Parrish, had come to meet Krystal. "Good morning, ladies. I assume you've come to meet Krystal?"

Hope grinned up at him and came inside, striding past him as he turned. "Absolutely! I hope we're not interrupting anything."

She wagged her eyebrows and giggled, a clear sign that it wouldn't have bothered her a bit to do just that.

"Hope!" Shaking her head, Charity gave Rafe an apologetic look. "Sorry about my sister. She's been downright giddy lately and more brazen than usual." She met Hope's grin with a raised brow. "I didn't think that was possible."

Hope giggled. "People *do* have sex, Charity. I don't know how you can be so shy about it married to that hunk of yours."

"Most people show a little discretion, Hope."

Hope shrugged, frowning at the recliners and the stacks of pillows and throws on them. "No reason to be shy." She glanced at Rafe. "Where is she?"

Amused, Rafe gestured toward the kitchen. "She's in the kitchen with Linc. Have you had breakfast?"

Charity nodded. "We have, but I wouldn't object to another cup of coffee."

Rafe followed them into the kitchen and introduced Krystal to the other women while Linc greeted them and poured each of them a cup of coffee.

Krystal seemed nervous but delighted to have company. "Hope, you're married to Ace, the sheriff, right?"

Hope grinned again and dropped into a seat at the table. "I sure am. This table's beautiful. The Prestons made it, didn't they? You can always tell their work."

Krystal beamed and took out the coffee cake they'd bought. "It's beautiful, isn't it? We just got it." She turned to Charity, her cheeks flushed. "And your husband is Beau. He owns the adult toy store in town."

Charity smiled and reached for her cup. "He does."

Linc retrieved plates from the cabinet. "And their parents, Gracie, Garett, Drew, and Finn own the diner."

Krystal smiled and cut into the coffee cake. "The place where you always used to eat breakfast. I hear the food there is delicious. I can't wait to try it."

"Thank you." Hope grinned and sipped her coffee, eyeing Linc and Rafe. "You two sure are easy on the eyes, but we came to talk to Krystal alone."

Rafe's smile fell. "Yeah, well, we're not comfortable doing that just yet."

Hope glanced at Krystal and nodded. "I know. Ace told me when I told him that Charity and I were coming here. We won't leave the house, and my husband and the others are only a phone call away."

Charity smiled in Krystal's direction. "We'll keep the doors locked, and I won't let anyone do anything stupid."

Krystal touched his arm, her eyes flashing with fury, and just enough panic to scare the hell out of him. "Please, Rafe. Don't do this. Kevin's not a threat to me, and I'm not going to be a prisoner here."

Although she kept her tone low and even because of their audience, Rafe read the threat in her eyes loud and clear.

If she felt like a prisoner, she would leave.

Inclining his head, Rafe smiled, determined to revisit the conversation later. "Of course you're not a prisoner. Linc and I will go to Tulsa and get you a cell phone. We'll be back in about an hour and a half."

He ran a hand down Krystal's back, deliberately patting her bottom in an unspoken threat of his own.

Linc finished his own coffee and set the mug in the sink. "Is that enough time for you to talk about us?"

Hope smiled and dug into her slice of coffee cake. "We're just here to invite her to the club. It'll be a chance for her to meet the others, and I'm sure she'll enjoy having a night out."

Charity laughed at that. "We all look forward to getting together, talking about our men, and then can't wait to get back home to them." She smiled at Krystal. "I'm sure you'll be no different than the rest of us."

Linc grinned and wrapped an arm around Krystal. "Good to know that you women appreciate your men."

Charity snorted. "Yeah. We're the only ones. The men in Desire are usually running over from the men's club as soon as we all start coming out."

Rafe grinned and kissed Krystal's head. "Very true. I don't suppose we'll be any different. We'll be back soon."

* * * * *

Krystal enjoyed making new friends and liked Hope and Charity almost at once.

Hope's outgoing nature made her laugh while Charity's calm and quieter demeanor made her feel as if she'd found a friend for life.

As soon as the men left, Charity leaned forward and patted Krystal's hand. "We're so sorry to hear about your parents. You've had a hell of a hard time."

Krystal shrugged, swallowing the lump in her throat. "Yeah. It's still hard to believe they're all gone."

Hope paused with a bite of cake halfway to her mouth. "*All?*" Lowering her fork to her plate, she glanced at Charity. "Don't you mean *both?*"

Irritated at herself for the slip of the tongue, Krystal grimaced. "That's what I meant."

Chrystal touched her arm. "You were also thinking about your brother, weren't you?" Lifting her hand, she waved it and shook her head. "I'm sorry. If you don't want to talk about it…"

Part of her wanted to avoid the subject while another part of her was relieved to have someone unbiased to talk to.

With a sigh, Krystal used her fork to pick at her own coffee cake, crumbling a corner of it onto her plate. "Kevin's kind of a sore subject between Linc, Rafe, and me. My brother's had some problems with drugs, and he's selfish, but he's always been that way. He was always Mom's favorite, and she spoiled him. He had everything."

Krystal's eyes welled with tears. "I don't know where he made a wrong turn or why, but he was always lazy. He never wanted to work but always had a get-rich-quick scheme. Somehow he got into drugs and ended up needing even more money."

She told them briefly about her conversations with her brother, both after the funeral and after she'd come to town.

Hope's eyes went wide. "He's after you for money?"

Nodding, Krystal set her fork aside. "I only have a little that I saved from my job. I don't have any of Mom's money. That all went for her care. I can't give him what I have because I might need it."

Charity took a sip of coffee, watching her over the rim. "Are you planning to leave?"

Krystal's stomach knotted at the thought. "No, at least not right now. I love Linc and Rafe, and I want to stay."

"But…" Hope waited expectantly.

Blowing out a breath, Krystal picked up her fork again. "But everything's happened so fast. I never really believed that Linc and Rafe loved me." She smiled humorlessly and glanced at each of them. "I never thought that they could be serious about me." With a shrug, she picked at her cake again. "I mean I thought they just wanted an affair. I couldn't understand how they could share me and want to be serious."

Charity smiled. "You thought they were just playing games. I can understand how someone who wasn't raised around ménage marriages could think that."

Krystal sat forward. "Your mother has *three* husbands? That's unbelievable."

Charity smiled, her eyes lighting up at the mention of her parents. "Yes. It is. They all love her so much. Hope and I grew up with a very happy mother and three happy fathers who all doted on us. They always had time for us. You can look forward to that with your children. Always someone around to help. Always someone around to count on."

Krystal frowned. "I have to ask. Why don't either one of you have that kind of marriage?"

Hope grinned. "The heart wants what the heart wants. You know what your heart wants, and now that you've seen that they're serious, are you still planning to leave?"

Krystal dropped her fork and reached for her coffee. "Hell, I don't think I could leave them if I wanted to." She rubbed a hand over her face, her stomach in knots. "I just can't believe they don't see that I've changed."

Charity smiled and dug into her cake. "They're not stupid men, Krystal. Do you really think they would have kept going back to see you if they weren't sure about how they felt about you?"

"Maybe they just felt bad breaking up with me when I was dealing with so much."

Hope blinked. "They felt so bad that they didn't even date anyone else in the last three years? Felt so bad that they kept going to see you even after you told them to stay away? Felt so bad that they raced to get to you as soon as they knew you needed them?"

Remembering the looks on their faces when they'd shown up at the nursing facility, Krystal blinked away tears. "I can't believe they waited for me."

Overwhelmed with love for them, she buried her face in her hands, unable to hold back tears. "Hell, I love them! I've always loved them. Who am I fooling? I only got through everything because I knew they were there. I always knew they were only one phone call away. I knew they would come if I called them."

She began to sob, the events of the past week catching up to her in a rush of emotion that clogged her throat. "If they change their minds about this—"

The scrape of chairs was her only warning before Hope and Charity closed in on either side of her, hugging her.

Hope laughed. "Don't be silly. They're not gonna change their minds. That's one thing you're gonna learn about the men in Desire. They *rarely* change their minds about anything."

Charity sighed and ran a hand over Krystal's hair. "Hope's right about that. They're stubborn as hell, and Linc and Rafe fit right in here."

Listening through tears she couldn't seem to shut off, Krystal couldn't help but laugh. "They're hard-headed. Won't even l-listen t-to m-me when I t-tell them that I need n-normal."

Hope giggled at that. "What the hell's that? Come on. Let's go to the spa. My treat."

Wiping her eyes, Krystal looked up at her. "I promised not to leave."

"I'll call Ace and tell him where we're going. Hell, my husband will know where I am anyway."

* * * *

Linc eyed the mug shot of Krystal's brother, his jaw clenching.

They'd stopped in at the station on their way out of town to touch base with the others about Krystal's brother and to let them know that it was still a sensitive issue with her.

Carter Garrison, one of the new deputies, searched Linc's features. "Your future brother-in-law has quite a rap sheet. He only served time a few months here and there, but never long. He got out again just recently a little over two months ago but already has three different warrants for his arrest. *Felony* warrants. Drugs. Burglary. Grand theft auto."

Linc shared a look with Rafe, furious with himself. "And we had him right in front of us."

Carter took a sip from his bottle of water. "You didn't know. Besides, you were out of your jurisdiction and at Krystal's mother's funeral. Does she know about him?"

Linc blew out a breath, but it did nothing to ease the tension inside him. "I don't think she knows the depth of it. If she does, she's in denial. He's her little brother, and she wants to protect him. He left her to deal with their parents alone, and she still wants to protect him."

Rafe grimaced. "I don't think she knows that he didn't come to visit for six months because he was in jail for drugs. He was busted with meth. She doesn't want to believe he does more than smoke pot."

Linc sighed and went to the refrigerator to retrieve a bottle of water, his stomach in knots. "We're trying to avoid any subject that upsets her for now, and her brother is definitely one of those. She's sleeping better, and her appetite is improving, but she's still too thin."

"Avoidance? That's not like either one of you."

Linc sighed. "Usually not, but I feel like I'm walking on eggshells around her. She sees the fact that we want to protect her from her brother as treating her like a prisoner."

Carter blew out a breath. "They just don't understand how important it is to protect them."

Linc grimaced, glancing at Rafe.

He knew that the woman Carter, Joe, and Marshall Garrison had shared a woman who hadn't been able to adjust to loving three men and, frantic about the criticism, had committed suicide.

Rafe studied Carter with narrowed eyes. "I hope you're not giving up."

Carter stilled when the front door opened and Talia came into the station, the tension emanating from him thick enough to be cut with a knife. "I'd like to, but don't know if I can. I couldn't stand it if I was responsible for another woman's death."

Carrying a box from the diner, Talia paused briefly, her eyes meeting Carter's across the distance before she gave Linc and Rafe a forced smile and set the box of food on the counter next to her desk.

Linc clapped a hand on the other man's shoulder. "You're not responsible for that."

"We should have known. We should have stayed the hell away from her." Carter glanced up again and, when he saw that Talia had her back to him, stared longingly at her. "It's better that way."

Rafe allowed a small smile. "So you and your brothers moved to a town where ménage marriages are accepted?"

Carter turned to Rafe with another shake of his head, his eyes unreadable. "Just because we can't live that way doesn't mean we can't protect those who do."

Rafe opened his mouth to speak, snapping it shut when his cell phone rang. He answered just as Ace came through the front door and paused when his own cell phone rang. "Delgatto."

"Put Krystal on the phone."

Kevin shouted into the phone so loudly that Linc could hear him clearly. Raising a brow, he gestured for Rafe to put it on speaker, not wanting to miss a single word.

Carter also listened, frowning as he took out his note pad.

After putting the call on speaker, Rafe held the phone out slightly. "Where are you, Kevin?"

"None of your fucking business. Put Krystal on the phone."

Rafe's eyes glittered with ice. "No."

Linc didn't like that Krystal's brother sounded so desperate and more than a little high.

Kevin cursed, his words slurred. "Listen, you asshole, you can't keep me from my sister."

Carter's eyes went wide and then narrowed on Linc's, his anger apparent.

Rafe's free hand closed into a fist. "It turns out that I can. She has nothing for you, and you've hurt her enough. Don't call again." He disconnected with a curse and looked like he wanted to throw his phone against the wall. "He's not gonna let up. I don't know what the hell kind of trouble he's gotten himself into, but he's desperate."

Carter nodded, tucking his notepad away. "I don't know what he usually sounds like, and it was pretty clear that he was stoned, but he sounded scared."

Linc blew out a breath. "Yeah. I have a feeling that he doesn't trust anyone but Krystal. He's been in trouble for years and usually depended on his mother and Krystal to help him."

Linc shared a look with Rafe while Carter spoke the words they were both thinking.

"If he's that desperate, and she's all he has, nothing's gonna stop him from showing up here."

He looked up as Ace finished his own call as he approached.

Ace tucked his phone into his pocket, his smile falling. "What the hell's going on?"

Rafe explained the phone call, along with the previous one, as well as their suspicions. "He'll show up here sooner or later, lookin' to cause trouble."

Linc scraped a hand over his jaw. "I'm sorry for bringin' trouble here, but we wanted her to be safe."

Ace nodded. "No need to apologize for wantin' to keep your woman safe. She's safer here than she was in California." He gestured toward the poster of Kevin that he'd had made and that hung thumbtacked to the bulletin board. "We'll all be on the lookout for him, and we'll let you two know if there's any sign of him."

His eyes narrowed. "I want you to contact me if you see him."

Linc and Rafe shared a look, both eager to get their hands on Kevin themselves.

Linc avoided Ace's sharp eyes and recapped his bottle of water. "Of course."

"I mean it. I don't want you dealing with him on your own."

Insulted, Linc met Ace's hard stare. "You think we can't deal with a punk kid?"

Watching both Linc and Rafe, Ace crossed to the coffee maker. "He's a little more than a punk kid, and the drugs make him unpredictable. Also, I don't want any conflicts coming up if something goes wrong."

Imagining the chance to confront Kevin, Linc smiled. "What could go wrong?"

Ace chuckled humorlessly. "Something always does. The phone call I got as I came in was from my wife."

Linc stiffened. "What's wrong? Did something happen with Krystal?" His heart pounded furiously with fear for her. "I knew we shouldn't have left her alone." He and Rafe started for the door, only to be stopped when Ace held out a hand. "They're all fine."

Shaking his head, he chuckled softly. "Do you really think I would be standing here drinking coffee if there was a problem? Hope called. Evidently, she and Charity got into a conversation with Krystal, and Krystal started crying."

"Hell." Rafe started for the door again, only to be stopped by Ace calling out his name.

Turning, Rafe all but growled, "What?"

"Jesus, you've got it bad." Ace smiled. "Hope and Charity decided that Krystal needed a spa day. They were already on their way. They'll be fine while they're there."

Linc nodded. "We were gonna go get her a cell phone. Shit. I wish she had one now."

Carter straightened. "I'll check in on them."

Ace nodded. "So will I."

Linc didn't doubt it for a minute.

Ace's protectiveness of his wife was well known and something Linc completely understood.

Ace sipped his coffee and grinned. "If I know my wife, they'll make sure they have the works and they'll be tipsy as hell when they leave. Don't worry. They'll be gone awhile, and the receptionist knows to call me when they're done. I'll put in a call to Beau, too, but I'm sure Charity already called him. You two should have plenty of time to get a cell phone. If she's done before you get back, Beau and I will take care of her."

Chapter Thirteen

Krystal took another sip of pink champagne and studied her freshly painted toenails, trying to wiggle her toes despite the bright pink toe separator holding them in place. "It's been a long time since I had painted nails."

"You deserve it." Hope giggled. "Once Rafe and Linc see your other surprise, I doubt if they're gonna pay too much attention to your toes. Is the champagne helping?"

Krystal grimaced and shifted in her lounge chair. "Yeah, but I think I need more."

The champagne had helped ease some of the discomfort of being waxed, the soothing balm applied afterward helping much more.

Hope obediently reached over to refill Krystal's glass, emptying the bottle. "Uh-oh. We need another one." She lifted a hand, and one of the women working there approached with a smile.

"Yes, Mrs. Tyler?"

Hope grinned. "Mary, someone drank all of our champagne."

Mary's smile widened. "So I see. I'll get another bottle. I'm just glad none of you are driving."

Hope winced. "Not a chance. My husband would beat my ass. Is Charity almost done with her wax job?"

Mary smiled again. "She'll be here soon. Oh, here she is now."

Holding the lapels of her robe closed at her neckline, Charity walked gingerly toward the seat on the other side of her sister. "Damn. I never get used to that. Thank God for that balm."

Hope grinned, wrinkling her nose at her sister. "Yeah, but it's worth it. Beau loves it."

Charity giggled. "Yeah. We both do.

Krystal chewed a bite of sandwich and washed it down with another sip of champagne. "I was told...she told me...the lady did...that I should buy some of the balm to take home." She pressed a hand to her head. "I'm getting fuzzy. I hope I remember."

Hope sat up and reached into her bag for her phone. "You should call Rafe and Linc and tell them. They won't forget. I'll call for you. Linc's number's first. I'll call him. Hey, the champagne's here."

Krystal reached out for another one of the small sandwiches on the tray placed between them that the spa offered, taking a small bite while she waited for Hope to place the call.

It took several tries, and apparently a few wrong numbers, but Hope finally managed to get Linc on the phone.

By then, Krystal had finished the small sandwich and accepted Hope's phone while picking up her glass of champagne again.

"Krystal?" Linc's slightly panicked tone reached her before she could get the phone to her ear.

"Hi, Linc. Jeez, you're impatient. I didn't even have the phone up to my ear yet. Guess what."

After a pause, Linc chuckled. "What?"

"My toenails are pink. Hope said I should get them painted. Charity agreed. Hope got red."

Charity saluted her with her glass and took a healthy gulp.

"I can't wait to see them."

Krystal smiled at the amusement in his voice. "Really?"

"Really."

"Did you get my phone?" Krystal took another sip of champagne, watching Charity pop a cracker into her mouth.

"We did. We're on our way back to Desire. I'm installing phone numbers into it now."

Nodding, Krystal decided that she wanted one of the crackers and set the phone and her glass down in order to spread some of the soft cheese on her cracker. "That's good. Did you put Hope's and Charity's in there?"

"I did. Krystal, what's wrong?"

Realizing that his voice sounded far away, Krystal looked down at the phone to see that she'd put it down. "Oh!" Hurriedly picking up the phone again, Krystal clumsily put it to her ear again. "Sorry. I was putting cheese on my cracker."

"Had a few drinks, darlin'?"

Smiling at the amusement in Rafe's tone, Krystal picked up her glass and sat back again. "Yeah. Hope and Charity brought me to the spa." Stiffening, she sat up again. "The sheriff told you, didn't he? Hope said he would."

"He did." Relaxing at Linc's reassurance, Krystal sat back again. "I didn't realize you had me on speaker."

"We're in the car, baby. We're both here and on our way back to Desire with your new phone." Linc's voice held an edge. "Hope told Ace that you were crying. We wanted to go to you, but Ace said that Hope and Charity had taken you to the spa. Why were you crying?"

Krystal shrugged and took another sip of champagne to wash down the lump in her throat. "Hope and Charity were asking about you."

Hope reached over and patted her hand before reaching for another sandwich and leaning back again. "Tell them that you're in good hands."

Giggling, Krystal relayed the message. "I hope you're not mad that I left."

"No, baby. We're not mad." Rafe's low tone held a hint of amusement. "You didn't have a phone, and we trust you with Hope and Charity. Besides, Ace and Carter have been checking on the three of you all day."

Krystal frowned, sitting up slightly. "They have?" She pulled the lapels of her robe closed, looking around for any sign of them. "I'm only wearing a robe."

Linc chuckled. "That conjures an intriguing picture, but they can't see you. They just keep driving past the spa to make sure there's no trouble."

Krystal sighed, her stomach knotting. "You're worried about Kevin."

"Yes, we are." Rafe's tone held a challenge as if he expected an argument. "It's our right to protect you. You still haven't told us why you were crying. You said Hope and Charity were asking about us. What about that made you cry?"

Krystal smiled and wiggled her toes again, finding that the champagne and the fact that she couldn't see them made it easier to open up. "When Hope and I talked about you, I told her that I was afraid of making a comment…" Frowning, she shook her head. "No. That's not the right word."

"Commitment?"

Nodding, she laughed softly. "Yeah. That's it. Thanks, Linc."

"You're welcome." Sounding suspiciously as if he was trying not to laugh, Linc cleared his throat. "So you're afraid of making a commitment…"

"I was because I couldn't believe that all of this is real." Feeling the sting of tears, Krystal downed the rest of her champagne and held out her glass when Hope pulled the bottle from the ice bucket to offer more.

"It's very real. You're not afraid anymore?"

Krystal met Hope's grin with a smile of thanks. "Terrified, but the champagne and talkin' 'bout it helps. When I was talkin' about leaving—"

"What?" Linc barked into the phone startling Krystal so much that she spilled some of her champagne. "You were planning to leave?"

"No. At least not right now. They made me realize that I hadn't really made a plan since I got here. Had one before. I figured I would have to in the future when you and Rafe realized that I'm not the same woman I used to be, but I didn't even plan it out. They said that meant I wanted to stay."

"The thought of turning you over my lap becomes more appealing by the minute." Linc's low teasing tone made her stomach flutter.

"You're just jealous because Rafe spanked me." She looked up at Hope and Charity, and although she'd kept her voice at just above a whisper, both women had obviously heard, staring at her and grinning. "And I'm not leaving. Hope made me admit that I can't leave."

"Why not?"

"'Cause I love both of you. Can't leave unless you throw me out."

Linc sucked in a breath, and a long silence followed.

Wondering if she'd accidentally hung up, Krystal lowered the phone to look at the screen but had trouble focusing on it. She lifted it to her ear again, hearing the faint sound of Linc and Rafe speaking in low tones but couldn't make out what they said. "Hey! You still there?"

"Damned right we're still here." Linc's voice had a huskiness to it that it hadn't before. "I have no reason to be jealous of Rafe spanking you since I have every intention of doing the same thing. And we both love you, too, and neither one of us has any intention of throwing you out."

Krystal took another sip of champagne. "That wouldn't be very nice. I mean to take me from California and bring me all the way to Oklahoma—to a strange town—and toss me aside as if I was garbage."

"Krystal—"

Ruthlessly cutting Rafe off, Krystal rose to her feet, surprised to find it difficult to keep her balance. "No. You made me love you. You said you love me."

"I do."

"*We* do." Linc cursed. "Damn it, Krystal. I'd hoped to have this conversation in person."

Dropping to her chair again, Krystal gingerly lifted her legs onto the end, careful to keep the toe separator in place. "If you change your mind, I'll kick your ass. Asses!"

Hope and Charity both lifted their glasses to salute her, both women nodding seriously.

Charity hiccupped. "Damn right."

Hope sat up abruptly. "Don't forget to tell him to remind you to get the balm."

"Oh, yeah. Linc, remind me to get the balm."

"The balm?"

"Uh-huh." Setting her champagne aside, Krystal picked up the cracker she'd coated with the soft cheese and nibbled on a corner. "I still have to go get my massage, and Hope said I'll probably fall asleep, and with all the champagne, I'm afraid I'll forget it."

"I'll remember. Baby, what's the balm for?"

Remembering Hope's words, Krystal giggled. "For my wax job. Are you going to pick me up, or do you want me to walk home?"

"I don't want you walking anywhere. We'll be there to pick you up." Linc grinned in stunned delight and glanced at Rafe, unsurprised that his friend's eyes widened and then his friend's slow, devious smile. "You got waxed, baby?"

* * * *

Shifting in his seat to adjust his jeans around his swollen cock, Linc smiled at Krystal's soft giggle.

"Hope said you would like it. Said I would like it, too, but it hurt. That's why I need the balm. They put some on me but said that I would need to keep appliping it for a day or two."

Linc chuckled. "Appliping it? I think you mean *applying* it."

"That's what I said."

Amused and delighted with her, Linc held back a chuckle. "Of course you did. My mistake. I'd be happy to apply it for you."

Rafe grinned from ear to ear. "Are you saying that you got that sweet pussy waxed?"

She giggled, a sound that tightened the fist around Linc's heart. Krystal lowered her voice even more. "I did. I don't think I would have done it if I hadn't had too much to drunk. I mean if I wasn't drink."

Lucas eyes filled with tears at the effort it cost him to hold back laughter. "I know exactly what you mean, baby. Did it hurt?"

"Like hell. Hope and Charity said that it'll be worth it. I'm startin' to think they were just teasin' me."

Rafe chuckled. "Oh, it'll definitely be worth it, especially if you don't mind having your pink toenails in the air and my mouth on your pussy."

"Rafe!"

Still smiling, Rafe glanced at Linc and leaned closer to the speaker. "Don't pretend you're shocked. A woman with a waxed pussy is just asking for trouble." Sobering slightly, he tightened his hands on the wheel. "So no more talk about leaving?"

"I'm willing to give this a chance. I just want you to promise me that you'll be honest with me about how you feel."

Linc let out the breath he'd been holding. "We will and expect the same from you."

"Okay." Krystal blew out a breath. "And no more talk about Kevin. Gotta go. Time for my massage." After she disconnected, Linc disconnected more slowly, breathing a sigh of relief as he slumped back in his seat. "It sounds like we're gonna have a very drunk woman on our hands."

Rafe nodded, more solemn that he'd expected. "At least she's finally in our hands—where she belongs."

* * * *

Struggling to see through eyes that continued to swell, Kevin pressed his arms against his sides to protect his ribs, making himself as small as possible between the two men on either side of him.

Despite that, when Roy, on his right, nudged him with an elbow, Kevin couldn't hold back a grunt of pain. "You'd better be right about your sister being able to get you the money. If not, you're in even bigger trouble."

"It's not my fault the cops took the drugs."

"Yeah, well, the boss sees it different. If you weren't dippin' into the merchandise, you wouldn't have been so stoned that you got caught. You gotta pay for what you used and what the cops took."

He'd been kidnapped by the two men when he'd walked out of his hotel room and, after searching him and the hotel room for money and finding only the twenty-seven dollars he'd stuck in his pocket, had beaten him until he'd finally admitted that he couldn't come up with the money.

When they'd cut off his pinkie finger, he'd told them about Krystal.

She was all he had left, and if she couldn't come up with the money he knew she had, they would kill him, but not without torturing him even more first.

Holding his throbbing hand in the other, which he'd wrapped in one of his T-shirts, he sat between them in the front seat of their pickup as they headed cross country to Desire.

He already regretted telling them about Krystal, but he hadn't known what else to do.

The pain had been excruciating.

They hadn't taken his cell phone, for which he was grateful.

If anyone could protect Krystal, it was Rafe and Linc.

The two big deputies were big and mean enough to protect his sister.

With his head down, he glanced out of the corner of his eye, swallowing heavily at the gun tucked into Roy's waistband.

He knew the driver, Al, also carried one.

If Krystal was telling the truth and there was no money, both of them would pay for his mistake.

Rafe and Linc were their only chance of survival.

He just needed to warn them.

Chapter Fourteen

Rafe attempted to pay for Krystal's spa treatments, only to be told that Hope had already paid for it.

He asked about the balm and bought two of them, holding the bag containing them and pacing back and forth as he waited for Krystal to emerge.

He paused, looking up when the door opened, and smiled when Beau Parrish came through the door. "I see you're here to pick up your tipsy woman, too."

Beau grinned, glancing toward the door to the back. "Tipsy hell! When she and her sister get together for a spa day, they drink champagne until they can barely walk."

Linc frowned, setting the jar he'd been looking at back onto the shelf. "Can we expect this to be a habit?"

Beau grinned. "If Krystal comes with Hope and Charity, you probably can. Neither one of them drink much, but when they come here, they like to let their hair down and make a day of it."

His smile fell, his eyes narrowing slightly in a look of concern. "When Charity called, she said that Krystal had something of a revelation about her feelings for you."

Rafe couldn't hold back a smile. "Because we wanted to share her, Krystal never quite believed that we were serious about her. Since coming to Desire, she's seen how well it can work, and I think we finally managed to convince her that we're serious. Who knows? Maybe Hope and Charity made her see it. If so, I'm grateful."

The door opened again, admitting Ace.

Smiling when he saw them, the sheriff nodded toward the woman at the register and approached, glancing at Beau with a knowing look before turning to include Rafe and Linc in his smile. "Welcome to the club."

Rafe smiled in return, his chest tightening with pride and love for the woman he waited for. "It sounds as if this could become a habit."

Ace chuckled. "I wouldn't be surprised."

Stiffening when his cell phone rang, Rafe retrieved it from his pocket, frowning to see that the call came from Kevin. He glanced at Linc, briefly considering not answering, but decided that it would be better to talk to him while Krystal wasn't present. "Shit. It's Kevin."

Ace's eyes went flat and cold. "Would you mind putting it on speaker? This guy's wanted."

"I know that." His good mood gone, Rafe answered, switching the call to speaker. "Delgatto."

"It's Kevin."

Surprised at the fear in Kevin's shaky whisper, Rafe stiffened, his gaze on Linc's. "What's wrong?"

"They kidnapped me. Beat me. Cut off my finger. I have to talk fast. We're on our way there."

Fear for Krystal, and anger at Kevin, tied knots in Rafe's stomach. "To Desire? Why? What the hell did you do?"

"I couldn't take it anymore. They beat the hell out of me. I had to tell them where to find her."

Rafe's stomach tightened painfully as he focused on Kevin's raspy, weakening voice. "Tell *who* where to find her?"

"Roy and Al. I owe money to their boss. As soon as Krystal gives it to them, they'll let me go. In bathroom. Had to call. Know you'll protect her. I'm sorry. Tell her I'm…" His voice trailed off.

Fury and terror warred inside him, both emotions so intense his hands shook. "Kevin!"

"Blue pickup."

"Shit. Kevin!"

But the call had been disconnected.

With a curse, Ace dug out his cell phone. "Pass the word to everyone." He turned away, speaking into his phone. "Talia, I need a BOLO on a blue pickup."

Rafe half listened to Ace direct Talia to tell Carter, Joe, and Marshall about Kevin and the trouble heading their way as well as to send the group text they'd established months earlier to pass the word about impending trouble.

Linc cursed, his hands fisted at his sides. "We don't know how far they are away, so we have no idea when they'll get here."

When Ace disconnected and rejoined them, Rafe turned to him. "As soon as we get Krystal home, I'll be in. We need as many eyes as we can out there."

He wanted to be on the street, determined to keep danger as far from Krystal as possible.

Ace inclined his head. "We'll meet at the station."

Beau cursed. "I'll bring Hope home with me. Let me know if you need anything."

* * * *

Krystal walked out to the waiting room, feeling looser and better than she had in a long time.

Since Charity had already told her that the men were all in the waiting room, she hurried out with Hope and Charity right behind her.

Expecting Rafe and Linc to be as happy and playful as they'd sounded on the phone, Krystal stopped short just inside the waiting room at the looks on their faces.

The tension in the room could be cut with a knife, a tension she picked up immediately despite having had several glasses of champagne.

Since Linc was closer, she went immediately to him, gripping his arm as she glanced at Rafe. "What's wrong?"

Linc shared a look with Rafe, his hesitancy scaring her. "We'll talk later."

"No." Looking from Linc to Rafe and back again, she gripped Linc's arm tighter while, out of the corner of her eye, watching Ace and Beau rush Hope and Charity out the door. "Tell me."

Linc shook his head and wrapped an arm around her, sweeping her from her feet and holding her high against his chest as he strode toward the door. "Not here."

Linc and Rafe both scanned the parking lot as they made their way to the SUV, Linc holding her close and leaning protectively over her.

Krystal didn't speak again until Linc tucked her into the back seat of the SUV and slid in behind her. "What's going on?"

Linc gathered her close and waited until Rafe slid into the driver's seat and closed the door behind him before answering. "Kevin called."

Krystal stiffened, pulling out of his arms slightly to look up at him.

Struck by the hard lines in his expression and the ice-cold glittering in his hazel eyes, Krystal gripped his arm tighter and looked around, glancing at Rafe. "What's wrong? Why are you so upset that Kevin called?"

Cupping her jaw, Linc turned her toward him. "I don't want you to worry. Rafe and I will take care of it."

Krystal's stomach dropped. "Take care of what?"

A muscle worked in Linc's jaw. "Your brother owes some very bad people some money. They kidnapped him and are heading here because he told them that you have it."

Shocked, Krystal momentarily forgot to breathe, fear for her brother and the knowledge that he was bringing trouble to the men she loved rendering her almost incoherent.

She stared into Linc's eyes, the anger and fear she found there leaving her momentarily breathless. "What? I don't have much money." She took a steadying breath, and then another to fight the dizziness. "Are you sure?"

Rafe started the engine and reached over to unlock the glove compartment and, to Krystal's shock, retrieved a gun, handing it to Linc before retrieving another.

She stared down at the gun in Linc's hand, feeling a dizzying sense of unreality.

She'd seen both of them wearing their guns in their holsters while in uniform, but she'd never seen either one of them holding a weapon in their hand.

It hit her suddenly that they'd always been armed but had carefully kept their guns out of her sight.

They'd always protected her.

Gripping the front of his shirt, she nodded and took another deep breath, staring at the gun in his hand. "What are we going to do?"

Linc pulled her against him, resting the hand holding the gun against his thigh. "We're taking you home. I'm going to stay with you while Rafe goes on duty. We'll switch off later."

Krystal took several more steadying breaths to clear her head. "You're in danger, and so are the others, because of me."

Rafe turned in his seat and slapped her knee. "Stop it. None of this is your fault. Your brother got himself into a lot of fucking trouble. Do you know he's got several warrants out for his arrest, including the one for stealing drugs from the nursing home?"

Ashamed, Krystal pressed her face against Linc's chest, blinking back tears. "I should never have come here."

Linc kissed her head, running his free hand up and down her back. "You didn't have a choice. Still don't. Your brother had enough faith in us to bring them here, knowing we would protect you and do our best to protect him."

Sitting back, he looked down at her, his gaze narrowed. "You don't trust us to protect you, darlin'?"

Krystal sighed. "Of course I trust you. I have no doubt that you'd take a bullet for me without hesitation. I just can't live with that."

* * * *

With Linc leading the way, Rafe followed Krystal into the house, scanning the yard and street before closing the door and locking it behind him.

Krystal's features had paled significantly since she'd come through the door of the spa, and she shook with the nerves. Her features no longer glowed and had a pinched, tight look to them while the happiness that had made her blue eyes sparkle had completely disappeared, leaving them darkened and flat.

Walking down the hallway toward the bedroom, he caught her around the waist when she would have turned into the kitchen. Pulling her close, he kissed her hair. "Don't worry, baby, We'll take care of this. They won't get anywhere near you, and we'll get your brother back."

Krystal sighed and slumped against him. "And then he's going to go to jail."

Unwilling to dump more on her when she was already dealing with so much, Rafe shared a look with Linc over her head. "We'll deal with that when the time comes."

Lifting her head, she looked up at him, her eyes and voice flat. "What else did Kevin say?"

Not about to tell her about her brother's injuries, Rafe gave her a smile of reassurance. "Just that they surprised him when he came out of his hotel room and wanted their money. He doesn't have it, but he told him that he could get it from you. They're hanging on to him until they get their money."

Krystal nodded and pushed away from him, going to the refrigerator. "So he decided to bring his problems here?"

Unsettled by her strange mood, and assuming it to be alcohol induced, Rafe blinked when she yanked the refrigerator door open hard enough to rattle the bottles on the shelves in the door. "He said that he knew we would protect you. He also said to tell you he's sorry."

"I wouldn't need any protection if he hadn't told them where I am." Straightening, she dropped her head back and closed her eyes. "He's in trouble and doesn't have anywhere else to go." Shaking her head, she bent again and searched the refrigerator shelves.

Linc turned from where he'd started a pot of coffee, his gaze narrowing on Krystal. "Your brother took a chance and called to warn us."

Krystal whipped her head to face Linc. "Why the hell are you defending him? You can't stand him."

Not giving Linc a chance to answer, she turned her sharp gaze on Rafe. "I'll fix you some sandwiches to take with you."

Rafe shook his head, his thoughts already on meeting the others at the station. "Don't worry about it. I'll grab something at the diner—"

"No!" Krystal slammed several packages of lunch meat on the counter and whirled on him. "Damn it! I said I'm fixing sandwiches!"

Rafe blinked, sliding a quick glance at Linc before giving Krystal his undivided attention. "Krystal?"

Fisting her hands on the counter, she lowered her head. "If you're going to be in danger because of my brother, you can at least let me fix you a couple of sandwiches."

Rafe glanced at Linc again as he closed in on Krystal from behind. Closing his hands over her clenched fists, he bent to kiss her ear. "Thank you. I'd love to take along a couple of sandwiches."

Nodding, she blew out a breath. "Okay. Will you call?"

Straightening, he kissed the top of her head. "I'll call and text and bore you to death. We don't think he's that close."

Krystal reached into the breadbox for a fresh loaf of bread. "But you're all worried that he could be, which is why the entire town is going to be on pins and needles until this is over."

Chapter Fifteen

Linc turned off the alarm as soon as it sounded, stilling when Krystal shifted restlessly beside him with a moan.

He lay motionless until she settled again, hoping she would sleep longer.

She'd been restless and jittery all evening and hadn't wanted to go to bed until Rafe came home and had only given in when she realized that he would be going in to work early in the morning and he had no intention of going to bed without her.

She'd slept in short increments, waking with a jolt over and over and reaching for her phone to text Rafe.

Not until Rafe crawled into bed in the early morning hours did she finally allow herself to fall asleep.

After making sure she'd settled again, he eased from the bed, hoping she would sleep longer.

After adjusting the covers over her again against the morning chill, he made his way in the darkness around the bed and to the bathroom to shower.

Minutes later, he left the bathroom as quietly as possible, the cloud of steam following him into the bedroom. He glanced at the bed as he passed it, his jaw clenching when he saw that Krystal was no longer in it.

Rafe shifted slightly on his side of the bed with a sigh. "She went out to fix your breakfast."

"Damn hard-headed woman."

Rafe chuckled softly. "That she is. Make sure she's back in bed before you leave. If not, wake me up."

"Will do."

By the time he'd dressed in his uniform and made his way out to the kitchen, she had coffee, juice, and pancakes waiting for him and was in the process of making sandwiches.

He knew better than to object.

Wearing only her nightgown and a pair of her new thick socks, she turned with a plate of pancakes and set it on the table before quickly turning back to the counter.

Moving in behind her, he wrapped his arms around her and kissed her hair, loving the feel of her warm softness in his arms. He breathed in the scent of lavender and smiled. "Good morning."

"Good morning. Eat your breakfast before it gets cold."

Sipping his coffee, Linc studied her over the rim, wishing he knew what was going on in her hard head. "You gonna talk to me?"

She kept her head bowed, spreading mustard on bread with jerky movements. "About what?"

Setting his cup aside, he cut into his pancakes, watching her closely. "I know you're scared for your brother."

Setting the mustard aside, she opened the package of sliced turkey. "There's nothing new about that."

Struck by the lack of emotion in her tone, Linc swallowed his bite of pancakes and stabbed another. "I'm sure that's true. We'll keep you safe, Krystal."

"I know that."

"We'll get him back for you."

"I know that, too." She slammed slices of turkey onto the bread, stacking them high before rewrapping the remainder. "I also know he'll go to jail."

Grabbing the cheese, she slapped several slices on top of the slices of stacked turkey. "He'll expect me to post bail for him, which would probably take every dime I have—money I'd planned to use to take refresher courses so I can get a job. He won't be able to leave town and won't have a damned place to stay, so he'll expect to stay here. You and Rafe will let him because you don't want me to worry. He'll steal from you. He'll lie. He'll lie around here and expect to live off of you and Rafe and probably get a kick out of thinking that he can get away with anything because of your feelings for me. He'll use you and expect to get away with it because of your feelings for me. He'll drive a wedge between us that we won't be able to overcome, and it'll be over."

She wrapped the sandwiches and stuck them in a paper bag before opening the refrigerator again to put everything away.

Something in her voice had him setting his fork aside and rising to his feet. "Krystal?"

"And that's the best outcome. The worst would be if someone got hurt or killed. I could never live here with that kind of thing hanging over me every day. The people who live here are good people, and because of me, someone they love could be hurt. No matter how you look at it, there's no good outcome to any of this."

Her flat tone scared the hell out of him, as well as the fact that she kept her gaze averted.

Turning her to face him, he wrapped his arms around her, lifting her chin as he pulled her close. "Baby, it'll be all right. I promise."

Shaking her head, she pushed away from him and went to the coffee pot. "It won't. Life isn't finished giving me shit yet. I should never have come here. It would have been better to have the memories of the good between us than the reality of how it all went to hell."

Fighting back fear, Linc caught her, yanking her against him. Fisting a hand in her hair, he tilted her head back to force her to look at him. "It's not going to go to hell. I won't let it."

"You can't control everything, Linc."

Linc bent his head to give her a hard kiss, one filled with frustration and anger at the circumstances that kept coming between them. Lifting his head, he stared into her eyes. "I can control my determination to keep you. I've waited too long for you to give up now, and I'll be damned if I let you give up on this either."

He released her, grabbing the bag of sandwiches. "Go back to bed."

"No. I think I'll just—"

Linc smiled coldly. "You leave me no choice then."

Krystal yelped when he flung her over his shoulder, and it gave him no small sense of satisfaction when she began to struggle. "What the hell are you doing?"

Linc slapped her bottom, smiling when she gasped and stopped struggling. "No longer walking on eggshells around you."

With just enough light in the room to make out Rafe's look of shock and then amusement, Linc opened the top drawer to the nightstand on Rafe's side of the bed where he'd placed his gun, badge, and handcuffs.

He slapped the key on top of the nightstand and grabbed the handcuffs before moving around to the other side of the bed. "I told you to go to bed so Rafe could get some sleep, but since you insist on being stubborn, I'll just take the decision out of your hands."

Chuckling, Rafe rolled to his back and lifted his right arm. "Cuff her to me."

Linc tossed Krystal to the bed, catching her left arm and closing one side of the cuff to it before she could react.

Rafe caught the other side of the cuff and attached it to his own wrist. "I've got her. At least now I can get some sleep."

"Hey! Are you friggin' kidding me?"

"Nope." Linc reached over to kiss her again, cupping her breast and running his thumb over her nipple through her nightgown before straightening. "You need a firmer hand than we've been giving you. That stops now."

* * * *

Krystal watched Linc walk from the room, once again struck by how sexy he looked in his uniform. "Damn it, Linc!"

Ignoring her, he kept walking, leaving her lying on the bed handcuffed to Rafe.

She listened to the front door closing behind him and, with a sigh, turned to Rafe to find him watching her but found it too dark to read the look in his eyes. She lifted her wrist, gesturing toward the handcuffs. "Would you please take these off?"

"No." Lifting her slightly, he lifted his arm above her head and around her so that she ended up facing away from him, his arm under her pillow holding hers in front of her. "I like you in handcuffs. Go to sleep. I need to go back in tonight."

Turning, she looked at him over her shoulder. "I want you to sleep because I want you to be sharp when you go back to work."

"Good." He pulled her closer. "Then go to sleep."

Krystal sighed, fighting to stay awake. "You can sleep while I cook. I want to do some baking."

She also wanted to stay in touch with Linc.

"You can bake later. I can't sleep if I don't have you close, so you're stuck here until I get a couple of hours sleep."

His deep tone had become even huskier, and with a sigh, she admitted defeat. "At least let me go back to the kitchen to get my phone so I can stay in touch with Linc."

"No. Go to sleep. He'll call me if something happens."

She let her eyes close against the grittiness, but she knew it would take some time to get her brain to shut off. "Linc let me stay in touch with you."

"And you texted me constantly, even after I told you I would let you know if something happened. Besides, Linc's nicer than I am, something you're going to find out if you don't shut up and go to sleep."

His threat might have had more impact if he hadn't cuddled her closer and pressed his lips against her hair.

Smiling, she snuggled against him. "You don't scare me."

"I will if you don't go to sleep."

"Shouldn't one of us stay awake to watch the house?"

"The house is being watched, baby. Hell, Caleb and Lucas came by last night and installed cameras on all four sides."

Krystal blinked. "I didn't hear them."

"You weren't supposed to. There are alarms set up that will go off on their phones, our phones, Ace's, and the other deputies'. But I doubt they'll even get that close. You're safe, baby. Go to sleep. We'll get up in a couple of hours, and you can text to Linc all you want to."

Warmed by his body, and exhausted from a nearly sleepless night, she let herself drift, promising herself she'd only sleep a little while.

When she woke up again, it was to bright sunlight and the realization that Rafe was no longer in bed with her.

Automatically pulling at her wrist, she found it free and sat up, scanning the room for any sign of Rafe.

Seeing the closed bathroom open, she slid out of bed just as Rafe emerged from the other room, fully dressed in his uniform. "Get dressed and make sure you put your sneakers on."

Krystal stood frozen, her heart pounding hard enough to leave her breathless. "Kevin?"

His features appeared as if carved from granite, the fury in his dark eyes turning them nearly black. "Yeah. Get moving."

He went to the nightstand, collecting the handcuffs and keys and tucking them away before opening the drawer and retrieving his handgun.

Once again, she experienced a sense of unreality, heightened by the fact that her brother was responsible for bringing trouble straight toward them.

Rafe slid his gun into his holster and paused, his gaze hooded, sharp, and impatient. "Krystal? You okay? Linc's on his way."

Seeing the concern growing in his eyes and realizing just how much he and Linc worried about her—babied her—she nodded. "I'm fine. I'll get dressed. So what's the plan?"

She threw off her nightgown, trying to ignore his appreciative gaze, and hurriedly dressed in jeans and a T-shirt and grabbed her shoes and socks before sitting on the bed and hurriedly putting them on.

"Carter caught sight of their vehicle just outside of town. He ran the plates to make sure and said he saw your brother in the back seat with one of them."

When his cell phone signaled a text, he pulled it out, frowning as he read the text. "Linc is coming this way, and the others aren't far behind."

She finished tying her sneakers and jumped to her feet. "Others? You mean the other deputies and Ace?"

Rafe reached out a hand and took hers as he started out. "Baby, in Desire, there are any number of people who live for this shit."

He paused in the hallway, pressing her against the wall and dropping a hard kiss on her lips. "Stay right here."

Krystal wrapped her hands around the corner, looking around it to watch Rafe move to stand closer to the front door, standing close to the wall between it and the front window. "Linc's here. Stay put."

From her position, she could see Linc get out of the SUV and rush toward the house, his features hard and cold as he scanned the street.

Rafe's cell phone rang, and without hesitation, he lifted the phone she hadn't noticed in his hand and answered. "Delgatto."

He turned to stare at her, holding her gaze. "Of course she's here."

He opened the front door to admit Linc, never looking away from her. "No. you can't talk to her. If you want the money, I'll get it for you."

Krystal stiffened and started forward, anxious to talk to her brother. "Let me talk to him."

Rafe shook his head sharply, his eyes going harder and colder. "Who am I talking to? Well, *Roy*, I'm afraid she's not going to meet you."

Krystal started forward again, only to have Linc stop her. Looking up at him, she kept her voice at a whisper. "He knows you're both cops."

Linc inclined his head. "Which is why we're both in uniform. We don't want any misunderstandings."

"Where are they?"

"Right outside of town."

Rafe moved to stand in front of the window, raking a hand through his hair in a rare show of stress. "Damn it! Fine. We'll be right there. Let me talk to him."

The sound of Kevin's cry sent a chill through him. "No. You talk to me right now."

They'd threatened to cut off another of Kevin's fingers, and listening to Kevin's scream of pain, Rafe wondered if they'd done it.

"Have her meet us at the end of Tyler Road. And, cop, don't try anything. I have a picture of her from his wallet, so I'll know if you try to pull anything."

Rafe stared at Krystal, his stomach knotting at the thought of having Krystal involved. "I don't want her involved. I'll make sure you get your money."

The soft knock at the back door startled a cry from Krystal, and she automatically pressed against Linc, who gathered her close and whispered to her before stepping away to go answer it.

"No. Send her alone and make sure she brings the money. All ten grand. Fifteen minutes."

Rafe cursed when the call disconnected and looked up in time to see Lucas Hart come through it and approach Krystal.

With a tender smile, he held out his hand to show her what he held. "This is a microphone and camera. It'll let us see and hear everything." He paused and looked up at Rafe. "I assume you couldn't talk them into meeting you or Linc?"

Rafe cursed and strode to Krystal, glancing at the duffel bag Linc dropped on the floor. "No. I couldn't. They also have a picture of her from Kevin's wallet, so there's no way Stormy could stand in."

Lucas nodded, his lips twitching. "My wife is gonna be disappointed, but we're prepared. I'm Lucas Hart, by the way. I'm here to help." He gave Krystal a reassuring smile, a sharp contrast to the fury swirling in his eyes. "The money's all there. Seems a hell of a lot of work for ten grand, but I guess it's worth it to them."

Rafe helped Lucas attach the equipment to Krystal. "Ten grand is a lot of money to some people. It sounds like they're getting a kick out of all the drama, which tells me that they're new at this. They want her to meet them at the end of Tyler Road."

Linc looked up from his cell phone. "They're sitting on the side of the road at the intersection. Carter is in the woods, keeping them in sight while Ace is watching them from the woods on the other side."

"Caleb and Devlin are on the main road to the south, and Marshall is on the road heading north. We'll take care of keeping them out of Desire." Lucas turned Krystal and clipped something to the waistband at her back while Rafe ran a small wire inside her bra in the front. "She needs a jacket."

Rafe nodded and met her gaze again. "It's on the recliner. You okay, baby?"

"I'm fine." Krystal smiled, relieved and surprised to realize that she was. "I think the time I spent working in the ER taught me how to handle the adrenaline."

"Joe and Hoyt have taken positions that give them the best shot." Linc moved away to retrieve her jacket and, after helping her into it, pulled her close, wrapping his arms protectively around her. "I don't like this."

Krystal turned in his arms, lifting her hands to his shoulders and staring up into his eyes. "I can do this, Linc. All I have to do is exchange the money for my brother."

Linc's eyes narrowed. "Joe is another deputy, and he's on the opposite side of the road, the side you're going to be on. I'm gonna be hiding in the SUV with you."

"Won't they see you?"

"No. At least not until it's too late."

Lucas handed both Linc and Rafe a small object that they each placed in their ears. "From now on, everyone can hear you. We're all communicating with these." He held out another one to her. "Put this in your ear, and you can hear all of us. You'll be on the opposite side of the road from them. They can't see, but they're surrounded."

She put the earpiece in but didn't hear anything.

Rafe closed in behind her. "And so are you. Slow down when you start to get close. Joe, are you there?"

"I'm here."

Krystal jolted at the sound of a stranger's voice in her ear.

Rafe turned her, lifting her chin. "What you're wearing will be used as evidence in court, but we'll all be communicating with you through your earpiece. Joe's a sniper, baby, and Hoyt is almost as good."

"Almost as good?"

Krystal jolted at the sound of another deep voice and couldn't help but smile at the outrage in it as she suspected he'd meant it to. "Wow."

Linc turned her back to face him. "Approach slowly and pull over to the side of the road. Joe will tell you when to stop so that you don't block his shot."

A cold knot formed in Krystal's stomach. "He's going to shoot them?"

Rafe inclined his head. "If necessary. We'd rather catch them on their way out of town, but it's up to them. Doc Hansen's in his office on standby."

Krystal blinked. "No hospital?" She remembered learning that the closest hospital was in Tulsa, something she'd learned when thinking about a job.

Lucas smiled faintly. "You don't know Doc Hansen's office. It's fully equipped and closer. Ready?"

* * * *

Aware that Rafe and Lucas rode in Lucas's SUV far enough behind them not to be seen, Krystal drove on the road out of town with Linc hidden on the floor behind her seat. "I see them."

"Slow down." Linc's voice sounded low in her ear, the calmness in it reassuring her.

Tightening her hands on the wheel, she slowed, easing the huge SUV to the shoulder.

Another voice sounded, one she recognized as the sheriff's. "Cut the chatter. Joe, you see everything, so you have the lead."

"Copy. A little more, Krystal. Slower." She slowed even more, obeying the commands of the man she recognized as Joe. "That's it. Stop."

Krystal hit the brake hard enough to jar her. "Sorry."

"You're doing fine, honey. They're watching you. Put your window down so Linc can take a shot if he needs to."

She obeyed him again, fighting the urge to look around in order to see the others.

"Don't turn the engine off. Just put it in park and get out. Slowly."

Krystal slid out of the SUV, automatically looking for traffic even though she knew they'd closed it off at both ends of the road.

She looked up, meeting the eyes of her brother, shaking even harder when she saw that her brother had a bloody nose and two black eyes.

He looked so terribly beaten that her anger fell away, fear for him adding to her nerves.

"Now walk around the front of the SUV so they can see you."

Once again, Krystal obeyed Joe, her knees so rubbery that she held on to the hood for support.

The driver got out, slamming the door behind him. "Where's the money?"

Krystal met the eyes of one of the men who'd kidnapped and hurt her brother, suddenly terrified at the evil in his eyes. "I'm getting it."

Her fear increased when he pulled a gun from his waistband and moved closer.

Joe's voice sounded low in her ear. "He pulled a gun. Has it pointed at her."

Hurrying to the passenger side, she opened the back door and retrieved the bag, surprised at the speed with which Linc slid out.

She closed the door again, and carrying the duffel bag, she rushed to the front of the SUV again, aware that Linc moved quickly to crouch by the front tire.

She could feel his sharp gaze—had gotten a glimpse of the fury and terror glimmering in his eyes—but forced herself to keep from looking at him.

"Tell him not to come any closer."

When the other man smiled, reaching out a hand, Krystal shook her head. "Don't come any closer."

Focusing on Joe's instructions, Krystal glanced at her brother again.

"Tell him to release your brother."

Krystal tightened her grip on the bag, locking her knees when they threatened to buckle. "Let Kevin go."

"Shit. Move to the left, honey."

Krystal tried to appear nonchalant as she moved closer to the hood again, shaking even harder when the other man got out of the passenger side and came around to stand at the back door where her brother sat.

The man standing in the center of the road gestured toward the bag. "I'm the one with the gun here. Toss the bag to me."

"Tell him to let your brother out first."

Krystal swallowed heavily, her throat dry. "Let Kevin out."

"When I tell you to duck, you hit the ground, Krystal."

Shaking, Krystal divided her attention between the two men holding her brother. "Let him go."

The man standing in the middle of the road took a step closer to her, his smile sending chills up and down her spine. "Your brother's a pain in the ass. What if I took the money and *you*? I wonder what those two cops you fuck would pay to have you back—after Roy and I finished with you, of course."

Law of Desire   *205*

Krystal swallowed again, her nerves stretched almost to the breaking point. "I think taking me would bring you more trouble than it's worth. Let my brother out, take your money, and go."

She had the feeling that they planned to take her with them anyway, which would make it harder for the sheriff and the other men to capture them.

They could hold the others off using her as their hostage, something she couldn't allow.

The man closest to her started forward again. "I think we'll take both of you *and* the money. You'd do anything to make sure we didn't hurt your brother anymore."

"Hit the ground!"

Krystal dropped to the asphalt, releasing the bag to put her hands over her head.

Expecting a flurry of gunshots, she stiffened when she heard nothing except groans and the sounds of both men falling to the pavement.

Almost immediately, she felt a hand wrap around her upper arm. "It's over, baby. Get up."

Lifting her head, she saw that both of her brother's kidnappers lay writhing on the ground and Lucas and Rafe approaching them with guns drawn.

Linc pulled her to her feet, wrapping one arm around her while holding a gun pointed at the other men with his other hand. "You okay?"

The sound of approaching sirens almost blocked out the voices in her ear, the noise deafening. "I'm fine." She started toward her brother, only to have Linc pull her back. "Not yet."

Taking the earpiece from her ear, she watched Rafe cuff first one then the other kidnapper, glancing at her with eyes that screamed of fear and rage. "She okay?"

"She's good."

Amazed to see that each kidnapper had been shot in the hand and the leg, she held on to Linc. "They're not dead."

"No." Once the two men had been handcuffed, he reholstered his gun and wrapped both arms around her, holding her tightly to him. "You did good, baby."

Several cars squealed to a stop, and before she knew it, she and the others were surrounded by grim-looking men, including the sheriff.

Rafe yanked her from Linc's arms, holding her close and burying his face against her neck. "Krystal."

"I'm okay. I want to see Kevin."

Rafe straightened and turned her slightly, both he and Linc closing protectively around her as another deputy helped Kevin from the SUV and brought him closer.

The other man inclined his head in her direction. "I'm Carter. You did real good, honey. Ambulance is on its way."

Krystal gasped when she saw that her brother looked even worse than she'd suspected.

Covered in cuts and bruises, with a bloody shirt wrapped around his hand, Kevin staggered closer with the support of the deputy. "Krystal, I'm so sorry."

"I know." Pulling away from Linc and Rafe, she unwrapped his hand to see that two of his fingers had been cut off, one bleeding heavily.

As if by divine intervention, another car pulled up and an older man got out, rushing toward the scene with a huge duffel bag.

He went to the men lying on the ground, and when he began to treat them, Krystal realized that he was the doctor they'd spoken of.

Gripping her brother's arm, she rushed toward the doctor. "Come with me."

Rafe followed Krystal, introducing her to Doc Hansen and hovering protectively over her as she treated Kevin's injuries with the supplies from the doctor's bag.

Once she'd cleaned and bandaged her brother's injuries and significantly slowed the bleeding from Kevin's hand, she pitched in to help Doc Hansen treat the others.

* * * *

Linc closed on one side of Rafe while Carter closed in on the other.

Blowing out a breath, Linc wiped the back of his hand over his forehead. "I can't stop shaking. Christ, when he said he was gonna take her—"

Carter chuckled. "You know damned well none of us would have let that happen. Look at her. She sure as hell looks like she knows what she's doing."

Rafe grinned, pride swelling his chest. "She worked in the ER in San Diego. When I got shot, that's where I met her."

Nodding, Carter sighed. "It's a shame about her brother. I have to put him in cuffs, you know."

"I'll do it." Linc pulled his cuffs from their holder. "I'll be thrilled to do it. What the hell?"

Krystal suddenly rose to her feet and approached her brother, who stood several feet away with Marshall, standing to the side and slightly behind him.

She said something to Marshall, something that made the much larger man smile faintly and shake his head.

Kevin began to speak hurriedly, his eyes pleading.

Krystal's scowl spelled trouble, a trouble Kevin must have seen since he held out his hands to her and continued pleading.

Intrigued, Rafe watched her, aware that, from either side of him, Linc and Carter stood equally fascinated.

Ace rose from speaking to the doctor and the men on the ground, turning toward the scene just as Krystal curled her hand into a fist, rearing back and punching her brother in the stomach hard enough to double the younger man over.

Rafe's jaw dropped in shock, and he and the others watched her storm over to him and Linc, stopping with her hands on her hips in front of them.

She looked so much like the sassy nurse he'd met over three years earlier that his chest tightened with emotion.

Brushing at the front of her shirt, she reached inside and pulled out the wire. "Forgot about this."

Rafe turned her, chuckling as he dropped a kiss on her hair. "Don't worry. We'll cut that part out."

He unhooked the pack from the waistband at her back and handed it to Ace before gathering her against him, loving her more than ever. "You want to tell me what that was all about?"

Shrugging, she leaned back against him, allowing him to take her weight as she met Linc's steady stare. "He wanted me to pay his bail. I told him that I wouldn't and that neither would you. He has to accept the consequences for his actions, and he's not to bring trouble around me again."

She turned to look at each of them. "Dr. Hansen offered me a job, and I took it. I can take refresher courses online while I'm training at his office. I can't have my brother coming by and started trouble. Once he gets out of jail and gets his life together, he can come see me."

Chuckling, Carter walked away. "I'll go put him in cuffs. They all need a trip to the hospital, and you've got a wildcat to deal with."

Chapter Sixteen

Linc refilled Krystal's coffee cup and looked over her shoulder, fresh from the shower. "Did you find everything you need?"

"Yep." Krystal grinned and reached for her cup. "I'm all signed up." She closed the laptop. "Between working at the doctor's office and taking my online classes, I'm going to be pretty busy."

Rafe stood, leaning against the doorway, sipping coffee and watching her, both men taking advantage of the time they could talk to her together before Rafe went to work. "For the next month, you're only working part-time."

"True." Krystal took another sip of her coffee. "He's going to let me take days off for Kevin's trial."

Linc dropped to the seat next to her, closed the laptop, and pushed it aside. "We'll be there with you. In the meantime, we want to marry you."

Krystal smiled, glancing at each of them. "No more eggshells?"

Linc inclined his head. "No more eggshells. You showed us yesterday that you're tougher than that."

Krystal eyed each of them. "You both know that I love you, but do we really need to rush into this?"

Linc shrugged, fighting not to show his impatience. "We've waited three years, Krystal. I don't think there's any rushing about it. We want a family with you."

Rafe straightened, moving to sit in the chair on the other side of her. "We're not in a rush for that. We want to spend time alone with you first, but you're ours, Krystal. We know it, and you know it."

Smiling, she reached out a hand to each of them. "Yeah. I know it." Shaking her head, she blinked back the tears shimmering in her beautiful eyes and met Linc's gaze. "It's really going to work out, isn't it?"

Linc smiled, feeling the knots in his stomach loosen. "Of course it is. I told you it would, didn't I?"

Closing his hand on hers, he pulled her onto his lap. "We've waited a long time to have you here like this with us, and we're not about to give you up."

She smiled up at him, the feel of her hand on his chest and her well-rounded ass on his lap making his cock spring to life. "Hope made me feel stupid for doubting that you and Rafe love me. I didn't think it could work, but seeing the love in this town, I'm starting to believe."

"Just starting to?"

Linc stripped her out of her shirt and bra and bent his head to take her mouth with his.

The feel and taste of her went to his head like straight whiskey, his hunger for her growing stronger by the day.

When he slid a hand to cup her soft breast, he couldn't hold back a groan at the feel of her beaded nipple against his palm, filled with delight when she moaned and slid a hand to his shoulder, pressing her breast more firmly against his palm.

Krystal jolted at the feel of another set of hands at her waist, moaning when Rafe slid her worn jeans and panties down and off.

Lifting his head, Linc stared down at her, sliding his hand from her breast to her waxed mound. "With everything that's happened, we haven't had the chance to explore you."

His eyes narrowed, a faint smile playing at his lips. "In the future, Rafe and I will take care of applying the balm. How does it feel?"

Stunned at the extreme sensation of having his fingertips on bare skin, Krystal shivered. "Dear God. It didn't feel like that when I smeared the balm on it."

Rafe chuckled, brushing his lips over her inner thigh. "I don't imagine it did." His hand replaced Linc's, who'd returned his attention to her breast. "I think we're gonna keep you this way. I like being able to see and feel everything, and I sure as hell like the way you react to it."

He brushed his lips over her mound, smiling when she gasped at the pleasure. "Yeah. I think we're gonna keep you this way."

Linc groaned. "I can't wait. Pick her up."

Krystal gasped again when they lifted her and laid her across the table with her head hanging slightly off the edge.

Linc smiled down at her as he unzipped his pants. "Looks like you're in trouble now, darlin'."

* * * *

Krystal reached for his cock as soon as he freed it, crying out at the sudden rush of pleasure when Rafe spread her legs and touched his tongue to her clit. "Dear God!"

Rafe chuckled. "Let's see if you can concentrate on sucking Linc's cock while I use my mouth on you."

Hungry for the taste of him, Krystal turned her head toward Linc's cock, opening her mouth wide to take the head of his cock inside.

Gripping his outer thighs, she drew his cock deeper, sucking gently and crying out again when he took her nipples between his thumbs and forefingers at the same time that Rafe stabbed his tongue into her pussy.

Linc groaned and began to move, fucking her mouth with slow, shallow strokes while toying with her nipples in a way that sent sharp currents of hot pleasure to her slit, making Rafe's attention there even more intense.

Spreading her folds wider, Rafe slid his tongue all around her folds. "When I get home from work, I'll be looking forward to fucking your ass."

Her bottom clenched, the awareness there adding to her arousal.

Rafe chuckled as if knowing what she felt and that his wicked threat would be in her mind all day.

Linc groaned and cupped her breasts, massaging gently. "I'll have her already lubed up for you."

He closed his fingers over her nipples again while Rafe slid his hands under her bottom and lifted her higher. "You're gonna marry us next weekend." He slid one hand to her cheek and stared into her eyes. "Aren't you?"

Krystal moaned and nodded, sucking him harder as the pleasure built.

Thrilling when he moaned again, she reached for his balls, using her fingertips to lightly caress them, earning another one of Linc's deep groans.

"You're a little too good with that mouth." He pinched her nipples lightly, his eyes flaring at her soft cry. "Christ, woman, I never stop wanting you. Fuck."

Realizing he was about to come, Krystal gripped the base of his cock to keep him from pulling away, moving her hand on it in time with his thrusts.

"Krystal!" Linc's harsh tone had an edge to it that always thrilled her. "I'm too hungry for you. Let go or I'll come in your mouth."

Rafe lifted his head slightly. "I'm good with my mouth, too. Ready to come, baby?"

He lowered his head again, sucking on her clit and using his tongue in a way that left her helpless to hold back.

Bucking on the table, Krystal tightened her hold on Linc, moaning when his cock pulsed, releasing his seed against her tongue at the same time that Rafe's attention to her swollen clit intensified, sending her over the edge in a rush of sublime pleasure.

Wave after wave washed over her, leaving her trembling with a pleasure made even stronger by the love she felt for them.

She stiffened, moaning in distress when Linc withdrew his cock. "No."

Cupping the back of her head, Linc lifted it slightly and stared down at her. "So fucking beautiful."

He watched her ride the waves of pleasure, his expression one of rapt fascination as he lifted her high enough for her to see Rafe lift his head and reach for the fastening of his jeans. "Looks like you're gonna get fucked good, baby."

Rafe pulled his cock free and hurriedly rolled on a condom before gripping her upper thighs, raising them, and pulling her closer. "She certainly is."

Krystal cried out when Rafe thrust into her, her cries growing frantic when Linc held her arms pressed against the tabletop and bent his head to take a nipple into his mouth.

They held firm, not letting her move her arms or legs at all, forcing her to accept the sharp pleasure.

Crying out, she trembled helplessly as Rafe thrust harder and faster while Linc switched his attention to her other breast, sucking and gently scraping his teeth over her already sensitized nipples.

Releasing one of her arms, Linc slid his hand over her quivering stomach muscles to her mound, lifting his head to look down at her. "So soft." Watching her eyes, he slid his finger lower, pressing it against her clit. "Come again."

Her inner walls clenched on Rafe's cock, making it feel even larger, so large that her inner walls had to stretch to accommodate it.

The light caress of her swollen and sensitive clit had her stomach muscles tightening in response, and when Linc lowered his head to suck her nipple into his mouth again, the pleasure once again consumed her.

Rafe's groan and the tightening of his hands on her thighs added to her pleasure, a pleasure that crested when he pumped into her with short, shallow strokes, before thrusting his cock deep inside her.

Lifting his head, Linc smiled down at her and slid his hand higher, caressing her belly. "Damn, you get hotter and more beautiful every day."

He bent to touch his lips to hers. "Kiss Rafe good-bye and you and I can go take a nap."

Krystal smiled, reaching up to cup his jaw. "Yeah."

She knew that both Linc and Rafe liked her to be in bed with them when they slept after their shift, a habit she knew she could easily adopt.

Straightening, he left the kitchen, leaving her alone with Rafe.

With another groan, Rafe gathered her against him, lowering himself to one of the kitchen chairs with her straddling his lap. Holding her against him, he rubbed her back, his face buried in her hair. "I love you, baby."

Impaled on his cock, she gingerly straightened, lifting her face to his. "And I love you. I've loved you ever since you kissed me in the ER."

His smile stole her breath. "Good. I'd hate to think I was the only one. You know, Linc was jealous as hell."

Loving the feel of his hands moving up and down her back, she arched, pressing her breasts against his bare chest. "It didn't take long for me to fall in love with him, too. I just spent more time with you because you were in the hospital."

Rafe cupped her jaw, running his thumb over her chin. "You used to come see me before and after every shift. You were so sweet. So bossy. I saw that woman again yesterday."

Using his thumb to keep her chin lifted, he watched her with narrowed eyes. "You're even stronger than you were then. You know that, don't you?"

Warmed by his praise, Krystal shrugged. "I don't know about that. I just know that I'm more confident now." She blew out a breath and smiled. "After dealing with Mom, Dad, and Kevin, I feel like I can handle anything. The biggest part of that is knowing that you and Linc were there. I was always afraid there would come a time when the two of you decided that the affair was over."

"And now you understand that it's not an affair to us."

Her breath caught. "And now I understand. I never realized that people could really live this way. When I got here, and saw that you'd purposely searched for a place where we could live like this, I couldn't believe the two of you quit your jobs and made it your mission to find such a place."

Rafe's lips twitched, and with a gentle hand, he tucked her hair behind her ear. "There isn't anything we wouldn't do for you, baby."

Blinking back tears, Krystal nodded. "I know. I just keep falling more in love with you. I never expected it to be this way."

Lifting her chin, he studied her features, his gaze hooded. "So you're gonna marry us next weekend?"

A raised brow promised retribution if she didn't give him the answer he wanted.

Krystal frowned. "Yes. I'll marry you, but how does this work? I mean I can't legally be married to both of you. What will my name be? Please don't tell me that I have to choose because, if so, we'll just leave things the way they are."

From the doorway, Linc chuckled. "You don't have to choose." He reached into the refrigerator for the orange juice. "So there's no getting out of it."

Rafe closed his hands on her thighs. "Since I'm older, tradition in Desire says that you'll be married to me legally, but according to the law of Desire, you'll be married to both of us. Your name will be Delgatto, but around town, you could be addressed by either name."

She turned to glance at Linc, pleased to see him smile. "This is okay with you?"

Linc inclined his head. "Yes. For all intents and purposes, you'll still be married to me. You'll use Rafe's name, but you'll be sleeping next to me at night, and any children we have will belong to all three of us."

"Children." Krystal smiled and let out a breath. "I'd like that, but I'd rather wait awhile."

He bent to kiss her and closed his hands on her waist to lift her from his cock. "Good. So would we. We want to spend some time alone with you before anyone else comes along. Now be good. I have to go to work."

Minutes later, she lay in bed next to Linc, her head pillowed on his shoulder. "I love you."

Turning toward her, he gathered her close. "I love you, too, baby. I'm just glad that you finally see what Rafe and I knew all along."

"What's that?"

"That you're a hell of a lot stronger than you give yourself credit for. The last couple of years wore you out, but they made you stronger." Sliding a hand down her back, he kissed her forehead. "Once you spend a couple of months resting up, you're gonna keep Rafe and me on our toes."

He kissed her forehead and sighed. "Very much lookin' forward to it."

Knowing Linc had to get some sleep before his shift, Krystal cuddled again him, smiling when he relaxed against her.

She didn't know how she'd gotten lucky enough to have two such wonderful men in her life, but she'd never again take love and security for granted.

With her head against his wide chest, she listened to his heart beat and made plans for the future.

* * * *

She'd surprised herself by falling asleep but had only slept a little over an hour before waking up again.

Eager to do some baking to fill the cookie jar, something she knew that both men would enjoy, she climbed out of bed and showered, quietly dressing in her new blue outfit while Linc slept.

After whipping up a batch of batter for chocolate chip cookies, she put the first two cookie sheets in the oven while getting the ingredients assembled for the fried chicken dinner she'd planned.

She'd realized that she would have to have plenty of food in the refrigerator to accommodate their schedules and hers and couldn't wait to get started.

She'd already finished the cookies and the fried chicken and had started the mashed potatoes before she heard the shower.

She'd boiled a dozen eggs to snack on and started a grocery list as more ideas came to her.

Pouring through another of her cook books, she looked up when Linc appeared at the doorway, already dressed in his uniform.

Using a piece of paper to mark her page, she closed the cookbook and sat back with a smile. "You look sexy as hell in that uniform."

Setting his hat aside, Linc smiled. "Glad you think so. You look sexy as hell in everything. Lookin' forward to seeing you in your nurse's uniform again. Gives me all kinds of ideas about playing doctor."

Giggling, she got to her feet and went to him. "You have time to eat, don't you?"

"Yep, and something smells delicious."

Pleased to watch Linc enjoy her cooking, she sat with him, picking at a piece of chicken while he ate. "I made cookies."

Looking up from his plate, Linc narrowed his eyes. "What kind?"

"Chocolate chip."

A slow smile lit up his features. "My favorite."

"I know."

Linc finished cleaning his plate and sat back, sipping the sweet tea she'd made. "See? We know each other a hell of a lot better than you remember."

Realizing the truth of his statement, Krystal nodded. "I guess you're right. You know, when you and Rafe showed up, I was shocked, but not really surprised. I don't know how else to explain it. Although I knew in my head not to expect you, when the two of you showed up, somewhere in the back of my mind, I thought…*of course they're here.*"

Sitting forward, Linc reached for her hand. "Of course we were there. We left as soon as we heard. We only stopped long enough to pick up the suitcases that we'd packed months ago. We'll always be there for you, baby."

"I know. You don't know what that means to me or how much I've come to rely on knowing that you and Rafe are always there."

He smiled again, lifting her hand to his lips. "And we always will be." He glanced at the clock. "I've got to get to work, but before I go, I've got to get you ready for Rafe."

Chapter Seventeen

Krystal stared at Linc, trying not to laugh while her body sizzled with the stirring of arousal. "You're not serious?"

Linc raised a brow, patting his thigh. "I'm damned serious. I told Rafe I'd have you lubed for him."

Crossing her arms over her chest, Krystal tried to ignore the tube in his hand, but her gaze kept returning to it. "Do you always do everything Rafe tells you to do?"

His brow went up again. "Rafe didn't tell me to do this. I offered because I knew both he and I would enjoy it. And don't try to pit one of us against the other. It won't work, especially regarding you. Now get over here."

"Or what?"

His slow smile sent a shiver of delight through her. "Then I'm going to take great delight in making you and spank your sweet ass as a reminder to you not to disobey me, and a bonus for me for you making me do this the hard way."

Krystal took a step back, trying hard not to laugh. "If you think I'm going to make it easy for you to shove lube up my ass, you'd better think again, Deputy."

As soon as he started to rise, she took off, running toward the living room, her laughter filling the air.

Going around the recliners, she stopped, waiting to see which way he would go.

He paused, the ominous tube still in his hand. "So we do it the hard way, and I get my bonus."

Krystal couldn't stop smiling, enjoying the chance to play. "Don't count your chickens, Deputy. You haven't caught me yet."

He took a step closer, a faint smile playing at his lips. "You know I do this for a living, don't you?"

"Yeah, but I just fed you a big dinner and you had seconds of everything. Besides, I'm slippery."

Smiling again, Linc lifted the tube of lube. "Not yet, but you will be."

Catching her off guard by pushing the chair she stood behind toward her, he effectively separated the two chairs, leaving her no choice except to back up or try to run past him.

He tossed the tube onto the chair and kept pushing it forward, giving her less and less space to maneuver.

Knowing she had to move fast, she darted to her left where there was more room, yelping when a hard arm hit her belly and lifted her from the floor.

Laughing, she tried to push his arm away, but it was made of solid muscle. "Damn it, Linc!"

He picked up the lube and flung her over his lap, his quick movements catching her off balance. "You're the one who chose the hard way, baby."

Sucking in a breath when he yanked her pants and panties down to her knees, she kicked frantically, unable to stop laughing. "You brute."

Pressing his forearm against her back, he ran his other hand over the cheeks of her ass. "Stop complaining. You had the chance to behave."

He slapped her ass several times in rapid succession, heating it until she wiggled on his lap. Pausing, he rubbed her hot flesh, spreading the heat. "Now I'm going to have to work an entire shift thinking about your gorgeous ass wiggling on my lap."

"Good." She smacked at his leg. "I hope you're hard all night. Ow!"

Several more slaps landed, covering every inch of her bottom before he paused again. "I'm not hurting you, and you know it. I'm just warming you up for Rafe. The next time I do this, it's gonna be for me."

Leaning closer, he slapped her ass again, slightly harder than before. "When I took your ass, it was your first time. Do you remember how it felt?"

Krystal moaned, fighting the awareness that his spanking and words inspired. "I hate you."

Chuckling, he uncapped the lube. "That's not a very nice thing to say to a man about to slide his finger into your ass."

His forearm pressed harder against her back, his fingers lifting and separating her ass cheeks. "So pretty. They waxed you good, didn't they, baby?"

Remembering how complete her waxing had been, Krystal was glad that her hair hid her burning face, the knowing of how well he could see her most private opening both arousing and embarrassing. "Yes, now stop staring!"

"Not a chance." Pressing his lubed finger against her puckered opening, Linc began to ease into her. "I remember the first time I did this. I knew you were a virgin, and the thought of being the first to take your ass almost had me coming in my damned pants. Did you use the balm here, too?"

"None of your business."

Linc pressed harder against one side, making her bottom hole sting. "Excuse me? Everything about you is very much my business, including this ass. Now answer my question."

Fighting not to clench on him and stunned that her pussy clenched, coating her inner thighs with her juices, Krystal gritted her teeth. "Yes, damn it. It hurt, and the balm helped. Oh!"

Linc thrust his finger deep, pressing against her inner walls to coat them with the lube. "Good to know. The next time you get waxed, Rafe and I will take care of spreading the balm on your mound and ass. Be still. I'm gonna add more."

Sucking in a breath when more of the cold lube began to enter her, Krystal fought not to clench on his finger, but the intense sense of awareness there made it impossible.

He did it again, and then again, until she began to writhe on his lap, lifting into the slow thrusts of his finger.

"There she is. The woman I fell in love with three years ago was sexy as hell, sweet as honey, and smart as a whip." Sliding his finger free, he bent to kiss her bottom. "And now she's even more." He helped her to her feet, pulling her pants and panties up before pulling her close. "You take my breath away, baby. You always have. Just knowing you're mine now makes me happier than you could ever know."

Krystal smiled, her throat clogged with tears. "And knowing you're mine makes me just as happy." Moving closer, she slid her hands up his chest. "How can you make me feel like crying when I'm horny as hell?"

"It's a gift. Rafe will be here soon."

After washing his hands and retrieving his hat, he came back into the living room, pausing to kiss her before he left.

The light kiss she'd been expecting deepened into something more. Something hotter.

With a curse, he broke off his kiss and slammed his hat onto his head. "It's gonna be a long shift."

Standing at the window, she watched him pull away, startled at the sound of her cell phone ringing.

Rushing to the kitchen where she'd left it, she grinned when she looked at the display. "Hello, future husband."

"I'm on my way, baby." He chuckled softly. "Linc's gonna have a long night."

"So he said. It's his fault."

"Do you know how badly I want you?"

"You want my ass." She shifted restlessly as the anticipation grew.

"True. Do you know why?"

"Because you're kinky?"

"That, too. There's another reason."

Intrigued, Krystal walked back to the living room to watch out the window for him. "Do you want to tell me what it is?"

"I took your virginity."

"I remember." She would never forget his tenderness or patience. "It's a night I'll never forget."

"Neither will I. Linc took your ass for the first time."

"I remember that, too."

"Before your father got sick, you told us both that you loved us."

"Because I did." Krystal smiled and dropped to the arm of the recliner Linc had moved. "I do."

"Linc had had all of you. I hadn't. I wanted to imprint myself on every inch of you. It didn't seem as important then. I was willing to wait."

Krystal stiffened when he pulled into the driveway, getting to her feet when he stared at her through the windshield. "Rafe?"

"And we suddenly ran out of time. It's the most intimate way a man can take a woman, and I hadn't been able to have that with you." He got out of the SUV and walked toward the front door, his gaze never leaving hers. "I want that. I want to take you in the most intimate way a man can take a woman. I want it slow. I want it now."

She didn't know how she could become so emotional about something so kinky, but she found she had to swallow the lump in her throat before she could speak. "So come take me."

Rafe came through the door, locking it behind him. Taking her cell phone from her hand, he tossed it and his into one of the recliners and lifted her in his arms, carrying her down the hall and to the bedroom.

Neither spoke as he gently lowered her to the bed, stripping her out of her clothes and using his lips, teeth, and tongue to explore every inch of her.

"Don't move." He stood briefly to strip out of his own clothes, the sound of his gun belt hitting the floor loud in the quiet of their bedroom.

His gaze raked over her in the waning light, his hands shaking as he rolled on a condom. "I want you so badly."

Lifting her arms in invitation, she smiled. "I'm yours."

Bracing a knee on the edge of the mattress, he rolled her to her belly. "I want you to say that when I'm inside you."

Instead of taking her the way she'd expected, he kissed his way up the back of her thighs, using his tongue and lips to awaken nerve endings all the way up her body.

He paused at her bottom, kissing her ass cheeks and using his teeth to scrape over them. "I missed this more than you can imagine."

Spreading her thighs, she lifted her bottom, moaning at the feet of his warm lips working their way up her body. "I missed this, too. Sometimes, I missed you so much I couldn't eat. Couldn't sleep. I would have done anything to feel your arms around me."

Rafe continued to work his way higher, wrapping his arms around her from behind to cup her breasts as he nuzzled the sensitive spot below her ear. "Like this?"

"God yes!"

Tilting her head to give him better access, she lifted herself slightly, her breath catching when he ran his thumbs lightly back and forth over her nipples.

The feel of his cock against the back of her thigh had her lifting again. "Please, Rafe. I can't wait any longer."

He shifted to the side and the back of his hand brushed against her bottom as he positioned his cock at her puckered opening. "Nice and slow. I've been waiting for this for a long time, and I want it to last as long as possible."

The head of his cock pushed into her, forcing her puckered opening to stretch wide to accommodate it. Pushing her knees wider with his, he covered her body with his, reaching up to close his hands over hers.

"Easy, baby." Nuzzling her neck, he slid a little deeper. "The most intimate way a man can take a woman. It's private, a little naughty, and very sexual."

His teeth caught her earlobe, nipping playfully as he slid deeper. "You're so hot. So tight. You're trembling with reaction at having my cock in your ass. Your tight ass is clenching on me as if it's trying to take me deeper."

Krystal moaned, her entire body shaking with an awareness that left her breathless. "I want you deeper. Closer. Hold me, Rafe."

Rafe groaned and pushed his cock deeper, tightening his hold on her hands and brushing his lips over her shoulder. "I've got you, baby."

He withdrew slightly and slid even deeper. "A little more. You can take more. Your ass is so damned tight."

The slow friction against her inner walls sent a riot of sensation through her, the combination of chills and heat making her shake and clench on him even harder. "I feel so full. God, Rafe! It's so intense."

With a groan, he withdrew almost all the way and slid deeper, so deep her breath caught. "Yes it is. Intense. Hot. My cock's deep in your ass. It's mine now, just like the rest of you."

His lips pressed against her hair as he linked his fingers with her. "My lover and, soon—my wife."

"Yes." Knowing what he needed, she gripped his hands tightly. "I'm yours."

He moved slowly, the decadence of the act made even more intimate in the slow, loving way he took her. Holding her hands in his, he kept his face close to hers, hearing every moan.

Every breath.

Using his elbows to keep most of his weight off of her, he continued to move, his body surrounding hers. "Mine. Ours. Forever."

"Yes."

The pressure inside her began to build, the pleasure so intense that she started to cry. "Rafe."

"I know, baby. I've got you. A little more."

His groan vibrated through her. "Ready for more, baby?"

Her clit was on fire, the erotic burn of her ass being stretched and the friction against her inner walls combining into something so powerful that she sobbed, her body shaking against his.

"Please!"

Sliding a hand under her, he moved slightly faster, his control over his movements further evidence of his strength. "Easy, baby. I'll take you there."

Lifting her head, she turned her face toward his. "I want to come together."

"Yes, baby. Come with me."

Krystal cried out when he moved faster, pressing her feet against the backs of his thighs.

One slide of his fingers over her clit shot electric currents of pure pleasure through her, sending her over in a rush of ecstasy and heat.

The sensation intensified when Rafe slid deep, the pulsing of his cock setting off another rush of pleasure that had her inner walls clenching on his cock even harder, the pleasure pouring over her in layers.

Aware of his lips against her neck, she held on to his hands and leaned into him, tears of release burning her eyes.

They lay that way for several minutes, the closeness between them never stronger.

Pulling his hand closer, she touched her lips to his knuckles. "I love you."

"I love you, too, baby." He slowly withdrew, dropping to the bed next to her. Smiling, he ran a hand through her hair. "I've spent a lot of sleepless nights missing you. There were times when I wondered if it would ever happen."

He rolled closer, kissing her shoulder. "I was afraid you'd meet someone."

Pressing her lips to his chest, she sighed. "I kept waiting for you and Linc to tell me that you'd found someone else. I still can't believe you didn't."

"I couldn't even think about touching another woman. Every time I closed my eyes, I remembered the look on your face the first time I kissed you." He smiled and leaned back to look into her eyes. "You still look at me like that every time I touch you."

Amused, Krystal grinned. "How do I look at you?"

Rafe smiled again. "You look at me with love in your eyes and a kind of wonder—like I'm every dream you've ever had rolled into one. Linc feels the same way."

Krystal sat up, running her hand down his chest. "That's because you are. You both are. I never expected anyone to love me the way you do. It's kind of scary sometimes."

"I know. You have way too much power over me, woman."

Krystal blinked back more tears. "You make me feel powerful. You have the same power over me, and it scared me, but knowing how much you and Linc love me gives me a kind of inner strength that I never thought I could feel. It's gotten me through the worst time in my life. You didn't even have to be there for me to feel your love."

Sitting up, Rafe wiped a tear from her cheek. "Well, from now on, you'll feel it even more because there's no way we'll ever be apart again."

Epilogue

Slightly tipsy from the margaritas she'd had with dinner, Krystal leaned against Rafe as they rode the elevator up to their room. "I can't believe it's the last night of our honeymoon."

Chuckling, Rafe wrapped his arms around her waist and bent to nuzzle her neck. "It might be our last night in the Bahamas, but the honeymoon is far from over."

Giggling, she eyed Linc, who leaned against the opposite wall, looking handsome as hell in a dark blue shirt and dark gray trousers. "You look more relaxed."

He smiled faintly, his gaze raking over her. "So do you. You put on a few pounds in the last couple of weeks."

Warm under his appreciative gaze, she faked a pout. "That's not a polite thing to say, especially if you're planning to get laid tonight."

"Oh, I'm getting laid." Linc's eyes narrowed. "Those pounds seem to have settled in all the right places. Your ass is even more lush than ever, and your bathing suit top barely contains you."

Rafe's lips touched her hair. "I spend every day glaring at other men who seem to enjoy ogling what belongs to us."

Leaning her head back, Krystal looked up at him. "Now you know how I feel with all those women looking at the two of you like they want to take a bite out of your asses."

Rafe chuckled again, his teasing and laughter more frequent since their wedding. "You're the only one allowed to take a bite out of our asses, baby."

Linc snorted. "That's easy for you to say. I think I'm still bruised from where she tried to take a bite out of mine."

Krystal laughed at that and straightened when the elevator stopped and the doors opened. "That's what you get for being so hot, and don't look for sympathy from me. You've tried to take a bite out of me a time or two."

Taking her hand, Linc led her from the elevator and started down the hallway toward their room. "That's it? I'd better ramp up my game."

"If your game gets ramped up any more, I won't be able to walk."

Rafe paused to unlock the door, turning to glance at her over his shoulder. "I have no problem carrying you."

As soon as they entered the room, Rafe reached for her, wrapping his arms around her and pulling her close. With a hand at her bottom, he lifted her against him. "Do you know how hard it was to sit there with you, knowing that you're wearing a garter belt and stocking and no panties?"

Wiggling against him, Krystal lifted a hand to his hair, gripping his shoulder with the other. "No. Why don't you tell me how hard?"

She moaned when he covered her lips with his, the hunger in his kiss sparking her own.

Linc closed in behind her, unzipping her dress and running his lips over the skin he'd exposed. "I'd rather show you."

Taking one arm and then the other, Linc worked the short sleeves of the dress down her arms to let it gather at her waist. "This bra should be illegal." He ran his hands over the cups, which just covered her nipples. "I have a better use for this."

Undoing the front clasp, he scraped his teeth over her shoulder, sending a shiver through her.

Rafe lifted his head, breaking off their kiss and lowering her to her feet. "Good idea. Hold her."

"With pleasure." Wrapping an arm around her waist, Linc shoved her dress down to puddle at her feet, leaving her dress in nothing except her light blue garter, stockings, and high heeled sandals.

Lifting her arms around Linc's neck, Krystal leaned back against him, a moan escaping at the feel of his hands closing on her breasts.

Watching Rafe strip out of his clothes and retrieve two condoms from their luggage, she smiled. "Nice tan lines, Deputy."

Fisting his hard cock, Rafe rolled on a condom, his gaze raking over her as he approached. "I like your tan just fine, but it's the white parts that fascinate me."

After rolling on the condom, he tossed the other onto the bed and took her bra from Linc. "Hands out in front of you."

Linc closed his fingers on her nipples, sending a sharp stab of heat to her slit.

She dropped her hands in front of her automatically, her heart racing when Rafe caught her wrists and tied them together with her bra. "You getting kinky, Deputy?"

He bent, slipping her bound wrists behind his neck, he gripped the cheeks of her ass and lifted her against him. "I just might."

With a hand at her bottom and one at the nape, Rafe sat on the edge of the bed.

Cupping the back of her head, he held her in place for his kiss, pressing against her lips to force them open with a determination that thrilled her.

Sweeping her mouth with his tongue, he slid his other hand lower, brushing her clit with his fingers, his hold tightening when she jolted.

Breaking off his kiss with a groan, he leaned her back and closed his lips over her nipple, sucking gently as he continued to stroke her clit.

Linc moved in behind her, already naked. "There's something real sexy about those garters and stockings, darlin'."

Rafe lifted his head, sitting up and pulling her with him. "Come on, baby. I want my cock inside you."

Rafe lifted her to her knees, and while Linc removed her shoes, slowly lowered her onto his cock. "That's better. I've wanted to be inside you ever since I saw these garters and stockings."

Sucking in a breath, Krystal used her bound hands to pull him closer. "You always want to be inside me."

Rafe smiled, a flash of white against his tanned skin. "True."

The feel of Linc's lips on her back again drew another moan from her, a moan that drew a smile from Rafe.

Touching his lips to hers, he sipped at them, nipping her bottom lip while closing his hands on her waist. "I never get tired of that look."

Knowing that he spoke of the love and need in her eyes, Krystal smiled, sucking in a breath when a lubed finger slid into her bottom.

"Oh God." Pressing her face against Rafe's shoulder, she shivered at the feel of Linc's finger moving slowly in and out of her, adding lube several times.

Rafe ran his hands over her back. "I know, baby. You get a little overwhelmed when we take you together."

He leaned back, taking her with him. "That look in your eyes gets me every time."

Her position made her more vulnerable to Linc, a fact that he used to his advantage.

He slid his finger free and positioned the head of his cock at her puckered opening. "Got her?"

Rafe watched her face, his gaze hooded. "Always." His hands tightened on her hips. "Hold on, baby. Let Linc inside."

Linc applied pressure, the hand at her waist tightening until, with a harsh groan, he pushed the head of his cock into her. Closing his other hand on her waist, he groaned again. "Fuck me."

Crying out when he thrust into her, Krystal couldn't even work up a giggle at his curse. "I think that's my line."

Rafe's chuckle became a moan when Linc pushed deeper. "Christ, she's so fucking tight that I'm always afraid of hurting her when we take her this way."

Her bottom and pussy clenched on them, the need to move incredible. "If you don't move, I'm gonna strangle you with my bra."

Rafe made a growling noise in his throat and began to move, withdrawing slightly to thrust deeper. "Can't have that."

Linc's lips touched her shoulder and with a harsh rush of breath, he pushed deeper as Rafe slowly withdrew.

Even though she knew what to expect, the sensations never failed to take her by surprise as they established a rhythm that made each stroke a combination of raw sex and loving hunger that never failed to overwhelm her.

Pressed against Rafe's, heat consumed her, every thrust of his hips going deep.

She felt every bump and ridge of their cocks, her pussy and ass burning all around them.

Even though she knew Linc would surge deeper with each thrust, the pure lust always stunned her.

She knew they would move faster, but could never wait for it.

Pressing her hands against the bed, she used her knees for leverage and began to move. "Oh God! Faster."

Frustrated that the hands at her hips and waist kept her from moving the way she wanted to, Krystal moaned in frustration.

Her inner walls shimmered at the friction, clenching on them in a way that made the sensation even more intense.

Her orgasm remained just out of reach, each thrust of their cocks promising completion, something she suspected they knew because they slowed their strokes.

"Please!" She struggled to move faster, throwing her head back and digging her knees into the mattress.

From behind her, Linc slowed his strokes even more, a groan rumbling from his chest. "I want it to last, damn it!"

"No! I need to come."

The movement of Rafe's hips had her clit rubbing against him with every thrust—the combination of sensations sending her over in a rush of heat that threatened to consume her. "Ahhh!"

Rafe cursed and moved faster. "Fuck."

Linc's hands tightened on her waist as he surged deep. "The way she clenches."

Caught up in the pleasure, Krystal threw her head back and squeezed her eyes closed, crying out again when the feel of her inner walls clenching on them, making the feel of their cocks pulsing inside her even more intense.

Rafe slid his hands up her body, sliding one over her back while fisting the other in her hair to lift her face to his. "You okay, baby."

Smiling at the feel of Linc's lips against her back, Krystal sighed.

She thought back to the first time she'd met Jesse, remembering the other woman's claim to never having felt such a sense of security.

Krystal had wondered if she'd ever feel such a thing.

It had become such an integral part of her life now, and had freed her to be herself.

Rafe cupped her cheek, frowning up at her. "Baby? You okay?"

To her embarrassment, tears filled her eyes. "Always. I'm always all right now that I'm with you and Linc."

* * * *

The warm breeze felt good against her skin, the beach umbrella protecting her from the powerful rays of the sun.

"Ready to go back to the room, darlin'?"

Krystal smiled, not bothering to open her eyes. "I'm staying here for the rest of my life."

Chuckling, Linc kissed her shoulder. "In the Bahamas?"

"In this chair."

From her other side, Rafe spoke in a voice just as drowsy as hers. "I thought we discussed that. We're not being apart ever again."

"So stay here with me. We can lie here forever and never move."

Rafe glared at a man who walked past and eyed Krystal. "I meant the chair." He reached out to touch her arm. "I'm too far away from you. You fill out that bikini a little too well."

Linc ran a fingertip up her arm. "You sure you never want to move again?"

His fingertips continued to move over her, tracing the edge of her bikini top before trailing over her belly. "You were moving pretty good last night when Rafe and I took you together."

Krystal gasped and jolted upright, looking around to make sure no one had heard him. "Linc!"

She couldn't hold back a laugh when she realized that everyone close to them had already left. "Damn it, Linc."

Grinning, he bent to kiss her. "Did you really think I would talk about our sex life with an audience listening?"

"I should have known better." She wrinkled her nose at him, grinning playfully. "They're going nuts here trying to figure out which one of you I belong to."

Rafe sat up, pulling on his T-shirt. "They should know by now that you belong to both of us." He glanced at his watch. "We have just enough time to shower and eat before we have to get to the airport." Reaching out, he took her left hand in his and kissed the set of rings he and Linc had placed there two weeks earlier. "Did you have a nice honeymoon, baby?"

They'd chosen a beachfront resort, where they'd done nothing more than eat, sleep, make love, and lounge on the beach.

She felt better than she had in her life and was madly in love with her new husbands.

Getting to her feet, she watched each of them gathering their things, filled with love and satisfaction each time she saw the glint of the rings she'd given them. "It was amazing. Thank you."

Linc helped her slip into her beach cover-up. "You're welcome. Ready to go home, darlin'?"

Krystal sighed and shook out her towel, stuffing it into her bag before slipping on her shoes. "I am. This was amazing, but home sounds wonderful."

She eyed each of them, the sudden rush of emotion bringing a lump to her throat. "Yes. Thank you for making a home for us."

Rafe reached out to take her hand in his. "You're welcome. It wasn't a home until you got there, though, baby."

Linc took her other hand in his. "Now that you're with us, we're never letting go of you again."

Krystal smiled. "I'm going to hold you to that."

With them, she'd found a dream far richer than any she could have imagined, and each day, she fell more deeply in love with them.

Each day, they showed her how much they loved her.

She thought of her mother and father and wished they could know that she'd found a love as deep as theirs had been.

She smiled to herself, knowing in her heart that somehow they did.

THE END

WWW.LEAHBROOKE.NET

Siren Publishing, Inc.
www.SirenPublishing.com